* * * * * * *

Suddenly the phone went dead. After I hung up my phone, I sat there looking at it. It wasn't because I expected it to ring again; it was because of the sound of Josh's voice and the fact he ended the phone call rather abruptly. At least I thought it was abrupt. He didn't even give me a chance to say goodbye. I thought it was a little strange.

In the years I had known Josh, he had always been rather laid back. I don't remember anything ever bothering him, yet he seemed upset about something. There was also the fact that I remembered he had always been the talkative type with a great sense of humor, but this time he seemed uptight and in a hurry. I wondered why?

* * * * * *

Other titles by J.E. Terrall

Western Short Stories	Western Novels
The Old West*	Conflict in Elkhorn Valley*
The Frontier*	Lazy A Ranch
Untamed Land*	(A Modern Western)
Tales from the Territory*	The Story of Joshua Higgins
Frontier Justice*	The Valley Ranch War*

Romance Novels	Mystery/Suspense/Thriller
Balboa Rendezvous	I Can See Clearly
Sing for Me*	The Return Home*
Return to Me*	The Inheritance
Forever Yours	

Bill Sparks Mysteries
  Murder in the Backcountry

Nick McCord Mysteries
  Vol – 1 Murder at Gill's Point
  Vol – 2 Death of a Flower
  Vol – 3 A Dead Man's Treasure
  Vol – 4 Blackjack, A Game to Die For
  Vol – 5 Death on the Lakes
  Vol – 6 Secrets Can Get You Killed

Peter Blackstone Mysteries	Frank Tidsdale Mysteries
Murder in the Foothills	Death by Design
Murder on the Crystal Blue	Death by Assassination
Murder of My Love	

* also available in Large Print Editions

MURDER IN THE DARK OF NIGHT

A PETER BLACKSTONE MYSTERY
by
J.E. Terrall

4

Printed in the United States of America
First Printing / 2018 – createspace.com

Cover: Front and back covers by author, J.E Terrall -
        Photo on back cover by Phyllis J. Terrall

Book Layout/
Formatting: J.E. Terrall
             Custer, South Dakota

MURDER IN THE DARK OF NIGHT

In memory of my friend and fellow co-worker,
Ken Noah, who was one of the nicest people I have
ever had the pleasure of working with and knowing.

CHAPTER ONE

WINTER HAD DECIDED TO COME a little early to Denver. I could see large wet snowflakes drifting down from the dull gray clouds that were hanging low over the city. The temperature was a little below freezing and the snow was just starting to stick on the window ledges of the twelve-story building. It was a good thing there was very little wind. With a good wind and a little heavier snow fall, it could easily become a serious storm that would snarl traffic to a point where no one would be able to go anywhere without some difficulty.

I was sitting behind my desk with my feet on the windowsill of my ninth-floor office while I looked out the window. I was watching the snow drift down from the sky. I wasn't really looking at anything special, just looking while sipping on my second cup of coffee of the morning.

I should have been working on sending out bills and writing out a few checks, but it was a good morning to just relax and enjoy the coffee before I dove into what I should be doing. The coffee was hot and it felt good to take a few minutes to relax and enjoy it in the quiet morning hours.

As I sipped on the hot coffee, I was thinking how nice it was to be inside where it was warm and dry when my phone began to ring. As much as I would have liked to let the answering machine take the call, I turned around, reached over and picked up the phone while setting my cup on the desk.

"Peter Blackstone Investigations. How may I help you?"

"Peter, you probably don't remember me, but I'm Josh Garrett."

"Sure. I remember you. It's been a long time."

"It sure has."

"I don't think I've seen you since college. What are you up to?"

"I've been working in the investment business."

The first thought to cross my mind was he wanted to sell me something, but I would give him a chance to tell me why he wanted to talk to me. Although I had known him in college, and we had played football together; we had never been what you might call "close friends". As I recall, we didn't socialize much outside of school. For the most part, the only time we were together was during football practice and the games, and maybe a party or two if most of the football players were there. However, I don't recall having any of the same classes with him.

"I was wondering if we could get together and talk, that is if you are not too busy?" he asked.

"That would be great. When did you have in mind?"

"Could we meet - - say - - this afternoon?" he asked, his voice sounding hopeful that I would be available.

Maybe it was my suspicious nature from all the years as a police officer and a private investigator, but something in his voice told me the meeting he wanted might not have anything to do with selling me some kind of an investment program, or stock in a company I never heard of before.

"Just name a time and place. Would you like to meet here at my office? I can put on the coffee pot and we can sit around and talk."

"Well, - - ah - - I was thinking more like maybe at a little coffee shop on Broadway downtown."

"Okay. Sure," I said wondering why he didn't seem to want to come to my office. "There are several along Broadway. Do you have one in mind?"

"There's a little coffee shop near the corner of Ninth and Broadway. Could we meet there? It's a quiet little place where we could talk without being disturbed."

"Okay. I know where it is. Say, is there something bothering you? You sound like, I don't know, like maybe there's a problem."

"No. No," he said rather quickly. "I just want to have a talk with you. There's nothing wrong."

With the quickness of his response and the tone of his voice, I got the feeling he was lying to me.

"Okay, but if you want privacy, you can come to my office; and we can lock the door and talk without being disturbed."

"No. I'd rather meet at the café. Could you meet me there at - - say - - two-thirty this afternoon? It shouldn't be very busy at that time," he asked.

"Sure. I'll meet you at the café at two-thirty. See you then. We'll talk then," I said.

"Great. I have to go now."

Suddenly the phone went dead. After I hung up my phone, I sat there looking at it. It wasn't because I expected it to ring again; it was because of the sound of Josh's voice and the fact he ended the phone call rather abruptly. At least I thought it was abrupt. He didn't even give me a chance to say goodbye.

In the years I had known Josh, he had always been rather laid back. I don't remember anything ever bothering him, yet he seemed upset about something. There was also the fact that I remembered he had always been the talkative type with a great sense of humor, but this time he seemed uptight and in a hurry. I wondered why?

The way Josh sounded made me wonder what was going on. If he wanted to talk to me in private, there was no better place than my office. I could shut the door and lock it, and let the answering machine take any calls. Maybe there was a reason he didn't want to talk to me in my office, but the only reason I could think of for not wanting to come to my office was he was afraid someone might see him come here. I couldn't think of any other reason for him to be afraid of coming to my office.

The more I thought about our conversation, something in the back of my mind told me that he didn't really want to see me about an investment program; but I have been wrong about those sorts of things before. However, I couldn't get over the idea he seemed relieved that I had agreed to see him, more relieved than if he had wanted to simply sell me something or talk about old times.

I took a look at my watch and found it was almost ten o'clock. I had about four and a half hours before I was to meet Josh and hopefully find out why he wanted to talk to me. Since there was nothing I could do until I talked to him, I might as well get some work done. I could spend the time getting some of my billing taken care of before I was to meet him.

Just the thought of having to do the billing made me think I should get a secretary. I disliked almost any kind of paperwork. A secretary would relieve me of those duties, well, at least most of them.

I HAD BEEN WORKING ON BILLING and the corresponding record keeping for about an hour and a half when there was a light knock on the door. I looked up to see a very nice-looking woman standing in the doorway smiling at me.

The woman standing in my door was wearing a winter coat and very nice boots with high heels. Even with the winter coat, I could tell she had a very nice figure. She was a rather sexy looking woman in her early thirties. I also knew she was very smart and a very caring person. She worked as a surgical nurse at one of the local hospitals,

Denver General Hospital. She was the nicest person I've ever had the pleasure of knowing. The woman was also my latest squeeze, Julie Archer. We had been dating for several months and our relationship had grown rather quickly.

"Hi. What brings you all the way down here?" I asked as I stood up and walked around in front of my desk.

"I have a couple of hours before I have to go to work. I thought you might like to take me to lunch."

"I would love to," I said as I stepped in front of her.

I reached out and put my hands on her narrow waist and drew her toward me. She put her hands on my chest then slid them over my shoulders and around to the back of my neck while leaning toward me until our lips met. It was not a real passionate kiss, but it was certainly a pleasant one. I liked the feel of her body up against me even if she did have a winter coat on, and I liked the feel of her in my arms.

"Wow! I didn't expect that. I guess I'll have to stop by more often," she said with a smile as she drew back a little and looked into my eyes.

"I certainly wouldn't mind," I assured her.

"Are you busy?"

"Not really. It has been pretty quiet around here this morning. I was just catching up on some paperwork. Where would you like to go for lunch?"

"I have to be at work by one-thirty. I have the afternoon shift," she said with a hint of disappointment in her voice.

"What time do you get off?" I asked.

"It will probably be late. I should get off before midnight, maybe a little later. The doctors have a pretty full surgical schedule today. If anything goes wrong, or we have an emergency, it could be pretty late. Do you want me to come by if it's late?"

"Are you sure you won't be too tired?"

"I'm never too tired to see you," she said with her sexiest smile.

"The only thing I have going on today is an appointment this afternoon with a guy I went to college with. I haven't seen him for a good number of years. I have no idea what he wants to talk to me about, but I'm sure I will find out. I'll probably be free the rest of the day," I said.

"Good. We could have a late dinner together."

"Okay. Would you like me to cook?"

"That would be nice," she said with a smile.

"How about coming to my place when you get off? I'll have dinner ready when you get there."

"Is this your way to get me to spend the night with you?" she asked with a sexy grin and a twinkle in her eyes.

"Would you like it to be?" I asked hopefully.

"I might. I'll let you know, but right now I'm hungry."

"Well, we can't have you going to work hungry," I said as I let go of her and reached for my coat.

I took my coat off the coat rack and slipped into it as we left my office. We took the elevator down to the parking garage in the basement. We got in my Tahoe and drove over to a restaurant where we could get a good meal. Since Julie would be going to work right after lunch, we decided to have a dinner instead of just a lunch, especially since there was a chance she would be working rather late.

We went to a very nice steak restaurant that I knew had very good food. We were seated in a booth in the corner where we could talk while we ate without being overheard. I couldn't help but watch her as she talked. She has a wonderful sense of humor. I always enjoy the time I spend with her.

After our dinner, I paid the bill and we left. I took Julie back to the parking garage so she could pick up her car. I walked her to her car and held the door for her while she got in.

"I'll see you as soon as I can get off work," she said. "Would you like me to call you before I leave the hospital?"

"You might want to do that. That way, I can have everything on the table when you get there."

"Okay," she said with a smile.

"Drive carefully," I said.

I leaned down and kissed her, then closed the door for her. I stepped back away from the car and watched her as she backed out of the parking space, then drove out of the parking garage onto the street.

As soon as she was gone, I turned and headed for the elevator. It took only a few minutes for me to get back in my office. I sat down at my desk and dove into my paperwork, picking up where I had left off. By the time I had finished my paperwork, I had several payments ready to be mailed and a couple of bills ready to send out.

Time had gone by rather quickly. A quick glance at my watch showed me it was about time to go and see what it was Josh wanted to talk to me about. I put on my coat, grabbed up the mail that needed to go out and left my office. There was a mail chute next to the elevator. I dropped the mail in the slot of the mail chute while I waited for the elevator.

As soon as the elevator arrived I got in and took it to the parking garage. I got into my Tahoe and headed out to meet Josh.

THE TRAFFIC WAS FAIRLY LIGHT in mid-afternoon as I drove downtown to meet Josh. The snow was wet and heavy making the street rather slushy. It was also starting to stick to the pavement in places where the street usually didn't get much sunlight, when the sun was out. I was only about eight or nine blocks from the café where I was to meet Josh when a police car and an ambulance went rushing by me, splashing slush and water on my Chevy Tahoe as they raced by. My thought was they were going a bit too fast for the condition of the street. It was only a minute or so before they were out of sight.

As I turned the corner onto the street where the café was located, I could see two police cars and an ambulance at the curb a couple of blocks down the street. Their lights were flashing, and there seemed to be people running all over the place.

The closer I got to them, the more I was beginning to think they were in front of the café where I was to meet Josh. It didn't take long for me to realize they were actually at the café, and the police were at the door. I immediately wondered what had happened. My first thought was that someone had either had a heart attack or had choked on something while having a meal in the café.

I pulled up to the curb and stopped a little way down the block since the ambulance was right in front of the café. I didn't want to get in the way. Before I could get out of my Tahoe, several more police cars showed up. I got out of my Tahoe and slowly walked toward the café while looking around for Josh, but I didn't see him among the people milling around. I glanced at my watch and saw it was about twenty minutes past two. I was about ten minutes early. Either he was not there yet, or he was inside the café waiting for me.

As I got closer to the café and looked toward the door, the EMTs were wheeling a gurney out of the café in a hurry. I didn't get a chance to see who was on the gurney. About all I could tell was it was probably a man. He had an oxygen mask over his face and two IV's in his arms. One of the EMTs, who was riding on the siderail of the gurney, was blocking my view. It looked as if he was working on the man while it was being wheeled to the ambulance. The patient had to be in serious condition. I stood back out of the way and watched as the gurney was put in the ambulance.

It never occurred to me that it could be Josh who was involved in some sort of an emergency. After all, Josh Garrett was a fairly young man, only thirty-three years old.

He had always been in good health and had taken good care of himself. We had played football in college and he was pretty good, not good enough for the pros, but still a good player. It had been a long time since we had seen each other, but we had kept in contact from time to time over the years. I had a picture of him from a Christmas card I received a few years ago. He looked to be in pretty good shape. As far as I knew, we were just meeting for coffee, and possibly a light snack, while we talked about old times.

While I watched the EMTs load the gurney in the ambulance, I felt a hand on my shoulder. I turned around and saw Captain MacDonald standing behind me. I've known Captain MacDonald for a good many years. I get along with him a lot better than I do with many of the other officers in the police department. We had grown to trust each other to the point where we would help each other from time to time. We had even worked on a few cases together. I had saved his life once.

"Pete, what are you doing here?" Mac asked.

He seemed to be surprised to see me. It took a few seconds for me to respond. I was about to ask him the same thing; but quickly realized that being a detective he was probably here to investigate what had happened in the café, and he didn't need me holding him up.

"Ah - - I'm here to meet an old college friend. Do you know what happened here?"

"Not yet. I just got here. I understand there was a shooting in the café. Two dead and one seriously injured."

"Any idea who the victims were?" I asked, hoping Josh was not one of them.

"Haven't heard. Like I said, 'I just got here'. What's the name of the guy you're here to see?"

"Josh Garrett."

"Give me a few minutes and I'll see what's going on. I might be able to find out something."

"Thanks," I said

I moved over close to the building to wait while I watched Mac go inside the café. Waiting was always hard for me and the thing I hate most. It always seemed longer than it really was, especially if you were waiting for news, good or bad.

It was shortly after the Coroner's van arrived when Mac came out of the café. I saw him looking around. As soon as he saw me, he walked up to me.

"I've got some bad news. It seems your friend, Josh Garrett, was just taken to the hospital. It looks like his chances of surviving are pretty slim. I'm sorry."

"Which hospital did they take him to?"

"Denver General."

"Thanks, Mac," I said as I turned and hurried back to my Tahoe.

I got in my Tahoe and headed for Denver General. Even with all the traffic and slushy streets, it took me only about twenty-five minutes to get to the hospital.

CHAPTER TWO

ARRIVING AT DENVER GENERAL, I parked my Tahoe and ran in the emergency entrance to the admission desk. The woman at the desk looked up at me and smiled.

"May I help you?"

"Josh Garrett was just admitted here. Can you tell me where he is?"

The woman looked at the screen of her computer, then punched a few keys. She looked at the screen for a moment more, then looked up at me. From the look on her face, I was sure it was not going to be good news."

"Mr. Garrett has been taken to surgery. I'm sorry," she said with a tone in her voice that seemed to convey a degree of sincerity.

"Can you give me some idea of his condition?" I asked, knowing she probably wouldn't tell me anything.

"Are you a family member?" she asked.

"No. I'm a friend of his, a very good friend."

"I'm sorry, but I can't give out any information on a patient. I'm sorry. I've given you more information than I should."

It was frustrating to me; but I knew what the rules were, and there was nothing I could do about it. She couldn't give out any information on a patient without authorization from the patient or next of kin. The only possible consolation was she looked like she really was sorry she couldn't tell me anything. However, it was of little consolation to me.

"Thank you," I said then turned around.

As I looked around thinking about what I should do next, I noticed there was a small waiting room off to one side. I decided to go there, sit down and wait. Maybe if I waited for a while, I might be able to get some information on Josh's condition and possibly on what had happened.

While I sat in the waiting room, I couldn't help wondering what had happened in the café. I knew from Mac that Josh had been shot, but I had no idea why, or any of the circumstances. I didn't even have any information on what Josh's position was at the bank.

It had been several years since I had actually talked to Josh. I had no idea what he was doing, other than what he had told me in his Christmas cards and on the phone earlier today, which was very little. It had been several years since I had received a Christmas card from him. Most of the cards were just signed, but a few of them had a little, very little, about what he was doing and where he worked.

All I knew from his cards was he worked in a small bank up in the mountains, but at the moment I couldn't remember where the bank was located, or the name of the bank. I didn't even know if it was a branch bank or the main bank. The only thing I could remember was it was some-where around Dillion. I wasn't even sure he still worked at the same bank. I would have to check my old Christmas cards from him to find out the name of the bank and where it was located, but that would have to wait for now.

While I waited, I thought about Josh and remembered one of his Christmas cards from a few years ago. In the card he told me that he was married, but gave no indication if he had any children. I couldn't remember getting any cards with photos of him and his family on the Christmas card. I vaguely remembered getting a card with a picture of him and his wife.

I couldn't remember for sure where he actually lived. If I remembered correctly, he lived somewhere around Dillon, but I wouldn't swear to it. Even if it was Dillion, I wasn't sure if he still lived there.

I HAD BEEN WAITING for a little over an hour with all sorts of thoughts going through my head when a woman walked into the waiting room. She looked to be about Josh's age. She also looked a little familiar. It took me a minute to remember where I had seen her before. It suddenly came to me. I had seen her in a picture on one of Josh's Christmas cards from a number of years ago. I got up and walked across the room to the woman.

"Excuse me, but are you Mrs. Josh Garrett?"

When she looked up at me, I realize that I had met her, but it had been some time ago. I got the impression she didn't recognize me, but then I didn't really expect she would. It had been a lot of years since I had seen her. In fact, I was in college when she first started dating Josh. It was in my senior year of college.

"Yes," she said with a hint of hesitation.

"I'm Peter Blackstone."

"Oh, I remember you. Josh has talked about you. He was going to try to get together with you today. I'm Barbara Garrett, Josh's wife."

"Yes, I know. Josh and I were to meet in a little café on Broadway."

"I take it from what you just said you didn't meet?"

"No, I'm afraid we didn't. I got there just as he was taken away in the ambulance."

"Do you know what happened?" she asked her eyes seemed to be pleading for information, any information about her husband.

"No, not yet."

"Do you know how Josh is doing? All they have told me was that he was shot and he is in surgery. I haven't had a chance to talk to the doctor yet," she said.

I could hear the concern for her husband in her voice. She seemed to be holding up rather well, considering.

"No. They won't tell me anything. All I know is he is in surgery. I have no idea what his condition is," I said.

She looked off toward the door as if she was waiting for someone to come in and talk to her. I was thinking about Josh. I wondered if she knew why Josh wanted to talk to me, but I was hesitant to ask. It seemed like an inappropriate time. However, I thought it was important enough for me to know if for no other reason than to find out why Josh was shot, and if there might have been some sort of problem where he worked.

"I'm sorry to ask this of you at a time like this, but do you know what Josh wanted to talk to me about?"

She turned and looked at me. From the expression on her face, I got the impression she wasn't sure what I had asked.

"Do you know why Josh wanted to talk to me?"

She looked at me for a minute as if she had to think about what I had asked her. I got the impression from the look in her eyes and on her face that she might have some idea of why he wanted to talk to me but was reluctant to say anything. It took a minute for her to respond.

"No. He just told me that he needed to talk to someone about the bank where he worked."

"What about the bank?"

"He didn't go into any detail. The only thing I know is he seemed very concerned about something," she said.

"I'm sorry, but can this wait? I'm afraid I have other things on my mind right now."

"Of course," I said. "I will leave you to your thoughts."

At that moment, a doctor in scrubs came into the waiting room. He asked for Mrs. Garrett. After she stood up, he took her aside and talked softly to her. The only thing I could hear from their conversation was that Josh had been taken to the recovery room. That bit of information told me that he had survived the surgery, but gave me no indication what his condition might be and what his chances were of survival. I decided to wait a few more minutes in the hope that Mrs. Garrett would let me know what the doctor told her.

After the doctor had talked to Mrs. Garrett for a moment or two, I saw him look toward me. He said something to Mrs. Garrett, then left her standing in the hall as he walked toward me.

"Mr. Blackstone?"

"Yes."

"Mrs. Garrett asked me to tell you that Mr. Garrett came through the surgery well, and is currently in the recovery room. He will undoubtedly be there for some time. Since only the immediate family can see him there, you will not be able to see him. It will be awhile before he will be out of the recovery room and you will be able to talk to him."

"Thank you, Doctor. I might as well go home. Would you tell Mrs. Garrett that I will contact her later, and my prayers go with her and Josh?"

"Certainly," he said with a smile then turned and left the waiting room.

It was good news to know that the doctor thought Josh would survive the shooting. I watched as the doctor walked down the hall with Barbara. He was probably taking her to the recovery room to see Josh and spend a few minutes with him.

There was no sense in hanging around the hospital. My time would be better spent trying to find out what had happened in the cafe. The best place to find out what happened was to find Mac and have a talk with him.

I WALKED OUT OF THE HOSPTIAL, got into my Tahoe and headed back toward the café. I had no idea if Mac would still be there, but I didn't think he would be finished looking for evidence or talking to witnesses. That part of an investigation usually takes time.

When I drove up to the café, I could see the forensic team was still going over the café. I didn't see Mac anywhere around. A quick glance at my watch told me it had been longer than I thought since I talked to Mac. He had probably gotten what preliminary information was available, and what information had been gathered by the other officers on the scene from possible witnesses. He would probably go back to his office to put it together while he waited for the preliminary forensic report, and the report of Josh's condition from the hospital.

I drove over to Precinct One where Mac's office was located. I parked in one of the visitor's parking spaces then went inside. Sergeant Russell was on the duty desk.

"Well, what brings you here?" Sergeant Russell asked.

"I'm here to see Captain MacDonald. Is he in?"

"Yeah, but he's kind of busy. I'll let him know you're here. Have a seat."

"Thanks," I said then walked across the room to a bench along the wall and sat down while I waited for him to call Mac's office. It only took a few minutes before Sergeant Russell called me.

"Pete, he'll see you now."

"Thanks."

Russell pointed to the hall leading to Mac's office. It wasn't necessary for him to point me in the right direction because I knew where Mac's office was located. When I got to the door to Mac's office, I knocked.

"Come in," Mac said.

I opened the door and walked into his office. He smiled when he looked up at me.

"Hi. I was thinking I might give you a call," Mac said. "Thanks for saving me the trouble."

"I hope I can help."

"Do you have any idea why Mr. Garrett was shot?" Mac asked.

"No, not yet. I talked to his wife at the hospital, but she was not much help. She's got a lot on her mind right now."

"I'm sure. You said you were at the café to meet Garrett. Is that right?"

"Yes, but he didn't give me any reason for wanting to meet me there. I assumed it was just to talk, but about what, he didn't say," I said. "I knew him in college, but haven't seen him for a long time."

"There were two killed in the café. We found a connection between the two who were killed, but no connection of either of them to Garrett. At least not yet. Do you know of one?"

"No. As far as I know, Garrett was to meet with me alone. Were all the victims sitting together?"

"I don't think so, but they could have been. The tables are small and pretty close together in that café," Mac said.

"I have not been told what the names of the two killed were, or anything about them. Do you know who they were?"

"One was Mrs. June Franklin and the other was William North. Recognize either of the names?"

"No, I don't think so," I said thoughtfully. "What is the connection between the two killed?"

"We're not sure, but one witness said they were talking very quietly to each other. The witness said they seemed pretty friendly. She indicated they were trying to keep what they were talking about a secret. Based on their ID's, they both live here in Denver."

"The last I heard, Josh Garrett works for a bank. I believe it's in Dillon. As far as I know he also lives in Dillion. I'm not sure which bank he works at, but if I remember correctly he sells some kind of investment income plans, stocks and possibly insurance. I'm not sure just what he does, but that was what he wrote in a Christmas card a couple of years ago. All he said about his work when he called me earlier today was that he works in the 'investments business', but didn't say where or with what company," I said.

"That doesn't help me make any kind of a connection with the other victims. We still don't know what Mrs. Franklin or North did for a living."

"Do you have any idea who was the real target?" I asked.

"No, just an idea at this time."

"What's your idea?"

"If I had to bet on it, it would be the two that were killed," Mac said.

"What's your thoughts on that?" I asked.

"If it was the two that were killed, it could be a jealous husband, maybe a jealous wife or girlfriend. This one could be a hard one to figure out. I still haven't seen the forensic evidence. All we know at the moment is a 9mm handgun was used and nine shots were fired. It may be a couple of days before I have anything to really go on," Mac said.

"Who took the most rounds?"

"It looked like North was hit five times, the woman twice and your friend took two. Whoever the shooter was, he didn't miss. We haven't found a single spent round that didn't hit one of the three. We were lucky in that regard. There were a lot of people in the café even though it was the middle of the afternoon," Mac said.

"I tend to agree with you. I hope Josh can tell us something. He was in the recovery room when I left the hospital, but from what I gather it is still touch and go. According to the doctor, his chances look good if he survives the night."

"I guess I'll have a talk with Mrs. Garrett and see if she can shed some light on this. Is she still at the hospital?" Mac asked.

"She was when I left."

"Are you going to be looking into this?" Mac asked.

"Yeah. I think I'll do a little nosing around and see what I can find out. I doubt I will be able to find out much until Josh is able to talk to me. I would like to know why he seemed so desperate to talk to me."

"Keep me posted if you find out anything," Mac said.

"Will do," I said as I stood up.

I LEFT MAC'S OFFICE and returned to my office. There was nothing for me to do at the moment but to think about what had happened. If the two killed were the target, was Josh simply collateral damage, or had he seen something the shooter didn't want him to see? Maybe the shooter recognized Josh and thought Josh might have recognized him. Maybe the shooter thought Josh had heard something he didn't want him to hear.

Were all three of the victims the shooter's targets? With what little information I had, there was no way to know for sure. The only thing that seemed to make any sense at the moment was the thought that Josh was not the target.

The one thing making me think Josh might not have been the target was the fact the other male victim took five rounds. Someone had to be really pissed off to pump five rounds at close range into the man.

It also crossed my mind that Josh might have been the target, even though I thought there was a slim chance of it. But if Josh was the target, why had the other two been killed? Had they just been in the way? Were they shot to make it look like Josh was not the target? Were they shot because they heard something that might identify the shooter? Or were they there for the same reason Josh was there?

There was something in the back of my mind that made me think Josh might have been the target. It was probably the phone call I had received from him only a few hours before he was shot. The tone of his voice, the subtle hint of relief when I told him I would meet him and the fact he seemed in a hurry to see me, all seemed to lead me to that conclusion.

Then there were the comments his wife made in the hospital. The way she answered my questions hinted at a problem Josh might have been having at work. Unfortunately, Barbara couldn't, or wouldn't, tell me what the problem was that caused Josh to want to talk to me.

At the moment, all I could do was speculate about what was going on. Since there was nothing else I could do tonight to get some answers, I thought I would go home. I would give Mac a call in the morning and see what new evidence he might have by then.

Since I was expecting company for a late dinner and I didn't have anything prepared, I would have to stop at the grocery store on my way home.

I ARRIVED HOME after stopping at the grocery store in plenty of time to prepare a nice evening meal for Julie. I went right to work fixing one of my favorite meals, a meal I was sure Julie would like. It was barbequed ribs cooked slowly in a thick barbeque sauce with side dishes of buttered whole kernel corn, Parmesan potatoes and corn bread, all freshly made, and honey butter for the corn bread. It was the barbeque that took time to prepare. I prepared the barbeque first then put it in the oven to slow cook until Julie arrived.

I received a call from Julie at about ten minutes to twelve telling me that she was leaving the hospital. That gave me time to fix the potatoes, corn, and corn bread.

It was about ten after twelve when Julie arrived at my apartment. I met her at the door, gave her a kiss, then took her coat and hung it up in the front closet.

"It sure smells good in here. What are we having?"

"You'll just have to wait a few minutes to find out," I said as I leaned over and kissed her lightly on her lips.

I guided her to the table and had her sit down while I put the finishing touches on the meal and put it on the table. After setting the food on the table, I sat across the table from her.

"Wow. This must have taken you half the day to fix. It looks and smells wonderful."

"It didn't, but I figured you would be hungry."

"I'm starving," she said with a grin.

"Then dig in."

I watched her as she put food on her plate. She sampled the ribs first, then looked up at me and smiled.

"This is really good," she said then stuck her fork into another piece of the tender meat.

It seemed we were both hungry. We dug in and finished off the meal with very little conversation. Once we were finished, we leaned back and looked at each other.

"How was your day?" Julie asked.

"It was good up until about two-thirty, then it all went to hell."

"Oh? What happened?" she asked as the expression on her face turned serious.

"Remember I told you I had a meeting with a guy at two-thirty?"

"Yes."

"Well, I went to the café where we were to meet and found he had been shot."

"I scrubbed for surgery about three," Julie said looking at me with a concerned look on her face. "It was a man in his mid-thirties who had been shot twice."

"It was probably Josh Garrett. He had been taken to Denver General."

"That was his name. I saw it on his medical chart. He survived the surgery and was taken to the recovery room. Last I heard he was critical, but stable."

"From what little the doctor told me, that was what the doctor had told Josh's wife. I know you can't tell me anything about him, so I won't ask. There is nothing I can do until he comes around. Since that is the case, what do you say we clean up this mess so we can get some rest?"

"Sounds like a good idea to me," Julie said with a smile.

It didn't take us long to clear the table and get the kitchen cleaned up. Once all the remaining food had been put away and the dishes were in the dishwasher, we went into the bedroom.

"I could use a shower," Julie said.

"Would you like your back washed," I asked with a grin.

"Yes, I'd like that," she said with a smile.

It didn't take but a few minutes before we were out of our clothes and in the shower. Julie was not only beautiful, she was passionate, too. Her body felt warm and soft, yet it was firm. We used up most of the hot water before we got out and dried off. We went right to bed, but it was almost three in the morning before we finally drifted off to sleep in each other's arms.

CHAPTER THREE

WHEN I WOKE, the morning sun was sneaking into my bedroom through a slight gap in the curtains. There was a warm body curled up against my back and an arm wrapped around me. It had been a long time since I had the pleasure of waking up with a beautiful and sexy woman holding me in her arms. I could hear the soft, slow rhythmic sound of Julie breathing. I closed my eyes and drifted off to sleep again.

Sometime later I woke again to the feel of Julie's fingers slowly running circles through the hair on my chest. She must have realized I was awake because she kissed me lightly on the back of my neck.

"If you don't stop that, I might not let you out of this bed until noon," I said with a whisper.

"I might not mind that," she replied with a slight chuckle in her voice.

I was about to roll over to face her when our moment was totally ruined by the ringing of my phone. I looked over my shoulder. Julie was smiling at me as if she knew what I was thinking. I turned back around so I could reach out and pick up the phone.

"Hello."

"Pete?"

"Yeah."

"I didn't recognize your voice. Did I wake you?"

"No. What's up, Mac?"

"I just got word that Josh Garrett died sometime during the night or early this morning."

"What?" I asked as I immediately sat up. "I understood he was critical, but in stable condition."

"I guess he took a turn for the worse, as they say."

I wasn't sure what to say at that moment. All I could think about was what went wrong. Why did Josh die if he was doing so well?

"Pete? You still there?"

"Yeah. Mac, is there any possibility he was the target of the shooting?"

"Not that I know of. Why? What's on your mind?"

"If there is even the slightest possibility he was the target, then I think it would be wise to perform an autopsy on him to find out what caused his death."

"You think he was murdered? He was in the recovery room. No one is allowed in there except for the family," Mac said.

"And doctors and nurses and other hospital personnel," I reminded him. "It wouldn't be the first time someone was killed in a hospital by someone posing as a doctor, a nurse, or some other medical personnel, such as a lab tech, or by someone on the hospital staff."

Now the phone was silent from the other end. I waited for a minute to give Mac a chance to think about what I said. While I waited, I looked over my shoulder at Julie. She was looking at me and wondering what was going on.

"You just might be right," Mac said thoughtfully. "Either way, it's murder. If he was murdered in the hospital, we will know he was the target."

"Right."

"I'll call the hospital and put a hold on the body for the coroner. Talk to you later," Mac said, then the phone went dead.

I hung up the phone and just looked at it. Was it possible someone had gotten into the recovery room and killed him? It certainly would not have been the first time that had happened, even though it was fairly rare. My thoughts were disturbed by Julie before I could answer my own question.

"Peter, what's going on?" she asked with a concerned look on her face.

"Josh died last night."

She just looked at me. I had no idea what was going on in her head, but I could see by the look on her face that whatever it was, it bothered her.

"Julie, how was Josh doing last night when you left the recovery room?"

"He was holding his own."

"What does that really mean? It really sounds sort of meaningless."

"He was breathing on a respirator; his blood pressure was stable and his pulse was good. He had a couple of tubes in his chest to prevent fluids from building up in his lungs, but he was resting quietly."

"What kind of a prognosis did he have when you left?"

"The doctor felt he would make it. He said the surgery went well, and that Josh looked like he was in good physical condition. It was a good prognosis."

"Well, it apparently didn't go so well," I said.

"I'm sorry," Julie said. "But those things happen."

"I understand that, but I think an autopsy should be done on him. I want to know if he died from the gunshot wounds, or if he died from some other cause."

"I agree with you because he was doing so well when I was there. Do you think someone might have gotten into the recovery room and killed him?" Julie asked.

"I don't know, but I think it would be good to know what killed him."

"I think we should get up and have some breakfast. I'm sure you will have a lot to do today," Julie said with a hint of disappointment in her voice.

"Yes, but I need a shower. It will give me a chance to think."

"I'll get breakfast ready while you shower. I can take a shower after breakfast."

I went into the bathroom and took a warm shower. The phone call from Josh yesterday had disturbed me a little. Now, it looked like I had reason to be disturbed. I needed to talk to his wife as soon as possible. After our short talk in the hospital waiting room, I believed she knew why he wanted to talk to me. I didn't know if it had anything to do with the shooting, but it might. Since I didn't know where they lived, I would need to find out, then get a phone number so I could place a call to Josh's wife.

Once I finished with my shower, I got dressed. I was slipping my 9mm pistol in my belt holster as I walked into the kitchen. Julie glanced at it but didn't say anything. I knew how some wives of policemen didn't like the fact they carried a gun, but to go out in the world I worked in without one would be next to committing suicide, the same as it would be for any policeman.

"Breakfast is ready," she said.

I sat down to a slice of ham, some scrambled eggs, orange juice, toast and coffee, not my usual breakfast. I looked over the breakfast as Julie sat down across from me. She was wearing my bathrobe that I almost never wear.

"Maybe you should come over more often and spend the night. I don't usually have this nice a breakfast and served by someone wearing my robe," I said as I looked her over.

"I figured you are going to have a busy day, and you would need a good breakfast."

"Thank you," I said looking at the food on my plate. "I didn't know I had all that in the refrigerator."

"You're kidding?"

"Yes, I am," I said with a chuckle.

We ate breakfast, but didn't talk all that much. It seemed we were both caught up in our own thoughts, plus I was sure that we were both hungry after last night.

Once we had finished eating, I got up and took my dishes to the sink. When I turned around, Julie was looking at me.

"You don't have to do that," she said.

"I thought I would clean up while you take a shower and get dressed."

"You need to go to work. I know you have a lot on your mind, and you need to follow up on things. I'll take care of the kitchen. When I'm done, I'll take a shower and get dressed. I'll lock up when I leave."

"Are you sure?" I asked.

"Yes. Now give me a kiss, then get out of here. I have a few things I have to do this morning, too. I'm on the late shift again tonight."

"Thank you," I said as I took her in my arms and kissed her.

I let go of her then looked at her for a minute.

"Get going," she said with a smile. "And call me later."

"I will. Love you," I said, then turned and left my apartment.

As I walked to the garage, I noticed the weather had turned warmer and the wet snow from yesterday was almost gone. It was not unusual when we had an early snow. I got in my Tahoe and headed for my office. I couldn't help but think of Julie as I drove. She was something special.

I ARRIVED AT MY OFFICE shortly after eight. I parked the Tahoe in the underground parking garage then took the elevator up to the floor where my office was located. When I got off the elevator, I saw a woman with a nice figure standing with her back to me. I couldn't see her face until she turned around and looked at me. It was Josh's wife, Barbara. She looked like she had been crying, which was certainly understandable after what happened yesterday.

"Mrs. Garrett, I'm so sorry to hear Josh passed away last night. Please come inside."

I unlocked the door and held it open for her. Once she was inside my office, I closed and locked the door. The last thing I wanted was to be interrupted.

"Please, sit down," I said.

She sat down on a chair in front of my desk, clutching her purse on her lap. Instead of going around and sitting at my desk, I sat down on a chair next to her. I gave her a minute or so to gather her emotions before asking her any questions. She finally looked at me. Her eyes were bloodshot and her nose was a bit red. It was clear she had been crying for some time. I could certainly understand that. As far as I knew, Josh and Barbara were very close.

"Barbara, do you think you are ready to talk to me?"

"Yes," she said, but not very convincingly.

"Do you know what Josh wanted to talk to me about? Was he in some kind of trouble?"

She looked at me for a moment or two before she answered.

"Josh worked at the First National Bank in Dillon. He worked in the investment and insurance section of the bank. He helped people invest in different businesses or buy stocks. He also sold different kinds of insurance. He told me he had discovered some irregularities in a couple of the investment accounts in the bank."

"Do you know what kind of irregularities?"

"I don't really know. He didn't tell me," she said, then paused for a moment. "I think it had something to do with the bank's use of the money invested from those accounts, but I'm not real sure. I don't really understand those things."

I wondered what kind of investments the bank might have made that would cause Josh to think there was something that was not right.

"Do you know if he had any evidence of these irregularities?"

"I think he did, but I don't know what kind of evidence he might have had, or where he might have hidden it."

"What makes you think he had any evidence?"

"He said he wanted to talk to you about what he had discovered. If you thought there was something going on that wasn't right, he would show you what he had. That's all he would say about it, except if you thought there was something going on, he would ask for your help in deciding what to do about it."

"He didn't tell you what kind of evidence he had?"

"No. He told me it was safer for me if I didn't know anything."

If Josh was the principal target of the attack in the café, then he might have had good reason to be careful. The problem was he had not been careful enough. It was beginning to look like someone found out he suspected something was going on at the bank that was illegal, or at the very least unethical; and someone wanted to stop him before he could tell anyone what it was he had found.

"Have you been home since Josh was shot?"

"No. I've been staying with a friend here in Denver. I wanted to go with him when he went to meet you, but he said he didn't want me to come along. I'm sure he thought it would be dangerous for me," she said.

"It looks like he was right, and it was a good decision on his part," I said. "If Josh had some evidence of wrong doing at the bank, do you have any idea where he might have hidden the evidence?"

"No," she said after thinking about my question for a moment or so. "I wouldn't even know where to start looking because he never said what it was."

"If you don't mind, I would like to drive out to your home and take a look around. Do you have a problem with that?"

"No, I guess not," she said. "Do you think he had the evidence at our house?"

"I don't know, but it seems the most likely place for him to hide it. I seriously doubt he would keep it in his office at the bank."

"I hadn't thought about that," she admitted.

"Could I have a key to your house?"

"Yes," she said as she reached into her purse then handed me a key.

I took the key and put it in my pocket. Barbara wrote down the address of their home in Dillon and handed it to me. I knew from the address that their home was located on the shore of Dillon Reservoir. I then leaned back in the chair to think. She was kind enough not to disturb me while I thought about what she had said.

There was no proof Josh had been the primary target of the shooting in the café, but it was beginning to look like he might have been. For someone to go to such extremes as to shoot him in such a public place with so many people around, he had to have found something very important and very incriminating to someone.

I also wondered if what he found might put Barbara in danger. If whoever killed Josh thought Barbara might know something, then there was no doubt in my mind she might be the next person they would attempt to kill. I couldn't let that happen.

"Barbara, do you have a place where you can stay for a few days, preferably here in Denver?"

"I guess I could stay with my friends for a few days."

"Does anyone know where you have been staying?"

"No one other than my friends. I didn't tell anyone where we were going, when we would be back, or where we would be staying. Josh thought it would be better if we didn't tell anyone," she said.

"Good. Are your friends acquainted with anyone who might guess where you are staying?"

"I'm not sure, but I don't think so."

"Good. I don't want you to tell anyone where you are staying. I want you to go there and don't go outside. In fact, don't let anyone see you there. Tell your friends not to let anyone know you are there. I want you to stay inside and don't answer the door or the telephone. It might be a good idea if you stay away from any windows someone could use to see inside the house."

"Do you think - - - ," she started to say but couldn't complete the question.

"I don't know, but it's better to play it safe. At least until we have an idea of what is going on. I'll need the name and address of your friends here in Denver."

Barbara wrote down the names of her friends and their address on a piece of paper, then handed it to me. I put the paper in my pocket.

"What about Josh? I have to make arrangements for his funeral."

"That can wait. Right now, I'm going to get a friend of mine to take you to your friends' house. He's a real nice man, but more importantly he is an excellent bodyguard. He will see you safely to your friends' house, and he will stay with you until I can get there."

"Will you be gone long?" she asked.

"I'm not sure. I'm going out to your house first. I don't know where that might lead me, but I will be back, probably before dark."

"Okay. I guess if Josh could trust you, I can trust you."

"Good," I said with a smile as I stood up and walked around my desk.

I picked up the phone and called George Archer. I had worked with him on a case a little while back, and I just happened to be dating his sister. I explained the situation to George and what I wanted him to do. He said he was free and would come over to my office and pick up Barbara then stay with her until I joined them at Barbara's friends' home.

While we waited for George, we talked about Josh and his work at the bank. I knew he worked in the insurance and investment department of the bank. From what little Barbara had told me about what he did at the bank, it didn't help me understand why anyone would want Josh dead. He must have stumbled onto something. Something that was not only important to someone at the bank, but something that could cause someone a good deal of legal trouble if word of it got out.

My first thoughts were someone was either embezzling funds from those investing with the bank, or someone was laundering money through the bank. Either way, it could very easily be reason enough to kill anyone who found out about it.

It hadn't been very long since I had called George when I heard a light knock on the door to my office. I had Barbara move over in the corner away from the door while I slipped my hand under my sport coat and over my gun. I opened the door and found George standing there. It hadn't taken him very long to get to my office. I motioned for him to come in while I checked the hall before closing the door. I saw no one in the hall so I closed and locked the door.

"Barbara, this is George Archer. He is a friend of mine and a very good bodyguard. George, this is Barbara Garrett."

"Nice to meet you. I wish it was under better circumstances," George said politely, then turned and looked at me.

"You know what I want you to do," I said to George. "Take her out through the parking garage and make sure no one sees you leave. Make sure you are not followed."

"Got it," he said then turned to Barbara. "Are you ready to go, Mrs. Garrett?"

"Yes," she replied softly.

I watched as George took Barbara by the arm and led her out of my office. She was in good hands now leaving me free to do what I had to do. As long as she was with George, it was one less thing I had to worry about. That would leave me free to look into what was going on.

My first stop was to drive out to her house and have a look around. I had no idea what I might find, but at the moment I couldn't think of any place else to start.

CHAPTER FOUR

THE DRIVE TO DILLON was pleasant. A trip into the mountains west of Denver was always a nice change of scenery for me, even if it was for business. The sun was shining and what little snow there was in the mountains was rapidly melting as the day was warm after a couple of days of cold wet weather.

As I drove along Interstate 70, I kept watch to make sure no one was following me. I had no idea who might have seen me at the café, or in the hospital, or who might know Josh had been in Denver to see me.

When I turned off the interstate at the Dillon exit, I thought it might be a good idea if I was to give Sheriff Tom Stillwell a call and let him know I was working in his area again. It had been my practice to talk to the local law enforcement agency when I worked on their turf. It could save some problems since I carry a gun. I had found the sheriff to be very helpful the last time I had a case that took me into his county.

When I turned onto the street where Josh's house was located, I pulled over to the curb and stopped. I did not park right in front of the Garrett house, but from where I parked I could see the front of it clearly.

There was nothing special about the house that caused it to grab my attention, so I called Sheriff Stillwell using my cell phone. It didn't take but a minute or so before he was on the phone.

"Well, Peter, what brings you back up here? You on another case?"

"I'm not sure what is going on, but I would like you to meet me at the Garrett residence over on Aspen Drive. I would like a little company when I go inside to look around."

"Are you expecting trouble?" he asked with a concerned tone in his voice.

"No. But if a neighbor should call about a stranger entering the Garrett home, I would like you to already know about it."

"Give me about twenty minutes and I'll be there," he said, then hung up.

While I waited, I looked at the house. It was a ranch style house with a two-car attached garage, but with a hint of Scandinavian style in the trim. It looked like it had been well maintained. There was a brick flower bed across the front which appeared to have been prepared for a long winter. If I had to guess, the house was probably less than twenty years old. The yard had the appearance of a well-cared-for yard and looked like it had been landscaped by a professional. I could see small areas of snow where the sun hadn't melted it away yet.

IT TOOK SHERIFF STILLWELL just short of twenty minutes to pull up behind my Tahoe in an unmarked sheriff's car. At first, I wondered how he knew it was me, but when I looked up and down the street it became obvious. My Tahoe was the only vehicle parked on the street for two blocks either side of Garrett's home. Stillwell got out of his sheriff's car, walked up on the passenger's side of my Tahoe, opened the door and got in.

"It's good to see you again, Stillwell. And thanks for coming."

"I think we know each other well enough that you can call me, Tom.

"Okay, Tom."

"I take it you've been watching the Garrett house since you called."

"That would be correct."

"Have you seen any action around the house?"

"None so far. There has only been two vehicles drive by the house since I got here. Neither one of them seemed to show any interest in the house or me. One was a minivan with a woman driving and two kids in the back. The other looked like some kid with his girlfriend in a rather expensive convertible. Probably his father's car."

"I'm sure. Are you expecting any trouble at the Garrett house?"

"I'm not sure," I said. "But I wouldn't be surprised if someone might want to get hold of Mrs. Garrett."

"You might want to explain what's going on," Tom said as he looked at me.

I spent the next few minutes telling him what I knew, which wasn't much. I then explained what little information I had from Mac and Josh's widow.

"I see your interest. I take it you want to go inside the house."

"That would be correct. I have Mrs. Garrett's permission. In fact, she gave me the key to the house just this morning," I said as I showed him the key.

"Why isn't she here with you?"

"I have only my gut feeling to go on, but I think she might be in danger. I have her staying with a friend of hers in Denver, and with a bodyguard friend of mine to keep an eye on her and protect her," I explained.

Tom sat there looking out the windshield of my Tahoe at the Garrett house. I didn't know what he was thinking, but if I had to guess it was about going into the house without a warrant, or at the least written permission from Mrs. Garrett. I knew Tom to be a by-the-book type of lawman.

"Well, do we go in together or do I go in alone?" I asked.

Tom looked at me for a moment before he commented, "Are you sure you have her permission?"

"Yes. As I said, she gave me the key herself while she was in my office this morning," I said as I held the key up again for him to see.

"Okay. Let's go in and see what we can find, but you're in big trouble if you don't have her permission," Tom warned me.

"I understand, but I do have her permission," I assured him.

I started my Tahoe and drove it into the driveway of the Garrett home and stopped in front of the garage. We got out and walked up to the front door. I put the key into the lock and turned it. It unlocked the door. I took a pair of surgical gloves from inside my sport coat pocket and put them on. Tom looked at me and smiled.

"I don't want to leave fingerprints all over the place just in case this turns out to be a murder case."

"Do you think it is a murder case?" Tom asked.

"I'm not sure at this point, but it very well could be. I would rather be safe than sorry. Besides, I don't know what we will find once we go in the house."

"Okay, let's go in."

I reached out and turned the doorknob and the door opened. I glanced at Tom, then stepped inside and got one hell of a surprise. From the entryway, I could see into the living room. The entire living room had been totally trashed.

"I guess this helps support your case for there being something amiss here," Tom said.

"It sure as hell does. I wonder if whoever did this found what he was looking for."

"I think I should get a forensic team out here."

"I'm going to look around a bit," I said as I held my hands up so he could see the surgical gloves I was wearing.

"I left mine in the car. I'll just follow you around and not touch anything."

Tom looked at me, I nodded and walked into the living room. I began a systematic search of the room, being very careful not to mess up anything that might contain a clue as to who had trashed the place, and possibly why. The hardest part of searching the house for something was the fact that I had no idea what I was looking for, but I hoped to find something that would give me a clue to what was going on.

"Do you have some idea what you are looking for?" Tom asked.

"No, not even a hint. It could be a tape, either voice or video, or it could be papers or a ledger, or a DVD or a flash drive from a computer. Frankly, I don't know what I'm looking for."

"That makes it kind of hard to find," he said as he looked around.

"While I'm looking around here, why don't you check out the other rooms? See if Josh had a home office or a work room of some kind. You get the idea."

"Sure."

As soon as Tom left the living room, I started looking for some place where Josh might hide something fairly small, although I had no idea how big it might be. There was no need to search the end tables that had drawers in them. The drawers were already pulled out and were on the floor empty. I didn't take but a few minutes to look over the insides of the tables for anything that might have been taped to the inside, but I found nothing.

I found a vase that had been smashed on the stone hearth of the fireplace. I couldn't tell if it was smashed out of frustration, or to find out if there was something inside it. The cushions from the sofa and chairs were all over the room, several of them had been cut open. Books that had been on the bookshelves had been pulled off the shelves and were lying scattered around on the floor below the shelves. Someone had gone to a lot of trouble searching the room. It appeared they had done a pretty good job of it.

Just then, Tom walked back into the living room. The look on his face told me that he had found nothing that would help me.

"Every room in the house looks just like this one. Whoever was in here did a thorough job of searching the place. He had to have been inside the house for some time to have searched every room, probably over two or three hours, maybe more. It would be my guess that whoever it was didn't find what they were looking for," Tom said.

"I would have to agree with you. Did you look in the garage?"

"Yeah. There's a car in the garage that was apparently searched, too. Even the freezer had been searched. There were packages of food torn open and scattered around the garage floor. There apparently had been two cars in the garage, but there is only one now."

"If there is one car in the garage, it would mean Mrs. Garrett was in Denver when Josh was shot," I said.

"How so?"

"Josh was at the café. He had to have either driven himself there, or Mrs. Garrett drove him there and returned to her friend's home with his car, or he took a cab from Mrs. Garrett's friend's home. If he drove there himself, Mrs. Garrett's friend would have probably driven her to the hospital, but I didn't see her with anyone. If Josh drove himself, I wonder where his car is now."

"Maybe you should call Mac and see if he knows. If he doesn't, he could put out an APB on it in the hope of finding it," Tom suggested.

"I was thinking the same thing."

I reached for my cell phone and placed a call to Mac's office. It only took a couple of minutes before Sergeant Russell answered his phone.

"Sergeant Russell, is this an emergency?"

"No, Sergeant. This is Peter Blackstone. I would like to talk to Captain MacDonald.

"I'll transfer you," he said.

"Captain MacDonald, how may I help you?"

"Mac, Peter."

"What's up, Pete?"

"I'm at the Garrett home in Dillon with Sheriff Tom Stillwell."

"What are you doing there?"

"I came in the hope of finding out why Josh wanted to talk to me. What I found was the entire house, including the garage, has been trashed."

"No kidding. Someone must have wanted something pretty bad. Do you think they might have found what they were looking for?"

"Neither Tom nor I think they found anything of interest to them. If they had found something, they would not have searched the entire house, garage and the car in the garage," I explained.

"I agree," Mac said. "What is your next move?"

"I plan to talk to Mrs. Garrett. But for now, I have a question for you."

"Okay, shoot."

"We found one of Garretts' cars here in the garage. Do you happen to know where the car he drove to the café is now?"

"No. I just assumed that Mrs. Garrett had it," Mac said.

"I would like to know where that car is. If he drove it to the café, it may still be parked near there. It might have something in it that would help us find out what is going on. He came to see me about some problems with the bank where he worked. He might have had the evidence of it in the car so he could at least show it to me, if I agreed to help him."

"I see your point. Do you know if Mrs. Garrett has the car with her?"

"No, I don't, but I doubt it. She left my office with my bodyguard. I would like you to put an APB out for the car. If you find it, impound it in a very secure place. I'm coming back to Denver to talk to Mrs. Garrett again," I said.

"Do you know where she is?"

"Yes. I have her in a safe place with a bodyguard."

"Good. I'll get right on it. Call me when you get back to town."

"Will do," I said then hung up.

I looked at Tom. He was standing in the doorway looking over the living room. He turned and looked at me.

"I take it you're going back to Denver."

"Yes. I need to talk to Mrs. Garrett. I don't think it is a good idea to tell her by phone what happened here. She's scared enough."

"I agree. I'll get a forensic team out here to see what we can find," Tom said.

"Good. I'll call you later."

Tom nodded as I turned and walked out the door. He followed me out of the house making sure the door didn't lock. As I got in my Tahoe, I could see Tom get in his car. He sat there for a moment or so. I could see he was on the radio. I was sure he would remain on the scene until the forensic team arrived.

I waved at him as I drove by on my way back to Denver. I didn't see anyone following me, and the scenery was beautiful. It gave me plenty of time to think about what I had seen in Josh's house.

I wondered what it was Josh had found at the bank that would cause someone to trash his home. Were they trying to scare him, or were they really looking for something Josh might have, or thought he had? I doubted they were trying to scare him since he was shot twice. I had a lot of questions running through my head, but I didn't have any answers.

CHAPTER FIVE

I ARRIVED AT THE HOUSE where Mrs. Garrett was staying. It was a large two-story house with a nicely manicured lawn and a few large trees. It had the look of a home that was owned by someone with money.

I had just stepped up on the porch when the front door was opened by George. He was slipping his gun back under his coat.

"Any trouble?"

"No. Just making sure it was you," he said with a grin.

"Anything going on here?"

"Mrs. Wallace is not very happy I'm here. I think Mr. Wallace understands, though. I guess Mrs. Wallace doesn't like guns in her house."

"I can understand that. I think it would be wise for us to move Mrs. Garrett to a different location," I said.

"I take it there's a reason for the move?"

"I think we need a more secure place. Mrs. Garrett's house in Dillon was ransacked, and I mean the entire house including the garage and car. I think Josh must have been onto something. I don't know what it is, but if whoever is involved thinks Mrs. Garrett might know something, she could be in danger. From the looks of this house, it is probably not all that secure. Plus, I don't think we want to put her friends in danger by hiding her here."

"Sounds good. How about I take her to my place?"

I had helped George move from his apartment to a house only a few weeks ago. I knew it would be more secure than his apartment would have been.

"Your new house is a lot more secure than it is here."

"I'll get her," George said, then turned and went back in the house.

I nodded then stepped into the living room. It looked as if it was decorated by a professional decorator. It was also spotless. The house was probably cleaned by a professional, or they had a live-in housekeeper.

I was interrupted in my looking over the living room when George returned with Mrs. Garrett. They were followed by a couple I assumed were Mrs. Garrett's friends.

"This is Mr. and Mrs. Wallace," George said. "Kathryn and John Wallace."

"How do you do. I'm Peter Blackstone."

"Mr. Blackstone, what is going on? I'm not thrilled with your bodyguard being in my house," Mr. Wallace said without acknowledging my introduction.

"I can understand that, Mr. Wallace. We will be taking Mrs. Garrett to a safe location until we find out what is going on. I have reason to believe she might be in some danger."

"What could possibly make you think that?" Mr. Wallace asked rather sharply.

"Excuse me, but at this point I would rather not say. I think the less you know the better it is for you and your wife."

"Well, maybe I should just call the police," Mr. Wallace said looking at me with squinted eyes.

"Mr. Wallace, you do what you think you need to do. If you insist on calling the police, you might want to talk to Captain MacDonald at Precinct One. He is handling the investigation of Josh Garrett's death. I'll give you his phone number, if you like."

"Peter," George said softly. "We have company."

I turned and looked out the window. A dark blue Cadillac sedan had just pulled up to the curb and two men were getting out of the car. They looked around then started up the walk toward the house.

"Mr. Wallace, do you know those men?"

Mr. Wallace looked out the window then turned and said, "No. I've never seen them before."

"George, duck into the dining room. Take Barbara with you. Mr. Wallace, take your wife and go upstairs quickly, and keep quiet. I don't want them to see you or hear you. It's for your own safety."

I slipped my gun out from under my sport coat and held it out of sight at my side. While Mr. and Mrs. Wallace went upstairs and George took Mrs. Garrett into the dining room, I moved over next to the door and waited for the two men to come to the door. They rang the doorbell, but I waited for a moment or two before I opened the door.

"Can I help you?" I asked.

"We're looking for a Mrs. Barbara Garrett. We understand she is staying here," the taller of the two men said very politely.

I noticed that the shorter man continued to look around the room.

"I'm sorry, but there is no one here by that name. You must have the wrong address."

"I don't think so. May we come in?" the tall man asked politely.

"Sure," I said as I stepped back, keeping the door in front of my hand holding the gun, then let them into the entryway.

As they walked past me, they were focused on the living room as if looking to see if there was anyone else in the house. I drew my gun away from my side and pointed it at them.

"I think that's about far enough," I said.

The two men turned around and quickly froze in place when they saw I had a gun on them.

"What's this all about?" the tall man said. "All we're doing is looking for Mrs. Garrett."

"You want to tell me why you are looking for her?"

"I don't think that is any of your business," the tall man said.

"I'm making it my business."

I noticed the shorter man had not said anything, but was looking very hard at my gun. I got the impression that he was thinking he might try to take it away from me. I thought it would be a good idea to discourage him.

"George, if either of these two men so much as twitches, shoot 'um," I said and looked directly at the shorter man.

When George didn't say anything, the shorter man started to grin and began to look like he might try to jump me. I was ready for him, just in case he tried.

"Do you want me to kill him, or just wound him," George asked calmly.

"Either way is all right by me," I replied without looking toward George.

The sudden realization that there really was someone behind them showed in the fear on the both men's faces. George's voice was enough to take any thoughts the shorter man might have had about relieving me of my gun. I also noticed that he was no longer grinning.

"Up against the wall and spread 'um," I ordered. "I'm sure you know the drill."

Neither of the two men hesitated. They reached out and put their hands on the wall. I patted them down while George kept his gun on them. The search resulted in finding three guns. The one doing the talking had a 9mm handgun under his coat. The short, silent one had a .45 caliber under his coat and a small .38 caliber pistol in an ankle holster. I placed the guns on a small table near the entryway.

"Gentlemen, I suggest you keep your hands on the wall. George gets a little nervous about holding a gun on guys like you."

I stepped back away from the two thugs, but didn't take my eyes off them. I reached down and picked up the phone on a small desk in the hall near the front door just outside the living room. I placed a call to Mac. It was quickly transferred to Mac.

"Captain MacDonald, how can I help you?"

"This is Peter."

"What's up, Pete?"

"I've got a couple of thugs who are looking for Mrs. Garrett. I would appreciate it if you would stop by and pick them up."

"Sure thing," Mac said. "Where are you?"

I told Mac where I was then hung up the phone. If I knew Mac, he would have a black-and-white police car sent to my location within minutes.

Since the thugs had not seen George, I decided it was time to get Barbara out of there before the police arrived. I leaned over next to the dining room door, close to where George was standing. While watching the two thugs, I mouthed what I wanted George to do. He nodded that he understood.

I stepped away from the dining room door to a position where I could see both the thugs and George. He had Barbara in tow as he quietly led her toward the back of the house and on out the backdoor. It only took George a moment to silently get Barbara out of the house. I knew where he was going to take Barbara, and I knew he would call me later to let me know that he had her secure at his home.

While I waited for the police, I saw Mr. Wallace sneak a peek down the stairs. I quickly motioned for him to get back. I didn't want these guys to see him.

After about eight minutes, I heard a siren. The next thing I saw out of the corner of my eye was a black-and-white police car pulling up in front of the house. Two police officers got out of the police car and ran up to the house with guns in hand. When they got to the door, they didn't knock. Instead, they called out to me.

"Mr. Blackstone, this is the police."

"Come in, officers, and don't shoot. I'm the one holding a gun."

The door slowly opened and two officers entered the house cautiously, with guns in hand. They didn't really know what they were getting into. When they saw the two men leaning against the wall, they relaxed a little. The lead officer, looked at me.

"Are you Blackstone?"

"Yes," I said as I held out my ID so he could see it.

"Captain MacDonald called us to come here to give you some assistance," the lead officer said. "He'll be along in a few of minutes."

"You can cuff these two," I suggested.

I stepped back and watched them cuff the two men. As soon as they were cuffed and searched, the lead officer gave them their rights while the other officer watched them. With everything under control and in the hands of the police, I slipped my gun back into my holster. It was only a moment or so after they were cuffed when Mac showed up.

"Well, Pete, what do we have here?" Mac said as he looked at the two men wearing handcuffs.

"It seems these two had it in mind to grab Mrs. Garrett."

"That's not true," the taller of the two men said.

"You shut up. I'll get to you later," Mac said.

"They marched in here carrying guns," I said as I pointed to the three guns on the table near the entryway. "You don't come to just talk to someone caring guns."

"I'll take them downtown and book them for unlawful entry of a private dwelling, carrying concealed weapons without a permit, and I'll figure out something else when we get them downtown," Mac said then turned to the two officers.

"Take them in and book 'um, for unlawful entry of a private dwelling and have their car impounded. I want that car gone over by forensic. Give them their rights, but don't question them or let them call for an attorney until I get there. I'll be there in a little while to talk to them," Mac said to the lead officer.

"Yes, sir," the lead uniform officer replied.

"And take their guns with you. Send them to the lab for ballistic tests. I want to know everything there is to know about those guns."

The officers nodded that they understood then took the guns and their prisoners out of the house. I could see them being put in the backseat of the police car.

As soon as the two thugs were taken away by the police, I called Mr. and Mrs. Wallace to come downstairs. I noticed when they came down the stairs, Mrs. Wallace was sort of hiding behind her husband. I guess I couldn't blame her. It isn't every day that you have some thugs arrested in your home.

"Mac, this is Mr. and Mrs. John Wallace. Mr. Wallace, this is Captain MacDonald with the Denver Police Department."

"What's going on Captain MacDonald? All these men coming into my house with guns," Mr. Wallace asked, but without the sharpness he had shown me earlier.

"First of all, we are not sure what is going on. However, we do think that Mrs. Garrett may be in danger," Mac said.

"Why would you think she is in danger?" Mrs. Wallace asked.

It was clear from the look on Mrs. Wallace's face that she was worried she and her husband might be in danger, too.

"Mrs. Wallace, we don't know why she might be in danger at this time, but we are not taking any chances," Mac said.

"It has to do with the death of Josh, doesn't it?" Mr. Wallace asked.

"I'm sorry, but we have told you as much as we can at this time," Mac said. "I would hope you say nothing about what happened here to anyone, not even your best friends or your neighbors."

"Are we in danger because Barbara was here?" Mrs. Wallace asked, her concern showing on her face.

"I don't think so," I said. "You have no knowledge of where Mrs. Garrett is so you don't know anything that would help them find her."

"But do they know that?" Mr. Wallace asked with a worried look on his face.

"I'm sure they do. The two men who were here knew that Mrs. Garrett was here. Now they know that she is no longer here. They also know that we would not tell anyone living in this house where she was taken. Therefore, they have no reason to come back here," I explained.

"If it would make you feel better, we will keep an eye on your house for a few days." Mac added.

"I would feel better knowing there is a policeman nearby," Mrs. Wallace said.

"You will be seeing police cars cruising the neighborhood much more often for the next week or so, especially at night," Mac said.

"Thank you," Mrs. Wallace said.

"Don't hesitate to call the police if you see anything that seems suspicious or doesn't look right. We will keep a unit in the area so they can respond quickly."

"Thank you. I'm sure we will feel more secure knowing the police will be around," Mr. Wallace said.

"I've got to be going," Mac said.

"Me, too," I said, then turned and left the house.

Once outside, I walked toward my Tahoe. Mac was walking beside me.

"I went to the Garrett home in Dillon," I said. "Someone was looking for something. The house was trashed. There wasn't a room in the house that hadn't been searched."

"Any idea what they were looking for?"

"None. The only thing I even have an inkling of is that it has something to do with First National Bank in Dillon. What it is, I have no idea."

"What did Josh do at the bank?" Mac asked.

"He had something to do with investments and insurance. At least that was the department he worked in. I'll need to talk to Barbara and see if she can give me more information about what he actually did there."

"Do you know where she is now?"

"No. My assistant took her from the Wallace house before you got here. He took her out the back way so the two you arrested didn't see them," I said.

It wasn't a complete lie. I did know where he was taking her, but I doubted that he had gotten there, yet.

"Let me know when she can talk to me. In the meantime, I'll see what I can get out of the two we have, but don't expect much. They're probably used to being arrested and won't talk to the police without a lawyer. Talk to you later," Mac said.

"I'll call you later," I said then turned and went to my Tahoe.

I got in my vehicle and started it as I looked toward the Wallace house. There were two things that bothered me. The first was how did the two men Mac arrested find out where Mrs. Garrett had been staying so quickly? The second was, who was it that trashed Josh's house in Dillon? Did something found in Garrett's house lead them to the

Wallace's home? Not having any answers, I drove away and headed back to my office.

WHEN I ARRIVED AT MY OFFICE, I sat down and checked my caller ID. It had two phone calls on it. The first one was from George. The second one was from a number I didn't recognize. I checked my answering machine and found only one caller had left a message. It was not George. I smiled to myself. George was smart enough not to leave messages where someone might be able to hear it.

I reached over and picked up my phone and called George's cell phone. It was answered on the second ring.

"Hi. I thought you would like to know we are here and we are safe."

"Sure thing. I take it Barbara is with you," I said.

"Yes, she is. She was a little shaken by the two men who came to her friend's home, but she has settled down a bit and is resting at the moment."

"Okay."

"She will be safe here. Those two at the Wallace house never saw me so they won't know who was behind them. Here, I can see anyone coming toward the house for some distance in most directions."

"Good. I don't want her to be seen by anyone."

"Got it," George said.

"Do you need anything?"

"No. We're all set for a while."

"Good. Call me if you need anything. I'll talk to you later," I said.

"Right," George said then hung up.

I decided I would check to see what the other call was all about. I pressed the button on the answering machine and listened to the message.

"Mr. Blackstone, this is Ralph Garrett, Josh's brother. I understand you know where my sister-in-law is. I would like to talk to her as soon as possible. Please call me back," the voice said on the answering machine, then left a number.

The number was from an exchange that was not familiar to me. It was not a local Denver area number. I looked through the telephone book, but didn't find the exchange number in it. The only thing I could think of was the call had been made on a cell phone, probably a no contract cell phone.

My thoughts turned to Josh and what I could remember about him and his family. I had met his only brother when we were in college, but I didn't think his name was Ralph. I couldn't remember his name, but I was reasonably sure it wasn't Ralph. The more I thought about it, it could have been Ralph, because I knew him by a nickname I couldn't remember at the moment. I would have to ask Barbara what Josh's brother's name is before I call back.

I reached over and picked up my phone. I placed a call to George's cell phone. The phone rang only a couple of times before it was answered.

"What's up, Peter?"

"I got a phone call from someone claiming to be Josh's brother. I need to talk to Barbara."

"Sure. Just a minute," George said.

I heard him set the phone down. It was just a moment or two before Barbara picked up the phone.

"Yes, Mr. Blackstone?"

"I got a call from someone claiming to be Josh's brother, Ralph. I didn't remember that Josh's brother's name was Ralph. Could you fill me in on him?"

"Josh did have a brother named Ralph, but he died in an auto accident about four years ago in California. If you knew him from when you were in college, everybody called him, Ruff."

"Ruff?"

"Yes. I'm not sure why or how he got the nickname."

"Thank you," I said as I thought about what she told me.

"Why would someone call you saying he was Ralph?" Barbara asked.

"I don't know for sure, but it might have been to find out where you are. Why, I don't know."

"Oh," she said, but I think she understood at least a little.

"By the way, how are things going with you and George?"

"He is really nice. He is taking good care of me."

"Good. If you need anything, he will get it for you."

"Mr. Blackstone, how long will I have to be here?"

"To be honest, I really don't know. We still haven't figured out what it was Josh discovered at the bank. Is there anything you can think of that might help us figure it out?"

"Not that I can think of," she said after taking a moment to think about it. "I have told you all I know about what Josh told me. However, if I think of anything else, I'll let George know. Would that be all right?"

"Yes, that would be fine. I'll talk to you later."

"Do you want to talk to George again?"

"Not unless he needs to talk to me."

"He says he doesn't need to talk to you right now," Barbara said.

"Okay," I said then hung up.

As soon as I hung up, my thoughts turned to the phone call on my answering machine. If Ralph had died about four years ago in California, the caller must have been someone who didn't think I would know that, or he didn't know it himself. It was probably a case of the caller not knowing about Ralph's death. The truth was I didn't know it until I talked to Barbara.

As I thought about the call, I was reasonably sure the caller had a pretty good idea that I knew where Barbara was, or at the very least I had contact with her. It had to be someone who knew Josh had talked to me, or was going to talk to me.

A quick look at my watch showed me it was getting late, and my stomach told me it was time to get something to eat. I knew Julie had to work late tonight. I thought about calling her, but I had no way of knowing if she would be in surgery. However, I remembered she had told me to give her a call. I reached over and picked up the phone. It rang three times before it was answered.

"Hi. Are you done for the day?" Julie asked.

"Yes. How are things going for you?"

"It looks like I might have a busy night. There was a car accident with several serious injuries on I-70. It looks like I will be going into surgery shortly. Would you be too upset if I don't come over tonight?"

"No. It's been a long day for me, too. I'll call you tomorrow," I said

"Not too early. I plan to sleep in."

"Okay. I'll call you sometime after noon, but don't hold me to that in case I get tied up with something."

"Okay. I've got to go, they're calling me to the OR. Love you," she said.

"Love you, too," I said, then hung up.

As soon as I hung up, I left my office and headed for home. I had a quick dinner, watched a little television then went to bed. It wasn't long and I was off in dreamland.

CHAPTER SIX

IT WAS A LITTLE BEFORE SEVEN when I woke. I hadn't planned to get up that early, but I had a lot on my mind. Josh had come to me for help, but I didn't know what kind of help he needed. Now that he was dead, I felt compelled to find out who killed him and why was he killed.

Since I was not going to sleep any more, I got up and fixed my breakfast. While I ate my breakfast, I thought about what had happened so far. It had become clear someone knew I was interested in what happened to Josh. I had no idea who it was, and finding out could prove to be difficult. I would have to keep an eye out for anyone following me.

My thoughts turned to Josh. While I was eating, I took the time to make mental notes of where to start looking for the reason Josh was murdered. I decided the best place to start was at the bank where he worked. I would like to find out who his friends were and what he did at the bank.

When I finished breakfast, I went out and got in my Tahoe. I headed for Dillon to pay a visit to the First National Bank of Dillion. It was a pleasant drive even though I kept a watch for anyone who might be following me. I didn't see anyone.

I ARRIVED AT THE BANK in Dillion a little after ten in the morning. When I walked in the front door, I noticed there were very few people in the bank at that hour. I looked around. I was looking for someone who might be willing to talk to me, but didn't see anyone who I thought might be a friend of Josh's. It wasn't until I noticed a young woman sitting at a desk in the corner that I thought just might be the one to help me. The fact that she was sitting very close to a door that had Josh's name on it might have been a clue.

The young woman wiped her eyes and then blew her nose. I couldn't be sure, but it looked like she was crying. However, she just might have a cold, or she was allergic to something. I decided to take a chance and walked over to her desk.

When I got to her desk, I just stood there for a moment looking at her. Her eyes were red, which was a pretty good clue she had been crying. She looked up at me and took a moment to wipe her eyes again before she spoke to me.

"May I help you, sir?"

"My name is Peter Blackstone. I would like to talk to someone who might have known Mr. Josh Garrett. Someone who worked closely with him here in the bank. Might that someone be you?" I asked, trying to speak softly.

She just sat there for a moment looking at me. From the look on her face, I got the impression she was afraid to talk to me. I could see her hands trembling and the fear in her eyes. With what had happened yesterday, I could certainly understand her fears.

"I have been a longtime friend of Josh and his family. You have no need to be afraid of me," I said softly in the hope of calming her fears while making sure no one else could hear me.

She looked around the room as if looking to see if someone was watching us. She then looked back at me and took a deep breath.

"Is Mr. Garrett really dead?" she asked afraid that what she had heard was true.

"Yes, I'm afraid so," I said quietly. "Did you know him well?"

"Yes. I'm, - - or was - - his secretary," she said with a sniffle.

"Is there somewhere we could go where we could talk privately?"

Just then I heard someone in street shoes coming up behind me. I also noticed the young woman in front of me looked away. I turned and saw a man in a suit coming across the room toward us. The expression on his face was one of concern, but for what reason I had no idea. His eyes kept going from looking at the young woman to looking at me.

"Is there something I can help you with?" he said rather sharply as he stopped only a few feet from me.

I had no idea why he was so sharp with me, and why he had such a serious look on his face. It was the kind of look a manager might have toward a customer who he felt was harassing one of his employees; or maybe someone who was afraid of what I had been told, or might be told, by the young woman at the desk.

"No. I was just asking her a few questions about an investment program since Mr. Garrett is not in this morning."

"Oh," he said looking at me as if he wasn't sure he should believe me. "I'm sorry to inform you that Mr. Garrett was killed in Denver. He was shot in a restaurant by some crazed man who shot him and two other people. He was just in the wrong place at the wrong time," he said in a very professional manner.

He sounded like he had rehearsed his statement. The man seemed to be going to great lengths to make it a point of telling me that Josh was collateral damage and not the intended target, but I knew better.

"Oh. Was that the shooting in the café in downtown Denver?" I asked.

"Yes, sir. Is there anything I can do to help you? I will be handling all his accounts until we find a suitable replacement."

"And you are?"

"I'm Wilbur Routh. I'm the assistant manager of the Investments and Insurance Department of the bank," he said with an air of importance. "If you have any questions about your account, I will be more than happy to check your file and discuss any concerns you might have," he said very professionally.

"Actually, I don't have an account here at this time. I was to talk to Mr. Garrett about opening an account this morning, and possibly look into some investments, if I found any that would interest me."

"Did you have an appointment? I didn't see an appointment on his calendar."

"No, I didn't really have an appointment. I had told him I would come in sometime today to talk about it. At the time I talked to him, I didn't know when I would be available to discuss an investment, just that it would be sometime today. As you can see, I found some time to talk to him this morning, but I guess I'm too late."

"I would be more than happy to talk to you about what we have to offer and open an account for you."

"I think I'll wait a few days. I want to think about it," I said.

Mr. Routh didn't look like he was too pleased with me, but then I wasn't interested if he was pleased or not.

"I understand, but I will be happy to help you with any investments or any insurance needs you may have when you are ready."

"I'm sure. I'll keep that in mind. Thank you, Mr. Routh."

I turned and nodded to the young woman, then left the bank. I walked to my Tahoe and got in. A quick glance at the front window of the bank showed me that Mr. Routh had moved over to the window and was watching me. I had no idea what he was thinking, but I was sure it had nothing to do with the kind of investments or insurance I might be interested in purchasing. He seemed to show a bit more interest in me than I thought was appropriate, under the circumstances.

I started my Tahoe and drove away. I drove down the street a couple of blocks then went around the block. I drove back a few blocks before turning back on the street that ran alongside the bank. I parked on the side street across from the bank. From my position, I could see the front door and the side door of the bank. I shut off the engine then tipped back the seat to wait and watch. I had no idea how long I would be sitting there, or what I expected to see while watching the bank.

I wanted to watch for two things. One was to see if the young woman left the bank. If she did, I wanted to talk to her away from the bank. The second was to see what Mr. Routh was going to do. Was he going to go somewhere after talking to me, or was he simply going to return to his usual duties in the bank? If I was a betting man, my bet would be on him leaving the bank. I didn't have the slightest idea where he might go, or why I thought he would leave the bank. It was just a hunch on my part.

It wasn't very long, five minutes at the most, when Mr. Routh came out the side door of the bank. He immediately stopped and looked both ways as if he wasn't sure which way he should go, or possibly to make sure he wasn't seen leaving the bank. He then turned and headed down the side street. His pace was that of someone who was in a hurry, but didn't want anyone to think he was. In short, he was walking rather fast.

I got out of my Tahoe and followed him from the other side of the street, at a distance. I half expected him to turn into the parking lot for a car, but he crossed the street instead. After crossing the street, he turned and went into a real estate office.

The real estate office was really a small house that had been converted to an office. The sign on the front said it was "Williams Realty". The sign also indicated that they dealt in both residential and commercial properties.

I turned the other way on the street and stepped around the corner of a building. From there I could see the front of the real estate office. I stood at the corner of the building and watched. I had no idea what I expected to see, but it was clear I had made Mr. Routh a bit nervous. The question was why was he nervous after talking to me? Did he know something about Josh's death? Did he know who I was? I had a lot of questions going through my mind while I waited to see what might happen.

TIME PASSED SLOWLY while I waited for Mr. Routh to come out of the real estate office. It was now a little past noon and I was getting hungry. I had seen a small sandwich shop across the street. I was thinking about leaving my post long enough to get a sandwich and a cup of coffee when the door to the real estate office opened.

Mr. Routh stepped outside and started down the steps to the street, but quickly stopped at the bottom step. He turned around and looked up at the door as if someone was standing inside the door just out of sight and had something more to say to him. I saw him nod, then turn back around and leave.

Mr. Routh had no more than gotten to the sidewalk when a man stepped out of the real estate office door. He looked around as if looking to see who might be watching him.

I took note of the man. He was probably in his mid-to-late fifties with thinning white hair and a thin almost white mustache. He was maybe five feet nine or ten inches tall, and looked to weigh close to three hundred to three hundred and forty pounds. He was wearing a suit with a coat and vest. The coat was open showing he had a fairly large pot belly.

After he looked around, he turned his attention toward Mr. Routh. He watched Routh walk down the sidewalk until he disappeared around the corner. As soon as Routh was out of sight, the man turned around and went back inside the real estate office.

I stood at the side of the building looking at the real estate office while thinking. What was so important that Routh had to see the man in the real estate office in such a hurry? It could have been something as simple as discussing a home or business loan for a piece of property a client was interested in, but I didn't think so. That would have been something Routh could have handled over the phone or by fax. It wouldn't have required him to rush out of the bank to the real estate office.

My thought turned to the young woman who had been Josh's secretary. She seemed very broken up over his death. Was it because she was afraid of something, or because she had grown close to Josh while working at the bank. None of my questions were going to get answered until I could talk to her.

I returned to where my Tahoe was parked. Across the street was a small café. I would be able to get something to eat while still watching the bank. I went across the street and got a sandwich and a soft drink then returned to my Tahoe. I sat eating the sandwich while I watched the bank. I was hoping to see the secretary leave the bank for lunch. Several people went in and out of the bank, but none of them were of any interest to me.

I began to think she might have left the bank while I was following Routh, or she had taken her lunch to work and would eat it in the employee's lounge. Either way, I was sure it was worth my time to wait in the hope of talking to her.

CHAPTER SEVEN

I HAD BEEN WAITING for more than an hour, but it seemed like forever. If I left without being able to talk to Josh's secretary, I might miss an opportunity to get some important information that would give me at least some idea what was going on. Taking the chance that she might still be at work, I decided to wait for a little longer.

It was almost three-thirty in the afternoon before Josh's secretary left the bank. She walked down the steps in front of the bank, then stopped and looked both ways. She put a handkerchief up to her face. It looked like she was blowing her nose. She then looked over her shoulder for a second before she turned and began walking down the sidewalk.

I had no idea where she was going, but it could prove interesting to find out. The fact it was rather late in the afternoon to be going for lunch, I thought she might be going to the little café for coffee during a coffee break, or she might have taken the rest of the day off since Josh was not there. If she went to a café at the corner of the block, I might get a chance to talk to her. I half expected her to turn the corner and go in the café, but instead, she walked to the corner, crossed the street and continued on.

Fortunately for me, she was going in the same direction I was facing. I waited until she was almost to the center of the next block before I started my Tahoe.

Just as I was about to pull away from the curb, I saw Mr. Routh step out of the bank with another man. The man who had followed Routh out of the bank was fairly tall. Even though he was wearing a suit, I got the impression he just might be more than a bank employee.

Routh quickly looked up and down the street, then tapped the man on the shoulder and pointed in the direction Josh's secretary had gone. It looked to me like Routh had pointed her out. The man immediately nodded then started down the street in the same direction Josh's secretary had gone.

I wasn't sure what was going on, but it didn't look good. I quickly pulled away from the curb and drove toward Josh's secretary. I quickly passed the man who was gaining on her. The woman turned the corner just as I got to it. I swung around the corner and rolled down the side window as I pulled to a stop. I called out to her.

"Get in," I yelled.

She looked at me as if I was crazy.

"Get in. You're being followed."

She turned and looked back toward the corner. She saw the man just as he came around the corner. He was hurrying toward her.

"Get in, damn it."

She turned toward my Tahoe, then quickly got in. She had just sat down and closed the door when I stepped on the gas and pulled away. In the rearview mirror, I could see the man stop and watch as I drove away. He had a very disgusted look on his face. I glanced over at Josh's secretary. She looked scared which was easy for me to understand.

"I'm sorry if I scared you, but when you left the bank and that man came out looking for you, I thought it best to get you out of there."

"What's going on? Why would he want me?"

"First of all, I would like to know your name."

"Mary Sullivan," she said softly, still looking scared.

"Well, Mary, I think it would be best if you don't return to work. I also don't think it would be wise for you to go to your home, unless you have someone with you."

"I don't understand." her voice trembling as she spoke.

"Did you know Josh was coming to see me in Denver when he was shot?"

"No," she replied while looking at me.

From the look of confusion on her face and the hint of fear in her voice, I had little doubt that she was telling me the truth. I could also see she was still trembling.

"I don't know if you know anything about why Josh was coming to see me, but apparently someone thinks you know something. Do you know who the man was who came after you?"

"No."

"Have you ever seen him before?"

"Yes. I've seen him in the bank several times, but he doesn't work at the bank."

"Any idea who he was seeing in the bank?"

"I know he has visited with Mr. Routh on several occasions. I think he has visited Mr. Sheridan once or twice."

"Who is Mr. Sheridan?"

"He's the president of the bank."

"Did he ever come to see Josh?"

"No, at least not that I know of."

"I don't want to scare you any more than you already are; but I think we should go to your home and pick up a few things as quickly as possible, then I'll get you someplace where you will be safe."

"Do you think that's necessary?"

"Yes, for your own safety. Where do you live?"

She looked at me and hesitated for a moment before she said, "I have an apartment in Frisco."

I headed for Frisco by the most direct route. While I drove, I placed a call to Sheriff Tom Stillwell, gave him Mary's address and asked him to meet us there as soon as possible. I also briefly explained why I wanted him there.

Mary looked at me as I talked to Tom. I could see she was still trembling a little, but I couldn't blame her. It was probably sinking into her mind that she really was in danger, even if she didn't know why.

"Tom, Sheriff Stillwell, is going to meet us at your apartment. Do you know Sheriff Stillwell?"

"Not personally, but I have seen him."

"Since you live in Frisco, how do you get to work?"

"I usually drive, but I rode with a friend of mine who lives in Frisco. I didn't feel like driving this morning."

"I understand. I take it you were going to meet her for a ride home?"

"Yes, but I was going to a little café across the street from where she works to wait for her. She works in a sporting goods store until five."

"When we get to your apartment, I want you to wait with me in the car until the sheriff arrives."

"You think someone might be in my apartment?"

"I don't know, but I'm not willing to take any chances."

"Are you a policeman?"

"No. I'm a private investigator. I wasn't kidding you when I said that Josh was a good friend of mine."

Mary turned and looked out the windshield. I don't know what she was thinking, but I hoped she was thinking about Josh and anything he might have told her about what he suspected was going on at the bank.

WE ARRIVED AT MARY'S APARTMENT just as Tom pulled up to the curb. I took a look around, but didn't see anyone. I got out of the Tahoe as Tom got out of his sheriff's car. I walked around to the passenger's side, looked around then opened the door. As Mary stepped out of the Tahoe, I watched for anyone who might be a problem for us.

"Let's get inside," I said as I took Mary by the arm.

Tom simply nodded and followed Mary and me into the apartment building. Mary led us directly to her apartment. I stopped her at the door.

"Give me your key, please," I said.

She glanced at the sheriff, he nodded that it was okay, then she handed me the key to her apartment and stepped back. I drew my gun from under my coat, put the key into the lock and turned it. I glanced back at Tom before I pushed the door open. He also had his gun in his hand.

Tom stayed with Mary while I entered her apartment. They waited outside while I did a quick search to make sure no one was hiding in her apartment.

Mary's apartment was a fairly small one bedroom apartment. The living room was clean and neat. The décor showed that a good deal of thought went into decorating it. The kitchen was small, but functional. The appliances were not new, but were not more than a few years old. Her bedroom was nicely decorated and looked like I would have expected a young woman's bedroom to look like. It had a few personal pictures on the dresser and a colorful quilt on the bed. I returned to the door after finding no one in the apartment.

"All clear," I said as I stepped over next to a window that looked out over the street in front of the building.

Tom had Mary by the arm as they stepped into the apartment. I glanced out the window in time to see a car coming down the street then slow down. I could see the driver was looking up at the window. As soon as he saw the sheriff's car parked in front of the building, he hit the gas and got out of there, but not before I got a good look at his license plate as he drove away. I quickly wrote the license number down in my pocket pad.

"Thanks for coming, Tom. This is Miss Mary Sullivan."

"Nice to meet you, Miss Sullivan.

"Tom, I just saw the same guy who was following Mary drive by. He took off like a scared rabbit when he saw your car."

"Did you get a license number?"

"Yes," I replied then gave him the number I had written down.

"I think we best get Mary out of here for her own safety," I suggested.

"I agree," Tom said. "Do you have a place in mind?"

"Yes. I have Mrs. Garrett staying with a friend of mine in Aurora. I'm sure she could stay with them. By the way, my friend is a professional bodyguard," I added mostly for Mary's benefit.

"That sounds like a good idea," Tom said. "What do you think, Miss Sullivan?"

She looked at the sheriff for a moment before she said, "I don't know what to think. Why would someone be after me?"

"First of all, it is clear someone didn't want you talking to me about Josh," I said. "The fact you were followed tells me they think you know something they don't want you to know, and certainly don't want you to tell anyone. They probably think you know why Josh was planning to visit with me in Denver."

"But why? I don't know anything that would cause anyone any trouble."

"That may or may not be true, but they apparently think you do. If they think you know something, then there is a possibility you do know something that could be a problem for them. You just don't realize it."

Mary looked at me for a moment then looked at the sheriff. It was clear she was not only afraid, she was also very confused. I could certainly understand her fears, as well as her confusion.

"Miss Sullivan, I think it would be a good idea if you packed up a few things you will need and go with Mr. Blackstone. He has a place where you will be safe until he can find out what is going on. I can assure you that I will be working on this end to help him in that quest. But until then, we want you to be safe," the sheriff said, his voice soft and comforting.

She looked at him, then nodded reluctantly that she agreed. Mary went to a closet and got out a small suitcase. She began to pack it with clothes and a few other things she might need while I stood next to the window and watched outside.

"Tom," I called to him, keeping my voice down.

Tom came across the room to me. I pointed out the window at a dark blue sedan parked on the corner of the next block. I didn't say anything, but I was sure he knew what I was getting at.

"You think that's the same car?" he asked quietly.

"Yes. Can you hold him up for a few minutes while I get Mary out of town?"

"Sure."

As soon as Mary had her suitcase packed, she looked at me. I walked over to her, picked up her suitcase then took her gently by the arm and led her to the front door of the apartment building. Tom followed us out of her apartment locking the door behind him.

When we got to the front door of the apartment building, we walked her to my Tahoe, Tom on one side of her while I was on the other side. Once she was safely in my Tahoe, I hurried around to the other side, got in and started it. I waited until Tom was in his car before I pulled away from the curb.

As I started down the street, Tom waited for a moment. When the car at the corner started to pull away from the curb, he pulled out in front of it. At the next corner, I stopped for a stop sign and Tom pulled up behind me. The car from the corner pulled up behind the sheriff's car. I pulled out into the intersection and turned the corner while Tom just sat there. We made it to the next corner before Tom turned the corner, forcing the car behind him to slow down giving me time to lose him.

Once I was sure that I had lost him, I hurried out of Frisco and took the interstate to Denver. I kept an eye out for anyone who might be following us, but saw no one.

Mary was quiet all the way to Denver. I was sure she had a lot on her mind, and she was still a little confused by all that had happened to her.

CHAPTER EIGHT

WE ARRIVED AT GEORGE'S HOUSE in Aurora, a suburb of Denver. His house was a single story ranch style house with an attached two-car garage. It was located in a middle-class neighborhood. The lawn was well groomed and the house had been nicely maintained. I pulled into the drive and stopped, then called George on my cell phone.

"Hi," George said. "I'll open the garage door on the left. It's empty."

"Okay," I replied.

In a matter of seconds, the garage door on the left opened. I drove into the garage and waited in my Tahoe until the overhead door closed. As soon as it closed, I got out of the Tahoe. I walked around to the passenger's side and opened the door. Mary got out and looked around. I took her by the arm and led her toward the door leading into the house. We were met at the door by George. He had a gun in his hand.

"Who do we have here," George said as he looked at Mary while slipping his gun in the holster on his belt.

"This is Mary Sullivan. She was Josh's secretary. She is going to stay with you for a while."

"Welcome," George said. "I take it you know Mrs. Garrett?"

"Yes, of course," Mary replied.

"Good. We have some very strict rules here, but before we get into that, come into the kitchen and sit down at the table, please."

Mary smiled at him, but it was clear by the look on her face she wondered what kind of rules this tall, nice looking man would impose on her. She followed him into the kitchen. I followed along with Mary's suitcase, closing the door to the garage behind me.

"Please, have a seat," George said. "Do you drink coffee?"

"Yes," Mary replied.

I pulled out a chair for Mary. She sat down, then I sat down at the table. I watched George while he made a pot of coffee.

"Where is Mrs. Garrett," I asked.

"She's resting. The loss of her husband has been very hard on her. It doesn't help any that she cannot make arrangements for her husband's funeral."

"I'm sure this is very hard for her," Mary said. "They were very close."

"I'm sure," I said just as George pulled up a chair and sat down at the table.

"Miss Sullivan. It is Miss, isn't it?"

"Yes, but you can call me Mary if you like."

"Okay. Mary, the rules of the house are for the safety of you and Mrs. Garrett as well as for me. They are simple rules. You do not go into a room if there are any windows someone could see in from the outside. You do not answer the phone, the doorbell or knocking on the door. You do not make any phone calls from here without first talking to me. If you feel you have to make a call to someone, I will provide you with the phone you will use. If you call someone, you are not, I repeat, you are not to tell them where you are. And most important of all, is you will do what I tell you to do when I tell you," George explained.

"The reason for the last rule is simple. If someone comes to the house, I will tell you to stay out of sight. I may have to tell you where I want you to go, and you are to go there, immediately. It is for your own safety and the safety of the rest of us. Do you understand?"

"Yes," Mary said, but looked like she might think it to be a little much to ask.

"Mary, I can assure you that George knows what he is doing. His job is to keep you safe until it is safe for you to return to doing whatever you want to do," I said. "He cannot do that without your complete cooperation."

"I understand," Mary said nodding her head.

"Josh was killed because he discovered something that apparently bothered him. You and Mrs. Garrett are in danger because they think you might know what Josh had discovered, and they don't want you to tell anyone what it was Josh discovered. If they think you have told someone, they will not want you around to be a witness against them in court. Do you understand?"

"Yes, I understand, but I don't know what it was he discovered," Mary said.

"It really doesn't matter if you know anything or not. What matters is if they think you might know something. The fact a man was following you from the bank is a good indication they think you know something, or might know something," I said.

Mary looked at me for a moment then nodded her head to indicate I might be right.

"Do you understand the rules?" George asked looking directly at Mary.

"Yes. I understand." Mary said more confidently.

"Good, because one breach of the rules could put us all in danger, even here."

I looked at Mary then at George. It looked like Mary understood.

"One thing I would like you to do while you are here is to take some time to think about everything you heard, saw, or thought you saw with regard to Josh over the past few days or weeks. Make a list of who he talked to, who he called, and anything he did that didn't seem to be normal for him during his time at the bank, especially over the past, say, couple of months. Also, anything he asked or told you that was out of character for him. I want you to write it down. It may help you remember. Do you think you can do that?" I asked.

"Yes, I'll try."

"Good. I think it's time for me to get back to work. The sooner I find out what is going on, the sooner you can get back to living your life the way you want," I said as I stood up.

I walked out to the garage and got in my Tahoe. George opened the garage door then closed it as soon as I backed out. I turned down the street and headed back to Denver and my office. I kept watch for anyone who might be following me, but again, I saw no one.

I ARRIVED AT MY OFFICE at a few minutes before five in the afternoon. I took a few minutes to check my mail. Most of it ended up being filed in the round file behind my desk. The rest could wait until morning for me to respond to it.

Just as I was about to get up and head for home, the phone began to ring. I reached over and picked up the receiver.

"Peter Blackstone Investigations. How may I help you?"

"Pete, Mac here."

"What's up, Mac?"

"I just got the preliminary autopsy report on Garrett from the ME. You were right."

"Right about what?"

"It looks like he was murdered. By that, I mean he was murdered in the recovery room of the hospital sometime in the middle of the night."

"What happened?"

"According to the ME, someone who either works in the hospital, or snuck into the recovery room, injected something directly into his arm by injecting it into his IV tube. That something is what killed him. The ME isn't one hundred percent sure, but he thinks it might have been either cocaine or amphetamines in a rather large dose."

"He was killed by an overdose of drugs?"

"Yeah. The ME said Garrett showed signs of having convulsions immediately before his death. The toxicology report isn't back, but the ME is convinced Josh was killed with an overdose of drugs. The ME is leaning toward cocaine as the drug, but isn't one hundred percent sure. He also said if Josh died from his gunshot injuries, or from any of the drugs normally used in the treatment of a case like his, he would have died without convulsing. The ME said there were no signs of large amounts of any other drugs."

"Well, I guess Josh had a very good reason to want to talk to me. It also looks like he was the target in the café."

"It sure does. That changes everything," Mac said.

"Maybe, but maybe not. Have you found anything to connect the other victims to each other, or to Josh?"

"Not yet, but I'm still looking into it."

"I hope you can find out if there is a connection."

"Why? What are you thinking?" Mac asked.

"There might be a reason one of the other victims was shot so many times. I would like to be sure we have covered all the bases."

"I'll see what I can find. Keep me posted on what you find."

"I went to visit the bank where Josh worked. I talked briefly to his secretary, but was interrupted by one of the bank officers. Shortly after I left the bank, the bank officer left the bank in one hell of a hurry. He went around the corner and down the street a couple of blocks to a real estate office. He was there for about an hour before he left and returned to the bank. He didn't have any files or a briefcase with him.

"An hour or so after he returned to the bank, Josh's secretary left the bank and was followed. I grabbed her before the man who followed her could catch up to her. I have her here with a bodyguard friend of mine along with Mrs. Garrett."

"What was the name of the real estate office?"

"Williams Reality. The sign says they deal in residential and commercial properties. I'm interested in what else he is dealing in."

"You think there's something going on there?"

"I'm not sure, but the guy from the bank didn't seem to want anyone to see him go to the real estate office. If it was normal bank business, why did he sneak out the side door of the bank and hurry over there? By the way, it was shorter to go out the front of the bank. And why no papers, if it was bank business?"

"I see what you mean," Mac said thoughtfully. "What about the guy that tried to grab Josh's secretary? Do you have a name for him?"

"No, not yet. But I can describe him for you. He was about six one, about two hundred and forty pounds, well built, looked like he spends a lot of time in a gym. He had brown hair cut in a crew cut and was clean shaven. My best guess, he was probably in his mid-thirties."

"That could be a lot of men," Mac said with a hint of frustration in his voice.

"Sheriff Tom Stillwell might be able to help identify the man. I got his license plate number. Tom is going to run a make on it and let me know the results."

"Good. Does Josh's secretary know who the man is?"

"No, but she told me that she has seen him in the bank on several occasions. By the way, she said that he doesn't work for the bank."

"Does she know why Josh was murdered?"

"No, I don't think so. She was pretty upset by his death. She was also upset with the man following her from work. I thought I would give her a couple of days to think about Josh's actions over the past few weeks, then talk to her again. Maybe she'll remember something."

"Okay. I will want to talk to her as soon as possible," Mac said.

"Okay, but I would appreciate it if you would wait for a couple of days. I think we will get more out of her if she can remember anything that might help."

"Let me know when you think she's ready to talk, but don't make it too long. I need information as soon as possible," Mac said.

"I'll have it for you in a couple of days. The other two victims, I believe you said they were June Franklin and William North."

"That's right."

"You also said they were just talking at a table together and being kind of secretive about it," I said.

"Right."

"Were you able to find out what they were talking about?"

"No, but it was obvious to a couple of the witnesses they knew each other rather well. They held hands while they talked."

"Were either of them married?"

"June Franklin was married. We have interviewed her husband, Robert Franklin, but nothing came of it. He had no idea why she was in the café, or why anyone would shoot her," Mac said.

"What was his reaction when you told him his wife was dead?"

"He broke down and cried. It didn't look like he was faking it, but as you know we can't always get it right."

"I agree. What did he say about his wife being with another man at the café?"

"We didn't tell him anything about it. I thought it would be better if we didn't say anything about it for the time being, at least until we have a better idea of what is going on."

"I think that was a good idea. What about North?" I asked.

"As for North, his driver's license was a new one. He hadn't had it for more than two weeks. We're checking to see where his previous driver's license was from. A couple of uniform officers went to the address on his license, but didn't get an answer. They checked with two of his neighbors in the apartment building, but they knew very little about him. About all they could tell the officers was he kept to himself and hadn't lived there very long. It appears he might have lived alone. There was no indication he was married or had a girlfriend," Mac said.

"Are you going over there to check out his apartment?"

"I was just about to go over to his apartment building to talk to all the people living in the building to see if I could find someone who might have known him. If that doesn't turn up anything, I'll talk to a judge and see if I can get a warrant to search his apartment."

"Mind if I look into it?"

"Have at it. Let me know if you find anything interesting. If you hit a dead end, I'll get a warrant and we'll go enter his apartment together."

"Okay. I probably will not get to it until tomorrow. I have my hands full right now," I said.

"No problem. I still have a lot to do here. By the way, we found Mrs. Garrett's car."

"Good. Where was it?"

"In your parking garage. One of the security guards in the building saw it and asked a policeman to run the license plate. The officer recognized the plate number and called it in. We went and got it. The forensic people are going over it right now looking for anything that might help us."

"Great. Let me know what they find out. I'll talk to you later," I said.

"Will do," Mac said then hung up.

I leaned back in my chair and thought about what Mac had told me. Finding Josh's car in the parking garage of my building was not a surprise. It had probably been driven there by Barbara.

My thoughts turned to the couple murdered in the café. I had no idea what I might find out if I contacted Mr. Franklin or talked to North's neighbors. All I knew for sure was I would like to know if there was some reason for the two of them to be murdered. It would also be interesting to find out why they were at the café together.

I spent some time thinking about Josh's murder. It quickly became clear that whoever killed Josh found out very quickly he had survived the attack at the café, and he was likely to survive the surgery as well. It had taken less than fourteen hours from the time Josh was shot in the café to the time he was murdered in the hospital. It seemed like a short time since he had spent a good deal of that time in surgery. It was only about six hours, eight at the most, after the surgery that he was murdered.

The more I thought about it, the more it looked like it might have been someone who worked in the hospital. Someone who knew he had survived the surgery. I was sure Mac would think the same thing and would be questioning all those who worked in surgery and the recovery room or had access to the recovery room.

It was clear Mac would be talking to Julie since she was the surgical nurse who had scrubbed for the surgery, and she had taken Josh from the operating room to the recovery room. From what she had told me, she must have checked in on Josh several times after he was in the recovery room and before she left work. I wondered what she would tell Mac.

Just the thought that the police would be questioning Julie seemed to bother me a little. I wasn't afraid of what she might tell the police, but I was a little concerned about what some detective working for Mac might think about her. If she was the only one to have been around Josh in the operating room and in the recovery room, the questionings could get rather pointed. If Mac questioned her, I was sure she would tell him that we have a relationship, something she might not tell anyone else.

It suddenly occurred to me that maybe I was being a little overly concerned for Julie. She was smart, she was able to deal with people and she could handle herself. Of most of the people I know, she was the one I should least be worried about when questioned by police. With that thought in mind, I decided it was time to go home. Besides, I probably couldn't get in touch with her now.

I left my office and took the elevator to the underground garage. As I walked to my Tahoe, I got the feeling I was being watched, but I didn't see anyone. I got in my Tahoe and drove home, being very careful that I was not being followed.

CHAPTER NINE

I HAD JUST WALKED IN THE DOOR to my apartment when the phone began to ring. I quickly walked across the room and picked up the receiver.

"Hello."

"Hi. Did I catch you at a bad time?" Julie asked.

"No. It's never a bad time for you to call me. What's up? Are you at work?"

"Yes. I just needed to hear your voice," Julie said sounding a little relieved.

The sound of her voice indicated there was something bothering her. It caught my attention and caused me concern.

"What is the matter, honey?"

"Oh, nothing really. I just spent an hour or so with some police detective who was asking me a bunch of questions about Josh's death. The thing that really got to me was he asked the same questions over and over again as if he didn't believe me. A few of his questions seemed to imply I had something to do with Josh's death, or at the very least I knew something about it," Julie said.

"I had a feeling something like that might happen. Mac called me earlier and told me the Medical Examiner thinks Josh was murdered while he was in the hospital."

"You didn't call me and tell me?" Julie asked sounding a bit surprised and maybe a bit angry.

"I found out less than an hour ago," I explained.

"Oh. I'm sorry," she said after taking a deep breath. "I guess his questioning bothered me more than it should."

"It's all right. Most people don't handle questioning by the police very well, especially if they are in a position to be considered a suspect. They tend to get flustered even when they know nothing about the crime the detective is investigating."

"Do you think I'm a suspect?"

"I don't, but they might think you are since you work in the area and had contact with Josh. They have to eliminate you as a suspect."

"I've been questioned before by the police about patients, but this detective seemed to be looking for someone to blame Josh's death on, rather than to get information that might actually lead him to the person who committed the murder."

"Sometimes the detectives get a little closed minded about things, especially when the murder takes place where access by outsiders is limited or is supposed to be limited. He's probably got someone on his back to find answers and find them quickly."

"I guess you're right. I'm sorry if I took it out on you."

"It's okay. I don't mind. In the course of his questioning did he tell you anything about what they suspected?"

"No, not really. He did say one thing that sort of surprised me, though. He said they knew Josh was killed in the hospital, but didn't know why. He then implied someone on the hospital staff had to have given him something that killed him. I told the detective nothing we gave Josh, before, during or after the surgery would cause him to have the kind of reaction he had just before he died."

"What did he say to that?"

"He asked me what kind of a reaction Josh had," Julie said. "I would have thought he would already know what kind of reaction Josh had."

"I would think so. What did you tell him?"

"I told him Josh had convulsions just before he died."

"How is it you know that? I only found out about it less than an hour ago."

"One of the lab staff told us the ME noticed signs of convulsions on the body. It was maybe an hour before I was questioned."

"The detective didn't know that?" I asked, a little surprised he wouldn't know that if he was looking into Josh's death.

"Apparently not. He just looked at me with a blank stare for a moment or two, then stood up. He told me I could return to work, then hurried out of the room. The look on his face was strange as if I had said something that actually upset him. I still don't know what I said to make him leave so quickly."

"Did you get the detective's name?"

"I think it was Hamilton. I don't think he ever mentioned his first name."

"I'll give Mac a call and ask him about Hamilton. I've never heard of him, but I don't know all the detectives on the force."

"Peter, can I come over tonight after work?" she asked softly. "I don't want to be alone tonight."

"Sure. What time do you think you might get off?"

"I'm not sure. It sounds like they are not going to do any surgeries that can wait until tomorrow. The police have upset the schedule around here, so I may get off early."

"Why don't you give me a call before you leave and I'll have something for you to eat here," I suggested.

"I'll do that. I love you."

"I love you, too," I said then hung up.

I took a minute to think about what Julie had said. It made me wonder if Detective Hamilton was looking to solve the case in order to get some brownie points with the lead detective, namely Mac.

From what Julie had told me, I couldn't understand Hamilton's reaction. It sounded more like a lack of professionalism on the detective's part. I wondered if he had suddenly become sick from what she had said, but that didn't seem logical. What didn't make any sense to me was the fact Hamilton didn't know the drug used to kill Josh had caused him to convulse. A call to Mac to find out if there was a Detective Hamilton working with him seemed like a good idea.

I reached over, picked up the receiver to my phone and placed a call to the precinct where Mac's office was located. It was answered by the desk sergeant, who immediately transferred my call to Mac's office.

"Captain MacDonald, how may I help you?"

"Mac, Peter."

"What's on your mind, Pete? Did you find out something?"

"Not really, but I have a question for you. Do you have a detective by the name of Hamilton working on Josh's case?"

"Hamilton?"

"Yes."

"No, not on Josh's case. I don't know any Detective Hamilton. Why?"

"Julie called me a few minutes ago and told me she had been questioned by a Detective Hamilton. He had upset her with his questions, but when she told him the drugs they used in surgery would not have caused Josh to have convulsions, he left in a hurry. She said he looked at her funny, then ended the interview abruptly and left in a hurry."

"What did she mean by 'he looked at her funny'?"

"She said he seemed surprised and had a strange look on his face as if he didn't understand what she was telling him."

"I think I better talk to Julie myself. I would like a description of this Hamilton fella. Do you know where she is now?"

"As far as I know, she is still at the hospital," I said.

"I'll get over there. Are you there now?"

"No, but I'll meet you there," I said then hung up.

I left my apartment immediately for the hospital.

I ARRIVED AT THE HOSPTIAL in about twenty minutes and parked in the lot just outside the receiving entrance. I quickly locked my Tahoe and headed for the door. Just as I was about to get to the door, I saw Julie coming toward me. I stopped and waited for her to come out.

"Hi. I didn't expect to see you here," she said with a pleasant smile.

"Is there some place where we can talk?" I said.

"Sure," she said looking a little confused. "What's the matter?"

I looked around as I turned her around and guided her back inside the hospital.

"We can talk in here," she said as she pointed toward a door.

I guided her into the room. It was an empty examining room.

"What's the matter?" she asked.

"I called Mac after you called me and asked him about Detective Hamilton. He said he didn't know of any Detective Hamilton. He is coming here to talk to you. I thought I should get over here as soon as I could."

"Do you think I'm in danger?"

"I don't really know; but I thought if this Hamilton fellow upset you, it might be a good idea for me to come here and make sure you got to my place safely."

"I can assure you that I have no objections. He scared me. I almost called you to have you come and get me."

Just then there was a light knock on the door. I gently pushed Julie behind me, then carefully opened the door. I found Mac standing there. I opened the door so he could enter the room.

"The nurse at the desk told me that she had seen you and Julie come in this room," Mac said as he closed the door.

"I thought it was best if someone was here to escort her home," I said.

"I think you're right. I did a quick check of the roster of police officers and found two Hamiltons. Both of them are uniformed officers, not detectives.

"Julie, can you describe the man who interviewed you?" Mac asked.

"I think so."

Julie sat down on a chair while I sat on the examining table. Mac just stood leaning against the door as if to keep anyone from barging in.

"He was about six-foot-tall with brown wavy hair, brown eyes, and a small scar that ran from the left corner of his mouth toward the lower end of his ear. The scar was only about an inch and a half long and straight. It looked like it might have been a surgical scar, but I don't know for sure. It was an old scar. He was wearing black slacks, a white shirt, and dark gray sport coat. His tie was black, red and gray in diagonal strips. His shoes were black dress shoes. If I had to guess his weight, I would say he was probably a little over two hundred pounds. He looked to be in pretty good physical condition."

"That's pretty good," Mac said with a hint of surprise in his voice. "Did he show you a badge and ID?"

"No, he just said he was a detective and needed to ask me a few questions. We all knew there had been police all over the place today, so I didn't think to ask him for ID. By the way, he had a small bulge in the left side of his sport coat like he might have had a gun under his coat."

"What was it about him that upset you?" Mac asked.

"His questions were pretty much what I would have expected until he asked me about Josh's surgery. I gave him a run down on what was done and what drugs Josh had received. When I mentioned the drugs we used would not have caused Josh to convulse, he turned pale, told me I could go, then almost ran out of the room."

"Did he look sick, like sick to his stomach?" Mac asked.

"No. It was more like he was surprised to find out Josh had convulsions before he died. That piece of information seemed to almost scare him half to death. I don't know why it would, but it did," Julie said.

"Thank you for your help," Mac said.

"Pete, are you going to see her home?"

"I plan to take her to my place."

"I think that's a good idea, at least until we find out what is going on. I'll be looking into this Hamilton character."

"Do you think I'm in danger?" Julie asked looking a little concerned.

"No, I don't think so. But it might make you feel a little better to have someone around," Mac said.

"It will do that," Julie said with a hint of relief.

"I'll talk to you later," Mac said to me, then left the room.

As soon as he left, I walked Julie out to my Tahoe. I was pretty sure her car would be safe parked in the parking lot near the emergency room entrance. There were always people going in and out all night long.

Once Julie was in my Tahoe, I drove directly to my apartment. I fixed us something to eat, then we turned in for the night. We were both very tired.

As we laid down in the bed, I drew her close to me wrapping her in my arms. It wasn't long before she was asleep. It felt good to have her close to me. It also felt good that she felt safe and secure in my arms. It wasn't long before I dozed off to sleep.

CHAPTER TEN

I WOKE SEVERAL TIMES during the night. I guess I had been more concerned for Julie's safety than I thought, and I felt the need to check on her. Each time I found her curled up against me, sometimes facing me, sometimes with her back to me, but always leaning against me. It was obvious that, although she had been sleeping, she still had a restless night.

It was around six-thirty when I woke and looked over at her and found her lying on her side looking at me. She had her head supported on her hand as she looked at me. She smiled.

"I'm sorry if I woke you," she said.

"You didn't wake me."

"You've been checking on me off and on all night, haven't you?"

"Yes," I admitted.

"Do you think I'm in danger?"

"I don't know, but it is possible. Mac is going to see what he can do to find out who the man was who questioned you last night. The description you gave Mac is very close to the man who tried to grab Miss Sullivan, Josh's secretary, in Dillion. I think your comment on the bulge in his coat concerned Mac as much as it did me. What you described indicated to us he was carrying a gun. If he was a cop, then I understand that; but if he wasn't, we both want to know who he was, what his intentions were and why was he carrying a gun in the hospital."

"Are you going to stay with me until you find him?" Julie asked with a hopeful look in her eyes.

"I can't stay with you and still find him. I think during the day I will have you stay with George. He is watching over Mrs. Garrett and Miss Sullivan."

"Can we stay here for a little while longer? I would like you to just hold me."

I didn't respond to her question. I simply reached over to her and pulled her up against me. She curled up against me, laying one arm across my chest, a leg curled over my legs and her head rested on my shoulder. Her warm naked body felt good against me. It wasn't long before she dozed off for a few minutes of peaceful rest.

However, I didn't sleep any more. I had too much on my mind to get any more sleep. The thought of what had happened to my last girlfriend kept running through my mind. I couldn't let it happen to Julie.

It was about half past seven o'clock when she woke and started running her fingers through the hair on my chest. I ran my hand over her smooth shoulder. It was a time to be close.

"You ready to get up," I asked after several minutes of just lying together.

"I would like to stay right here, but I guess you have things to do?"

"I wouldn't mind staying here with you, but you are right. I do have things to do if I'm going to find out why Josh was murdered."

Julie rolled onto her back. I sat up on the edge of the bed and looked over my shoulder at her. The sheet was down almost to her waist. Seeing her lying there looking at me was almost enough to make me change my mind and lay back down with her.

Just as I was about to stand up and go into the bathroom, my phone began to ring. I reached over and picked up the receiver.

"Hello."

"Pete, Mac here. I got a call from the ME just a few minutes ago. He said the toxicology report shows Josh was killed with a lethal injection of cocaine 'large enough to kill a horse'. The ME's words, not mine. It caused Josh to have convulsions for only a few seconds up to a couple of minutes before he died. It was injected through his IV tube directly into the vein. Whoever did it wanted him to die a violent death, but still fairly quickly. Most likely, whoever it was didn't know what might happen when he shot such a large does of cocaine directly into the vein. Josh couldn't have been saved even if a doctor had found him within a few seconds of the injection."

"It is clear Josh was onto something that was probably illegal," I said.

"I would think so. Do you think his secretary might know what Josh had discovered?"

"With the attempt to grab Miss Sullivan, someone must think she knows something."

"That would be my guess. I would sure like to talk to her," Mac said, his voice sounding hopeful that I would tell him where she was being hidden.

"I think I'll go have a talk with her myself."

"Will you let me know what she has to say?" Mac asked.

"Yes, of course. Just as soon as I'm done talking with her, I'll give you a call."

"Okay, be careful out there. We still don't know who we're dealing with. There's a pretty good chance they know you're involved," Mac said.

"I'm sure you're right. I'll be careful. Talk to you later."

"Okay," Mac said then the phone went dead.

I set the phone down as I thought about what Mac had said. My thoughts were suddenly disturbed by Julie.

"I take it that was Mac," Julie said as she sat up in bed.

"Yeah," I said as I looked over my shoulder at her. "Josh was killed with a very large overdose of cocaine injected through his IV tube."

"No wonder he convulsed," Julie said.

"When did you see Josh last?"

"I looked in on him before I left to come here. It must have been about quarter to twelve, maybe a few minutes earlier."

"Would there have been anyone staying with Josh?"

"Yes, I'm sure there would have been. There would have been a duty nurse who would check on him every fifteen minutes at least. In fact, there were two nurses on duty at the time I was there. Josh seemed to be doing okay. I checked his chart. His vital signs were good and had been stable for well over an hour," Julie added.

"What I mean, was Josh under constant watch while he was in the recovery room?"

"Probably not. There would be someone with him almost all the time until his vital signs were stable and had been stable for at least an hour. After that he would be checked on frequently. In addition to the two nurses on duty in the recovery room that night, there were at least two more nurses just outside on the surgery ward in case the recovery room nurses needed help.

"When I left the recovery room, there were three nurses in the room. All the patients were doing well. With that many patients, there would be times when the recovery room nurses would have to take vital signs of other patients, or do other things in the recovery room," she said.

"Like what?"

"Oh, change IV's, check on dressings to make sure they are dry, check a patient to be sure he was not bleeding, check on drainage and empty drain bottles, get a medication, log in activities in the patient's charts, things like that."

"So, there would be times when the nurses would not be watching him?"

"Yes. I doubt he would have been left alone for more than the fifteen minutes between the vital signs, most often it would be less. If he was left alone for even a moment, the curtain around his bed would have been left open so any of the recovery room staff could see him. That's required," Julie explained.

"To be honest, do the nurses always leave the curtain open when not at the patient's side?"

"I'm sure there would be times when a nurse would not open the curtain, but it would be very brief, and hopefully rare."

"A couple of minutes, at the most, would be all it would take to inject the cocaine into the IV tube. I think I need to talk to the recovery room staff," I said thoughtfully. "Someone might have seen a stranger, or a person who didn't belong in the recovery room just before Josh died. Possibly a staff member who worked in the hospital but wasn't assigned to the recovery room. Someone who might have been seen checking his IV just before he died."

"Wouldn't the police have already done that?"

"I'm sure they would, but I would like to know what happened during the hours Josh was in the recovery room, and I would like to hear it from the staff."

"Oh. The same recovery room staff won't be there until this afternoon."

"In that case, I need to have a talk with Miss Sullivan."

"Can I go with you?" Julie asked hopefully.

"I'm certainly not leaving you here alone."

Julie smiled and said, "I guess I should get dressed."

"I think that would be a good idea. Let me get dressed, then you can have the bathroom to yourself."

It didn't take us very long to get dressed and have our breakfast. When it was time to leave, I walked to the door and had Julie wait inside my apartment until I checked around outside. As soon as I was sure it was clear, I drew my gun and walked her to my Tahoe. She got in while I kept an eye out for anyone or anything that didn't belong there. Once she was in the Tahoe, I quickly ran around and got in behind the wheel. I started it then drove out onto the street.

WE HADN'T GONE VERY FAR when I noticed a dark sedan that seemed to be following us. Since I didn't want to be followed, I started to form a plan in my mind on how I was going to ditch him.

"We've got company," I said. "The dark sedan three cars back."

"Are you sure?" she asked as she looked in the outside rearview mirror.

"No, but I'm about to find out. Snug up your seatbelt, it could get to be a rough ride."

As soon as she snugged up her seatbelt, I started looking for just the right place to make my move. Since I knew the streets in the area well, it didn't take me long to form a plan. I came to a street I knew had an alley a half a block down from the cross street. I made a quick turn down the street and immediately stomped on the accelerator. When I came to the alley, I hit the brakes, turned sharply into the alley and hit the accelerator again. I sped on down the alley, then turned out onto the next street, sped on down the street to the next alley and quickly turned into it. When I came to the end of the alley, I turned out onto the street and sped to a used car lot. I quickly turned into the lot and parked the Tahoe behind a row of used cars.

"Get down," I said to Julie as I shut off the engine and jumped out of the Tahoe.

Before the salesman could get out of the office, I had the hood up as if looking at the engine. What I was really doing was watching to see if the car we had tried to lose was still following us.

"Got a problem with your Tahoe?" the salesman asked as he approached me. "This might be a good time to trade it in for a more dependable vehicle."

I stepped around behind my Tahoe and looked around it to the street. There were two rows of cars in front of where I had stopped. I looked over them as the salesman walked around toward where I was standing. From my position, I could see any cars that drove by the used car lot.

"What do you think my Tahoe is worth?" I said while keeping an eye out for the car that had been following us.

"Well, I have to know what's wrong with it, and how much it would cost me to fix it, but the body is in very good condition."

I kept the salesman talking about my Tahoe until I was sure I had lost our tail. As soon as it was clear and safe for us to continue, I told him that I would have to think about it. I closed the hood and got back in. Julie sat up as I got back in my Tahoe.

"I saw the salesman look inside," Julie said with a grin. "From the look on his face, he was a little surprised to see me lying across the seats."

"He never said a word. He's probably seen worse things than that over the years."

"I'm sure he has," she said with a grin.

As I pulled out onto the street, I looked both ways. There wasn't any traffic and I didn't see the car that had been following us, so I headed for George's house in Aurora. We didn't see the car again.

WHEN WE ARRIVED AT GEORGE'S HOUSE, I pulled into the drive and honked the horn. Within a few seconds, the garage door opened and I drove into the garage.

We remained in the Tahoe until George closed the garage door. We got out and went into the house.

"Hi, Sis," George said as we entered the house. "What brings you two here?"

"I think we might have a problem. It seems someone posing as a detective questioned Julie. He was surprised by what she told him. Mac and I think she might be in danger, at least until we find out what the guy was up to."

"You're going to stay here?" he asked Julie.

"Peter thinks it would be a good idea."

"Well, welcome. What's one more woman to keep an eye on," George said with a grin.

"How are the others doing? Are they getting along okay?"

"Yes. They are in their rooms at the moment."

"I'd like to talk to Mary, somewhere private?"

"I'll get her. You can use my office."

"I'll make some coffee," Julie said.

I waited in the kitchen while George went to get Mary. I watched Julie as she made a pot of coffee. She knew her way around George's kitchen. She was his sister and had helped him move into the house when he bought it. She had probably been in his house on any number of occasions since then.

"You wanted to talk to me," Mary said as she walked into the kitchen.

"Yes. Let's go to George's office to talk. I have a few questions for you."

Mary didn't say anything. She simply followed me to George's office. Once in his office, she sat down on a sofa while I sat down on a chair.

"Mary, when I dropped you off here, I asked you to think about Josh and how he acted and what he said that might give us an idea what was going on at the bank. Have you thought about that?"

"Yes, I have."

"Did you think of anything that might give us a clue to what was going on?"

"Yes, I think I have, but I'm not sure how much help it will be."

"Why don't you tell me? I'll figure out how much help it is."

"Okay. About two weeks ago, Josh had been working on some account statements that had to do with investments that some of his clients had made through the bank. Maybe I should back up a little.

"I walked in on Josh while he was going over the account statements. I had no more than walked into his office when I heard him say something to the effect of 'what the hell'. I asked what the matter was, but he just looked at me for a minute then took a deep breath. He seemed a little surprised, but quickly rebounded and said, 'Oh, nothing'.

"He then asked me what I wanted. I gave him the papers I had for him to sign and waited. He looked at them for a moment before he signed them and gave them back to me. When I left his office, I glanced back at him. He was again looking at the account statements."

"Did you happen to see whose account statements he was looking at?" I asked.

"No, but I noticed he had the files for three different companies."

"Did you get the files for him?"

"No. He had gotten them himself so I don't know whose files they were."

"Were you able to see any of the names on the files?"

"Just one. I think the account statement he had been looking at when I surprised him was for Williams Reality, but I'm not really sure."

"Do you have any idea why he would be looking at Williams Reality's account statement?"

"No," Mary replied thoughtfully.

"Is there anything else you can tell me about Josh's attitude or his behavior from that time on?"

"He seemed more distant, you know, not as talkative or outgoing. He didn't seem to be as friendly after that day. I'm not sure if anyone else would have noticed, but I did. I have worked closely with him for the past four and a half years. I've gotten to know him pretty well."

"One more question. Was Williams Reality one of his accounts?"

"No, I don't believe it was. I had never seen him working on it before."

"Do you know whose account it was?"

"I'm not sure, but I believe it was one of Mr. Routh's accounts."

"Any idea why Josh was looking at it if it was someone else's account?"

"Not for sure. I saw him pick up a number of file folders just before he went into his office. He might have gotten it by mistake. That's the only reason I can think of for him to have that file folder," Mary said.

"What do you mean when you said 'he was going over the account statements'? What would he be looking for?"

"He would be looking over any activities the account had had, and checking the statements in the file to make sure that everything was in order, you know, payments had been listed, withdrawals shown, things like that," she said.

"Thank you. You've been very helpful. I want you to keep our conversation between us. I don't even want you to mention it to Barbara. Do you understand?"

"Yes, I understand."

"How is Barbara doing?"

"I'm not sure. She spends a lot of time in her room. She seems worried about what happened to Josh. I'm sure this has been hard on her. They were very close, you know."

"Yes, I know. I think we are done here for the time being. Be sure to let George know if you think of anything else."

"I will," she said with a smile.

"How are you getting along with George?"

"He's nice," she said with a smile. "Who was the woman who came in with you? He seemed glad to see her."

"That is George's sister, Julie."

"Oh," she said with an even bigger smile.

I smiled as I stood up. I got the feeling she might like George and may have thought Julie was George's girlfriend.

We left George's office. I returned to the kitchen while Mary went down the hall to her room.

As I walked into the kitchen, I saw George and Julie sitting at the table. I pulled up a chair and sat down with them.

"How did it go with Mary?" Julie asked.

"She did well. It seems Josh might have seen something in one of the accounts at the bank that he wasn't supposed to see."

"Any idea what it might be?" Julie asked.

"No. Mary didn't know why he was even looking at that particular account folder. It was apparently an account Mr. Routh normally handled."

"Wasn't Mr. Routh the man you followed to the real estate office?" Julie asked.

"Yes. I think I'll see what I can find out about Williams Reality. But first I want to talk to Barbara."

"She's in her room. I'll get her for you," George said as he pushed back his chair and stood up.

I picked up the cup of coffee and took a sip of it while I thought about what Barbara might be able to remember and be able to tell me. I wasn't sure if she would keep anything from me that might be important in finding out why Josh was murdered.

It wasn't but a few minutes when George came into the kitchen with Barbara. She looked a little better this morning than when I had brought her here. Her eyes were not red from crying, and her nose showed no sign of being wiped often.

"Good morning," I said as I stood up.

"Good morning," she replied as she looked at Julie.

"This is Julie. She is George's sister," I said.

"Hi," Julie said. "I'm sorry to hear about your husband."

"Thank you," Barbara replied then looked at me. "I understand you wish to talk to me."

"Yes. Let's go into George's office."

I led Barbara to George's office. As soon as we entered, I pointed at the sofa. Barbara sat down on the sofa and looked at me as I sat down on a chair.

"Barbara, I have a few questions to ask you."

"Okay," she said.

"The first thing I would like to ask is in the weeks or months before Josh was shot did you notice any change in him. By that I mean did he seem distant, irritable, or restless? Anything like that?"

"He did seem a little irritable during the last week before - - he - -."

"I understand. Did he give you any idea why?"

"Not until he decided to call you."

"How long was it from the time you noticed he was irritable until he decided to call me?"

"I guess it was about a week, maybe a day or two more."

"How long was it from the time when he decided to call me to when he actually did call me?"

"Only a couple of hours. He called you that same morning," she said.

"So, you didn't know anything was wrong until the day he called me, is that correct?"

"I knew something was wrong at least a week before that, but he wouldn't talk about it. I tried to get him to talk to me about what was troubling him, but he wouldn't talk about it."

"Did he tell you what was troubling him on the morning he did call me?"

"The only thing he said was there were some sort of discrepancies in a couple of the investment accounts at the bank."

"Did he tell you which accounts had the discrepancies?"

"No. That was all he told me. He said he wanted to talk to you to see what he should do about them."

"Did he say why he thought I could help him?"

"He thought you would know what he should do about it. He said you were the only person he could trust to give him advice on what he should do."

I took a moment to think about what she had said. With so little information on what he had discovered in the investment accounts, I wasn't sure what advice I would have been able to give Josh. I do know I would have to have more information than I had at the moment.

"Is that what you wanted to know?" Barbara asked interrupting my thoughts.

"Ah, yes. I have just a couple more questions. Tell me how you got to Denver and how you got to the Wallace's home."

"Josh and I drove into Denver in his car. He dropped me off at Wallace's home and took the car to the café while I waited."

"Who notified you that Josh had been shot and he was in Denver General Hospital? It didn't take you long to get to the hospital."

"I got a call from the hospital and they told me Josh had been admitted with gunshot wounds," she said then started to cry.

I gave her a few minutes to gather herself. When she looked like she was ready to talk again I asked her another question.

"How did the hospital know to call you at the Wallace's?"

"Their number was in Josh's pocket. He had it in case he needed to call me while he was with you."

"How did you get to the hospital since Josh had the car with him?"

"John, Mr. Wallace took me."

"How did you get to my office?"

"I took a cab from the hospital. Josh had taken the car. I guess I didn't think about the car."

"I can understand that. I think that will be all for now. You can return to your room if you like," I said as I stood up.

I waited for Barbara to stand then followed her out of George's office. I noticed she went down the hall to her room. I returned to the kitchen.

"Did you find out anything helpful?" George asked.

"I think so."

"What's your next move?" George asked.

"I think I'll pay Mac a visit. I have a few questions to ask him."

"Will I see you later?" Julie asked.

"Yes. I'll come by about five o'clock," I said. "I'm going to talk to Mac. I'm not sure what I will be doing after that, but I'll be going to the library sometime soon."

I leaned over and kissed Julie, then went out into the garage. As I got into my Tahoe and started it, George opened the garage door. I had no more than backed out when he closed the door. I turned down the street and headed for Mac's office in Denver.

CHAPTER ELEVEN

I ARRIVED AT MAC'S OFFICE mid-morning, about ten o'clock. Russell was on the front desk as usual. He didn't say a word, he simply pointed toward where Mac's office was located. I smiled and walked on down the hall. When I got to Mac's office, I knocked on the door.

"Come in," Mac said.

As I entered his office, he looked up.

"What brings you here so early?"

"I had a talk with Mrs. Garrett this morning," I said as I sat down in front of his desk. "I'm a little puzzled by one of her statements to me."

"Oh. What did she say?"

"Mrs. Garrett told me that Josh and she came to town in Josh's car. Josh dropped her off at the Wallaces' home, then he drove to the café where I was to meet with him, and where he was shot. Mrs. Garrett told me that Mr. Wallace took her to the hospital, but he apparently did not go into the hospital with her. At least, I didn't see him. She said that she came to my office in a cab from the hospital."

"So? What's your problem?" Mac said looking a little confused.

"The problem is how did Josh's car get from the café to the underground parking garage where my office is located? Josh certainly didn't drive there, and Mrs. Garrett said she didn't drive it there, so who did?"

"That's a good question," Mac said thoughtfully.

"Have you got an answer?"

"No. I don't know how it got there."

"Do you still have the car?"

"Yes. Our forensic people are going over it."

"Good. Let me know if you find any evidence that someone else might have driven the car. Something like fingerprints that shouldn't be in the car, or fingerprints that are not there that should be."

"I'll make sure they check it over completely," Mac assured me.

"Thanks. I'll get back to you later."

"What's your next move?"

"I'm going over to the hospital and talk with the recovery room staff who were on duty the night Josh died."

"Okay. We talked to them but got nothing of interest. Let me know what you find out. We can compare notes. You might be able to get them to talk to you," Mac said. "They didn't seem too cooperative when they talked to me."

"I will. By the way, I was followed this morning by a dark blue Cadillac sedan. I wasn't able to get a license plate number. If I get one, will you run it for me?"

"Sure. If someone is following you, it might be someone we would like to have a talk with, too."

"I'll see you later," I said as I stood up and walked out of Mac's office.

AS I WALKED OUT of the police station, I noticed a dark blue Cadillac sedan parked across the street from the parking lot. I wasn't a hundred percent sure if it was the same car that had tried to follow me earlier, but it certainly looked like it. With the dark tinted windows, I couldn't see if there was anyone in the car, but I could see one of the lights on the front of the car was on. I knew most brands of GM cars that had been built in the past few years had lights that were always on if the car's engine was running. It didn't take a genius to figure out there was probably someone in the car and I was about to be followed.

Since I had no desire to be followed, I stopped, looked down at the pavement in front of me for a moment, then turned around and went back inside the police station. I had done my best to make it look like I had simply forgotten something.

I returned to Mac's office and stuck my head in the door. Mac looked up at me.

"Did you forget something?"

"No. There's a dark blue Cadillac sedan parked across the street with the engine running. I think it is the same one that tried to follow me this morning. I need you to do me a favor."

"Okay."

"I would like someone to see if they can get the license plate number when it pulls away."

"Sure thing. I'll have an officer walk out to one of the cars in the lot. You get in your car and leave. He'll get the license plate number when the car pulls away from the curb. As soon as I get it, I'll run it."

"Thanks," I said.

Mac picked up his phone and called the front desk. He told the desk sergeant to have a policeman walk out of the building like he is walking out to a car. He told the desk sergeant that he wanted the officer to get the license plate number of the dark blue Cadillac sedan parked across the street when I left in my Tahoe.

Mac didn't hang up the phone. It was clear he was waiting to make sure there was an officer ready to go out as soon as I started to leave the building.

I waited next to his office door. When Mac nodded they were ready, I turned and left his office.

As soon as I got to the door, an officer walked out of the building only a couple of steps in front of me. I walked to my Tahoe, got in and started it. I backed out of the parking space, then drove out to the street. After looking both ways,

I turned out onto the street and headed away from the police station. A quick look in my rearview mirror showed me the dark blue Cadillac sedan had pulled away from the curb and was following me.

I took my time as I drove out to the Interstate. I turned onto the Interstate and headed north toward Thornton. The blue sedan followed me as if he was on a leash.

It wasn't long and I was getting tired of him following me. I had a friend who owned an automobile dealership in Thornton. I was sure my friend would think it was fun if he could help me ditch someone who was following me.

I pulled off the Interstate and drove the short distance to the dealership. I drove in and pulled up in front of the quick service bay. The door opened and I drove in. As the service door was closing, I got out of my Tahoe and watched for the blue sedan. I saw it turn into the parking lot of a Circle K convenience store across the street. He parked next to the building, but didn't get out of his car.

"What can we do for you today," one of the servicemen asked.

"Is Randy in?"

"Yes, I believe he is."

"Good. You can pull my Tahoe out in back and park it. Don't take it around in front. I'm going to see Randy."

"Yes, sir," he said, but looked a little confused by my request.

I left the service bay and walked out to where the offices were located, just off the showroom floor. I saw Randy sitting at a desk behind a glass partition. As I walked toward the door, he looked up and saw me. He waved for me to come in.

"Hi, Peter. What brings you way out here? Have you decided it's time for you to get a new set of wheels?"

"Not really. The Chevy Tahoe is running pretty good. I need a favor."

"Sure. What can I do for you?"

"You can loan me a car for a few hours. It doesn't have to be a new car."

"No problem."

"I would like you to have it brought around back so I can leave without being seen."

"Are you playing cat and mouse with someone?" Randy asked with a grin.

"Yes. I have a guy on my tail and I want to ditch him."

"No problem. My Ford F-150 is sitting out back," he said as he handed me the keys. "It has a full tank of gas and is ready to go. I take it you are in a bit of a hurry?"

"Yes. Here are the keys to my Tahoe. You might as well service it while it's here."

"We'll take good care of it."

"Thanks. I'll fill you in on what's going on when I come back."

"No need. I know what you do for a living. If you return it after we are closed just leave the truck out back. I'll leave your car out back. The keys will be under the floor mat."

"Thanks, Randy. Leave me a bill and I'll send you a check."

"Okay."

I turned and left out the backdoor of the shop. I found Randy's pickup, got in and drove away leaving my tail sitting in his car at the Circle K. I headed for Denver General Hospital.

Since it was a little after twelve noon, I decided to stop at a restaurant and have lunch on my way back to the hospital. I took my time because the recovery room personnel I wanted to talk to would not be there until about two. When I finished a leisurely lunch, I left the restaurant and drove back to Denver to the hospital.

I ARRIVED AT DENVER GENERAL HOSPITAL shortly after one. I got there just as the shift for the recovery room personnel I wanted to talk to were coming to work. I asked a nurse just outside the recovery room if she could point out the afternoon supervisor. She told me it was Rose Williams and pointed her out to me.

Rose Williams looked to be in her mid-to-late fifties. She was fairly short and a little on the heavy side, but carried herself well. Her short gray hair looked nice on her and was cut in a style I was sure would be easy to manage. She didn't wear very much makeup, but then she really didn't need it.

"Excuse me, but are you Rose Williams?" I asked as a nurse walked by.

"Yes."

"I'm Peter Blackstone."

"I know who you are," she said with a smile. "You're the young man who is dating Julie Archer."

"Yes," I said with a grin.

"I also know you are investigating the death of Josh Garrett," she said as the smile faded from her face.

"Yes. It is my understanding you were on duty the night he died."

"That would be correct. It's always hard when you lose such a young man."

"I'm sure it is. I'm interested in knowing if you saw anyone go in or out of the recovery room who didn't belong there. Please take a minute to think about everyone you saw that night."

"I don't remember seeing anyone who was not a staff member," she said thoughtfully. "We were pretty busy. We had had a full surgery schedule, plus one emergency surgery. That would have been Mr. Garrett," she said with a hint of sadness in her voice.

"What about visitors. I know family members are the only ones allowed in the recovery room. Did Josh have any visitors, other than his wife?"

"Why, yes. I almost forgot. His brother stopped by for a little while. As I recall, he wasn't there very long."

"His brother?"

"Yes," Rose said as she looked at me.

"That would be Ralph?"

"Yes. I believe his name was Ralph. I remember him because he came in rather late, about one a.m., maybe a few minutes after one. I was told later he had just flown in from, ah - - California, I believe."

"I need you to think real hard. What did Ralph look like?"

"Well, he was about six foot tall," she said thoughtfully.

"He was just a little shorter than I am?"

"Yes. I think he would be a little heavier than you, maybe two hundred twenty to two hundred and forty pounds. Not as muscular as you are though."

"What was he wearing?"

"He was wearing a mask and gown. That is required here with so many patients with fresh wounds. It helps reduce the chance of patients getting an infection, but I guess you would know that."

"Yes. I understand, but could you tell what he had on under the gown," I asked, hoping she might have noticed something that would help.

Rose looked at me. The look on her face told me that she was wondering where I was going with my line of questions.

"I guess I didn't notice what he had on under the gown. However, I did notice he was wearing cowboy boots."

"Cowboy boots?"

"Yes. They were those fancy kinds with silver tips on the toes and fancy stitching on the sides. The shoe covers we ask visitors to wear didn't fit them very well," she replied.

"The reason I'm asking the questions is because Josh's brother, Ralph, died in an auto accident several years ago, in California."

"Oh, my God. You mean we let someone in here who might have killed Mr. Garrett?" she asked as a shocked look came over her face.

"I'm afraid you are correct. I don't blame you, or whoever it was who let him in. I got a call from a person who told me he was Josh's brother, and I knew Josh had a brother named Ralph. It wasn't until I talked to Mrs. Garrett that I found out Ralph had died several years ago.

"I'm going to leave for now. I need to get in touch with Captain MacDonald of the police department and tell him about this. Please don't talk to the other staff members about our conversation until I have had a chance to talk to them. By the way, who cleared the visitor who came to see Josh on the night he died?"

"That would have been Mary Spencer. She works on the desk just outside the recovery room entrance. It's that glass window over there," she said as she pointed to a window next to the doors to the recovery room.

"Thank you," I said then turned toward the window.

I walked up to the window next to the recovery room door. There was a woman about thirty years old sitting behind the window. There was a computer in front of her. She was working on something on the computer. I waited in front of the window to see how long it would take her to look up and acknowledge my presence. It was a minute or so before she looked up at me. It was easy to see where someone could get into the recovery room without anyone noticing if she was busy.

"May I help you," the woman said as she looked up from the computer.

"Yes. My name is Peter Blackstone. Are you Mary Spencer?"

"No. I'm Kate Hunter. Mary called in just before noon that she wasn't feeling well."

"Do you know what was wrong?"

"No. I was sent here by my supervisor. She was the one who told me that Mary called in sick. I was told that Mary thought she was coming down with a cold. We don't expect her back to work for a couple of days. Is there something I can do for you?"

"No, thank you," I said then turned and walked down the hall.

I didn't bother to ask the woman at the window if she knew Mary's address. I was sure it was policy not to give out the addresses or any other information on hospital employees. The only way I might be able to get her address is to talk to the hospital administrator.

I took the elevator to the floor where the administration offices were located. It only took a couple of minutes to find the office I needed. I opened the door and went inside.

There was a nice looking young woman sitting at a desk typing something on a computer. She looked up at me and smiled.

"May I help you," she said in a very pleasant voice.

"I'm looking for some information on one of the employees," I said as I took my Private Investigator's badge and ID out of my coat pocket.

"Oh," she said as she looked at the badge.

"Who do I have to talk to about one of your employees?"

"Just a moment, please," she said as she picked up the phone and pressed a button.

She placed a call to someone, but didn't even hint at who it might be. If I had to guess, it was probably the hospital's Human Resource Administrator. It wasn't but a couple of minutes when a tall slim man wearing a dark suit came into the office. He looked at the woman at the desk, then at me. He walked up to me.

"Is there something I can do for you?" he asked.

"Yes. I'm Peter Blackstone," I said.

When I showed him my badge and ID, he hardly looked at it.

"What is it I can do for you?"

"I'm investigating the death of Josh Garrett. I would like to talk to Mary Spencer. I understand she is not at work today. She apparently called in sick and isn't expected back at work for a few days. I would like her home address, please."

"I'm sorry, but we can't give that information to just anybody," he said with a holier-than-thou attitude.

I wasn't about to let him brush me off so easily.

"What is your name, sir?"

"Nathan Waterman, I'm the Human Resources Administrator."

"Well, Mr. Waterman, your attitude seems to convey a lack of cooperation in a criminal investigation involving this hospital. How long do you think you will have your job if I were to make a call to a judge and get a warrant to search your files for the information I want, and might add, need? There's also the fact that there would be police officers all over the place."

"Are you threatening me, officer?" he said sharply.

"Oh, no, not at all. You see, I don't believe in threatening people, it never gets you anywhere. I only make promises, just promises, and I always follow through on my promises."

I almost smiled at the expression on his face. The attitude he started with seemed to fade away rather quickly. I got the impression he was beginning to believe I could cause him a lot of problems that would make him look bad in the eyes of his boss. From the look on his face, I got the impression he would not like that.

"That won't be necessary. I'll get her address for you," he said then turned and left the office.

I watched him as he left the office. As soon as he disappeared, I glanced over at the secretary. She had a grin on her face. I smiled and winked at her, but quickly lost the smile when I heard the door Nathan had left through start to open. Nathan walked in and stood in front of me. He gave me Mary Spencer's home address and home telephone neatly printed on a small piece of paper.

"Is there anything else I can do for you, sir?" he asked with a pleasant tone in his voice.

"Not at this time. Thank you for your cooperation, Nathan," I said with a smile.

I immediately left the office and headed for my friend's pickup truck. I got in the pickup truck and left the parking lot of Denver General Hospital.

CHAPTER TWELVE

I DROVE ACROSS TOWN to the address Mr. Waterman had given me and arrived at a little after three. I parked in the street across from the house.

The house was a small brick house which was probably built in the mid-fifties or early sixties. It looked as if it was in good repair. There was a one car detached garage with the garage door open. There was a four or five-year-old small Dodge in the garage.

As I looked at the house, I wondered what I was going to find behind the front door. I had no idea how old Mary Spencer was, or anything about her.

I got out of the pickup truck and walked across the street toward the house. Just as I stepped up on the front porch and was ready to knock on the door, I heard the side door of the house bang shut. I quickly stepped off the porch and ran to the side of the house. I caught a glimpse of someone running around back. I saw enough of the person to know it was man, but that was about all.

I took off after the man, but by the time I got to the back of the house, a car in the alley was making tracks out of there. With the tall bushes along the fence, I was unable to see much of the car, or get a license plate number. About the only thing I could see was it was the dark blue top of what was probably a fairly late model car. My first thought was it was a Cadillac, but that might have been because I had had a dark blue Cadillac follow me earlier. I couldn't be sure what make of car had been in the alley.

Since there was nothing else I could do, I turned around and walked back to the house. I tried the side door and found it was not locked. I decided to enter the house. I had no idea if Mary Spencer was home or not, but with the suspicious happenings I thought it was wise to check to see if she was home.

I stepped inside the side door and called out to Mary, but didn't get an answer. I moved into the kitchen. On the kitchen table, I found the remains of a sandwich on a plate, a cup of coffee and a glass of water on the table. My best guess was that it was probably her lunch, what was left of it. I put my hand over the partial cup of coffee to see if it was still warm, it was cold and from the looks of the inside of the cup, it had been there for some time.

I looked around, then called out again. Once again, I didn't get an answer. It seemed a little strange someone would run out of the house and speed away if nothing was wrong. I decided to walk through the house, being careful not to touch anything.

There was nothing in the living room that grabbed my attention. It appeared to be neat and clean, and nothing appeared to be out of place. I continued down the hall and took a quick look in the bedroom. The bed looked like it had been made and then had the covers pulled off it as if someone had been dragged off the bed. There were clothes that looked as if they had not been worn, but looked like they had been dumped on the floor when the covers were pulled off. There was also a robe lying on the floor. I wondered what had happened there.

When I took in the entire bedroom, it had all the classic signs of a struggle having taken place there. The small lamp on the bedside table was lying on the floor along with an alarm clock. Pictures that had been on the dresser had been knocked over with a couple of them on the floor.

I walked down the hall to the bathroom and slowly opened the door. The first thing I noticed was it was a mess. The floor was wet and a small throw rug in front of the sink was bunched up as if it had been pushed around. I stepped inside the bathroom and looked around the door. I was a bit surprised to see a hand hanging out over the side of the bathtub. It appeared to be the hand of a woman. I moved closer and pulled back the shower curtain. There was a woman wearing just her bra and panties lying in the tub which was full of water. Her head and face were completely under water. It was obvious that she had been beaten. Her eyes were practically open making it clear that she was dead. I couldn't be sure, but the woman looked to be in her late fifties or early sixties. There was blood in the water giving it a pinkish color. From the position of her head, it appeared that her neck might have been broken.

It was obvious there was nothing I could do for her. It was time to get the police involved. It was also time for me to get out of the house.

I left the bathroom and walked outside. I walked around to the front porch and sat down on the steps. I took my cell phone and dialed Mac's office. It didn't take long before Mac answered the phone.

"Captain MacDonald, how can I help you?"

"Mac, Peter."

"What's up, Pete?"

"I need to report a murder."

"What?

"Mary Spencer, at least that's who I think it is, was murdered. I came to her house to talk to her and some guy ran out the side door and around back and sped away. I didn't get a good look at him. I went into the house to investigate and found a body in the bathtub, under water. If I had to guess, I would say that her neck was broken, too."

"I'll get a unit out there right away. What interest is Mary Spencer to you?"

"She was apparently the one who let a visitor into the recovery room to see Josh, a visitor who should not have been allowed in."

"Give me that address," Mac said. "I'll be out there as soon as I can. I'll get a black-and-white unit out there to secure the area."

I gave Mac the address and told him I would wait for him. I hung up the phone then remained sitting on the steps to the front porch to wait for the police.

IT TOOK ONLY ABOUT TEN MINUTES before I heard the first police siren. It kept coming closer until a black-and-white police car pulled up in front of the house. I stood up and walked out to the curb in front of the house to meet the officers. Two officers got out of the police car.

"Are you Peter Blackstone?" the older of the two officers asked.

"Yes."

"I'm Officer Frank Norbert. I've heard of you. You're a private investigator now?"

"That's right."

"What have you got here?"

"There is a woman who looks like she was probably beaten then drowned in the bathtub. I'm not a hundred percent sure, but I believe her name is Mary Spencer."

"What's your involvement with her?" the younger officer asked.

I turned and looked at the young officer. The tone of his voice and his posture made it clear that he didn't like private investigators. He seemed a bit young to have developed an opinion about PIs so soon.

"I have no involvement with her, as you put it. I came here to question her about a case I'm working on."

"I'll bet," he said sarcastically.

I turned and looked at Officer Norbert. He was just shaking his head.

"How long has he been out of the academy?" I asked Officer Norbert.

"Not long," he said with a hint of frustration.

I turned back toward the young officer and looked at him for a moment.

"Young man, you might find it to your advantage to keep your mouth shut and pay close attention to your partner. At least until you have some idea what is going on."

I noticed the look in his eye and the way his body tensed. He was trying very hard to make me think he was ready to arrest me if I even tried to challenge his authority.

"It might be a good idea if you listen to Mr. Blackstone," Officer Norbert said. "He's been around a lot longer than you, and probably seen more than most officers. Besides, he was a police officer once, and I'm told he was a damn good one."

The young officer just looked at his partner. When he didn't say anything, I was sure Norbert was the young officer's training officer, and the young officer was fresh out of the academy. This was probably his first murder case. Maybe his first anything except for having written a traffic ticket or two.

"Can you tell me what happened from the time you arrived here until we arrived, Mr. Blackstone?" Officer Norbert asked.

I told him everything I could about why I was there, what I saw before I entered the house and what I saw after I went into the house. Office Norbert made notes of every-thing I said.

"Did you touch anything inside the house?"

"No. Ah, yes. I touched the bathroom doorknob, on the outside of the bathroom, before I knew there was a body in the bathtub. As soon as I saw the body, and it was obvious she was dead, I immediately walked out of the house and called Captain MacDonald."

"Captain MacDonald called dispatch and they called us to come and secure the scene. Has anyone else been in the house since you arrived?" Officer Norbert asked.

"Only the guy I saw running around to the back of the house. I think he came out the side door when I was about to knock on the front door. Since I didn't actually see him leave the house by the side door, it's just a guess on my part, but I did hear the side door slam shut. I didn't get a chance to see what kind of car he was driving because of the hedge row along the alley. About all I can tell you is it was a late model dark blue sedan, and it got out of here in a hell of a hurry. Since it left so quickly, there may have been someone else in the car with the engine running."

"Thank you. Captain MacDonald is on his way here. I'm sure he would like you to stick around."

"I'm sure. I have no intentions of leaving until I talk to him."

IT ONLY TOOK MAC about twenty minutes from the time I called him to when he pulled up in front of the house. By the time he arrived, an ambulance was just getting there. He was immediately greeted by Officer Norbert.

"I take it the area is secure?" Mac asked the officer.

"Yes, sir."

"Have you been inside?"

"No, sir. We were waiting for you."

"Pete, have you been back in the house since we talked?"

"No. I just waited on the front porch steps for these officers to get here. I talked to them about what I found, then sat back down and waited for you."

"Let's go in and take a look around."

I nodded then followed Mac into the house. We went in the side door. As soon as he stepped into the kitchen, he stopped and looked around.

"The coffee on the table was cold when I got here."

Mac didn't say anything, he simply nodded that he had heard me. I followed him into the bathroom. He stood just inside the bathroom and looked around. After a minute or so of just looking, he leaned over and looked at the body in the bathtub.

"Is she just the way you found her?"

"Yes. I didn't touch her. It was obvious she was dead and there was nothing I could do for her. I immediately walked out of the house the same way I came in and didn't touch anything but the doorknob on the bathroom door. By the way, the bedroom looks like there had been a fight in it."

"Okay. I'll get a forensic team out here to go over the entire house. Let's get out of here."

I followed Mac outside. I waited while he went to his car and called for a forensic team and the coroner. When he was done, he returned to where I was sitting on the front porch steps. He took a deep breath and sat down beside me.

"How much do you know about the woman in the tub?"

"I've never met the woman before. If it is the woman who is supposed to live here, her name is Mary Spencer. She worked for Denver General Hospital. I'm not sure of her position at the hospital, but one of her duties was to screen people who went into the recovery room. She was the one on duty the night Josh was killed. It is my understanding she let the person in who may have killed Josh."

"How so?"

"The way it was told to me by the recovery room supervisor, Rose Williams, Mary Spencer let some guy in to visit Josh. The guy claimed to be Josh's brother. Josh had only one brother, Ralph, but Ralph died in an auto accident about four years ago in California."

"No one checked him out to see if he was really a close family member?"

"Apparently, he either wasn't checked out to verify that he was a close relative, or he was allowed in knowing what he was there to do," I said as I looked at Mac for his reaction.

"You think this Spencer woman let him in so he could kill Josh?"

"I'm not sure 'let' is the word I would use. She might have been bought, or she might have been threatened somehow," I suggested. "Either way, it's just speculation on my part."

"I think a look into her background is in order," Mac said thinking out loud.

"That sounds like a good idea. If you're done with me, I think I'll head on out. I've got a few things to look into myself."

"Yeah, you can go. I'll talk to you later," Mac said.

I nodded, then stood up and walked across the street to the pickup truck. I got in and looked toward the house before I drove away. As I left, I noticed Mac was watching me as I drove off. I was sure he wondered if the brand new pickup truck was mine.

When I got to the end of the block, I turned just as the CSI truck turned the corner. I wondered what they might find in the house. Whatever they found, I hoped Mac would let me in on it.

I glanced at my watch and decided there was not much I could do at the hospital. Those working in the recovery room would be on duty. They would not have time to talk to me. I would have to try again some other time.

I did have time, however, to go to the library to see what I could find out about several people. I headed for the library to look up anything I could find on Mr. Wilbur Routh, Williams of Williams Reality, and Rose Williams.

Thinking of Mr. Williams of Williams Reality and Rose Williams at the same time made me think about something else. Was it possible they were related? Rose was old enough to be Mr. Williams' wife, or possibly his sister. I also knew there were other possibilities, one being that they were not related at all.

The more I thought about it, the more I didn't think it was likely they were related. There had to be a lot of Williams in Denver and the surrounding areas. Still it wouldn't hurt to check it out.

IT DIDN'T TAKE LONG to get to the library. I parked the pickup truck in the library parking lot and walked into the library. I went directly to the area of the library that was mainly for references. I started out looking for information on Williams of Williams Reality. Since I had no idea what his first name was, it took me awhile to find the right Williams. I discovered his first name was Anthony. I found several references to an Anthony Williams and Tony Williams.

One of the references to an Anthony R. Williams, said that he was a realtor in Dillion. That's when I knew I had the right one. I wrote down the information it provided so I could run criminal and financial background checks on him. I would do that in my office as I didn't think it was a good idea to run those kinds of reports on the library's public computers.

What I would run on the library's computers was anything I could find on him in the newspapers. I like to use newspapers for information on people. I would do it at my office, but my only connection was to the local newspapers, namely the Denver newspapers. I had a feeling I just might find some of the smaller newspapers in the area might have something on him.

After a bit of searching, I found the Summit Daily Newspaper covered most of the towns in Summit County. I began searching for articles on Tony or Anthony Williams. I quickly discovered there were two Anthony Williams living in Dillion. Based on their ages, it appeared they might be father and son, but I found nothing to connect them, such as the younger one being a junior.

I did a search for a picture of the younger Williams. The only picture I found was of Anthony Williams, the elder, which showed me I had the right Williams. In the background, there was a man who looked a lot like the man who had followed Miss Sullivan out of the bank and tried to grab her. Since it was not a very good picture, I couldn't be sure it was the same man. The article didn't give any information on anyone other than Anthony Williams, the elder. I still didn't know the name of the man who followed Miss Sullivan.

The thought of Miss Sullivan caused me to remember that I had not heard from Sheriff Tom Stillwell. Since I had not been in my office for some time, I thought it might be a good idea if I stopped by and checked my answering machine. I was sure Tom would try to contact me as soon as he knew the name of the person who was driving the car I saw outside Miss Sullivan's apartment in Frisco.

I took a minute to read the rest of the article that went with the picture. It was about the Grand Opening of Williams Reality. The date was just over three years ago. It did not identify the man in the background.

I decided to return to my office and look up what I could find on the two Anthony Williams. Maybe I would be able to get the kind of information I wanted in the privacy of my office.

I shut off the computer, got up and walked to the pickup truck. I got in and started it, but sat there for a minute to just think. My thoughts were about the truck I had been driving.

If I went to the dealership and returned my friends pickup then returned to my office with my Tahoe, whoever it was following me would know I had returned. If I took the truck to my office, I might be able to slip into my office without anyone knowing I was back. I put the pickup in gear and drove back to my office.

CHAPTER THIRTEEN

WHEN I ARRIVED AT MY OFFICE, I drove into the underground parking garage. I made it a point not to park in either of the two parking spaces reserved for me, one for my vehicle and one for a client or guest that might be visiting in my office. Instead, I parked in a space some distance from mine. The space where I parked was reserved for a man who I knew would not be using it for a week or so because he was out of town on vacation with his family.

I got out of the pickup and carefully walked toward the elevator, keeping an eye out for anyone who might be hanging around in the parking garage. I was being especially watchful for a dark blue Cadillac sedan like the one that had followed me. I didn't see any Cadillacs in the garage, or anyone hanging around.

As I worked my way between the cars parked in the garage, I noticed a small red sports car with two people in it. I smiled to myself when I saw them kissing. The young woman broke off the kiss and looked around as if she was afraid someone might see them necking. When she saw me, she looked a little embarrassed by the fact I had seen her necking with the young man. I immediately recognized her as one of the secretaries who worked in an office on the floor below the floor where my office was located. I winked and smiled then continued on my way. She smiled sort of an embarrassed kind of smile then looked away.

When I got to the elevator, I pressed the call button. The elevator opened immediately. After making sure there was no one in the elevator, I stepped in and pressed the button for the seventh floor. The door closed and the elevator started to go up. When it slowed for the fourth floor, I stepped back in the corner, slipped my hand over my gun and waited for it to stop.

As the door opened, I saw a woman with a young boy. I took my hand off my gun and let my coat fall over it. From the look on the woman's face, she must have seen my gun. The woman just stood there looking at me for a second before she spoke.

"We're going down," the woman said as she gently pushed the young boy behind her.

"I'll send it back down for you," I said politely, then pushed the button to make the door close.

When the elevator reached the seventh floor, I pressed the button to send the elevator back to the fourth floor, then got off and walked to the end of the hall. I took the stairway on up to the ninth floor. I had no idea if anyone would be planning anything, but it was just my way of making sure I was not surprised.

Once I reached the ninth floor, I looked out the small window of the fire door and saw the hallway was empty. I stepped out of the stairway and walked on down the hall to my office. I unlocked the door and went into the outer office, then closed and locked the door behind me.

I entered my office, hung up my coat, then walked around behind my desk and turned on my computer. While my computer was booting up, I sat down and checked my answering machine for any messages. There was one message from Tom. I pressed the button to hear the message.

"I guess you're not in your office. This is Sheriff Stillwell. I got a make on the license plate number of the car you saw at Miss Sullivan's apartment. It belongs to an Anthony Williams who lives here in Dillion. I hope this helps you. Talk to you later."

That was the only message on my answering machine. The thought ran through my mind, was the car registered to Anthony Williams, the elder and someone else was driving it, or was it registered to the younger Williams and he was driving it? It was a little late to call Tom and ask him which Williams it was registered to.

By the time the message had finished, my computer was ready to use. I turned around in my chair and rolled up to the computer.

I went to a program that allowed me to do background checks on people. I typed in Anthony Williams with the identifying words of "Dillion, Colorado". It came up with two Anthony Williams. I typed in additional identifying information which clarified for the computer that I wanted the elder Williams, Anthony. I then requested a criminal record for him. It took a few minutes before it came up with a criminal record. I wasn't sure if it took so long because it couldn't find his record; or if it took so long because he had such a long record, it took awhile to get it up on the screen.

Once it came up, it showed Mr. Anthony R. Williams had an arrest record that was quite lengthy. It included charges of extortion, bribery, and money laundering, plus numerous other charges that seemed minor by comparison. It seems his record went back almost thirty years. The one thing I noticed was he had never served any time for even the major crimes he was accused of. In fact, he had never even gone to jail for more than a night or two. I found that interesting.

The record also showed me that he was in his mid-fifties which fit the man I saw at Williams Reality. As I scrolled down the screen, I found a picture of him. It confirmed that it was the man I saw at Williams Reality.

It seemed a little strange he had been able to get a Realtor's License with his long arrest record. The only reason he might have gotten one was the fact he had never been convicted of a crime in a court of law.

The charge of money laundering was the most interesting charge to me. He would not be the first one to launder money through a bank, but it usually required someone in the bank to help in the operation. That caused me to think Mr. Wilbur Routh just might be the one helping.

Another thing I noticed from the report was all the charges had not been made in Colorado. Three of the major charges, one for bribery and two for extortion, took place in Reno, Nevada, and had to do with two of the large casinos. It appeared the casinos dropped the charges. It was apparent that those running the casinos probably didn't want that kind of publicity.

There was also a charge of money laundering that took place in Las Vegas. The charge there was also dropped. He apparently left shortly after the charge was dropped and moved to Dillion, Colorado. I wondered if the move out of Las Vegas was agreed to in exchange for dropping the charge. It was beginning to look like Anthony Williams had decided to set up shop in Dillion.

I sat back in my chair and thought about what I had found out. It didn't help much with my case, but it did give me something to think about.

It occurred to me that the younger Anthony Williams might be related to him. I closed out the files on the older Williams report and typed the identifying information on the younger Anthony Williams. The criminal report on the younger Williams cleared up one question. The report listed him as Anthony R. Williams, Jr., but noted that he used the first name of Tony. From the looks of his criminal report, Tony had followed in his father's footsteps. He had almost an identical criminal record as his father with the same criminal charges at or about the same times. The only major difference was he had several charges for assault, ranging from simple assault to assault with intent to do bodily harm. There was one of the assault charges as assault with a deadly weapon. There was even one that charged him with assaulting a woman. And like his father, all the charges had been dropped. With his background of violence, his victims were probably threatened in order to get them to drop the charges.

The report didn't show a picture of Tony, but it gave a description of him. The description matched the man who had followed Miss Sullivan out of the bank and tried to grab her off the street. It also matched the general description of the man who had posed as Ralph Garrett in the hospital, but that one could have matched a good number of men in the Denver area.

I sat back and thought about the reports. If I had to guess, Tony was the muscle, while Anthony Williams handled the family business. The only questions I had were what was the family business? What had Josh found out at the bank that led him to suspect there was something illegal going on there?

I couldn't see any answers to my questions on the computer, but one thought did come to mind. How did they discover Josh was on to them? Who found out? Was it Routh, or was there someone else in the bank involved? It suddenly occurred to me that if they were laundering money through the bank, where was the money coming from, and why did they need to launder it?

My first thought was it was drug money, but I had no way of knowing that for a fact. Nothing in their criminal records indicated they had anything to do with drugs. However, Josh had been murdered using a large dose of cocaine. Someone had to get it someplace.

It might prove interesting to find out if Williams was actually selling property, or if the business was just a front to take in money, then deposit it in the bank in things like stocks, bonds, various securities, or into properties that would be resold legitimately to people unaware of their origin. Putting the money into property then reselling it could work, but there was a greater danger of someone discovering it. Stocks, bonds, and securities seemed to me to be less risky because fewer people would be involved. The stocks or other securities could be purchased in one place, then sold off almost anywhere in the country.

Since Josh worked in the investments, securities and insurance department of the bank, it seemed likely the money was being laundered through those types of services. Things like securities could be purchased and turned over rather quickly.

The more I thought about it, the more it seemed logical that the real estate business was a front. The money would be used to buy securities then cash them out at a later date, or the securities would be sent to some other location where they could be cashed out without any questions, plus it would be a little harder to trace.

I was beginning to think there had to be more than just the few people I suspected of wrong doing. If they were laundering money, it seemed to me it would take more than just the three or four people I knew about so far.

A quick glance at my watch showed me it was getting on toward dinnertime. I had told Julie I would come and get her. I was beginning to think it might be best if she stayed with her brother.

I shut down my computer, locked up the office and went to the underground parking garage. Leaving the parking garage, I drove to the dealership where I had gotten the pickup truck. I returned it to where it had been parked, but discovered my Tahoe was gone. I checked with one of the salesman and was told Randy had already left for the day in my Tahoe. He also told me that Randy had left a message for me. He handed me an envelope. I opened it and read it.

The message said he had taken my Tahoe to his home and I could return his pickup truck anytime tomorrow at the dealership.

I smiled at the note. Randy was giving me a little more time with his new pickup truck in the hope of selling me one.

I thanked the salesman for the message and left. I drove to George's home in Aurora.

I ARRIVED AT GEORGE'S HOME at quarter to seven. When I drove in the driveway, I phoned George. I knew he would not recognize the pickup I was driving.

"Yeah," George said.

"It's me in the fancy new pickup in your drive."

"Okay," he said.

The garage door began to open almost immediately. I drove into the garage then waited in the pickup until the door closed.

"Where'd you get the fancy truck?" George asked as I stepped out of it.

"I borrowed it from a friend of mine. It came in handy in ditching a tail."

"Pretty fancy," he said with a smile.

"Yeah, it's pretty nice. How are the girls getting along?" I asked as we walked into the kitchen.

"They're doing okay. Mrs. Garrett spends most of the time in her room. She doesn't seem to want to socialize with the others, but then she just lost her husband," George said as we sat down at the kitchen table. "I sent them to their rooms when I saw the pickup pull into the drive. You want me to get them?"

"Before you say anything to get them out of their rooms, I've got a couple of questions to ask you."

"Go for it."

"Has Mary Sullivan said anything to you that sounds a little strange, or maybe like she is seeking information on what I might know?"

"No. In fact, she hasn't said much of anything to me. About the only questions she has asked me are about what I do for a living, what I do for a living when I'm not being a bodyguard, and what I like to eat," he said with a grin. "She hasn't said much at all about her life, nor has she asked me anything about your investigation."

"What about Mrs. Garrett?"

"Like I said, she spends most of her time in her room. I've checked in on her a couple of times without her knowing. She has been doing a lot of crying. I think she was pretty close to Josh."

"I think you're right. Has she talked at all to you?'

"Only at the table with the others around. It seems she doesn't want to talk about the death of her husband. I think she might be having trouble dealing with it."

"Has she talked to Julie?"

"She might have, but not that I know of. I do know she is concerned that Josh will be buried and she won't be there."

"I'll talk to Mac to make sure that doesn't happen."

"Good. Does she know that?"

"I had assured her that she would be there to help arrange for his burial."

"Okay. Are you ready to talk to my sister?"

"Yes. I don't think she will be happy with what I'm going to say."

"Really? What do you plan to tell her, if it's any of my business?"

"I'm going to tell her that I want her to stay here with you."

"I think she will be disappointed that she will not be with you tonight."

"I'd rather have her disappointed than end up like my last girlfriend."

"I understand. I think she will also understand, though she may not like it," George said as he stood up. "I'll get her for you."

It didn't take Julie long to come into the kitchen. I stood up as she entered the kitchen. She had a smile on her face and looked like she was glad to see me. As soon as she saw the look on my face, the smile faded away.

"What's the matter?" she asked as she stepped up in front of me.

I took her in my arms and gave her a kiss. It was a nice kiss, but I could tell she knew something was not right. After the kiss, she leaned back and looked up at me.

"What's the matter, honey? Did you have a bad day?"

"Well, sort of, but I need to talk to you."

"Okay," she said as she drew me closer to the kitchen table.

I pulled out a chair for her. She sat down then I sat down beside her. I just looked at her for a moment before saying anything.

"I want you to stay here for a couple of days."

"I'm not going to be staying with you tonight?"

She sounded disappointed, but I don't think she was too surprised. She knew about my former girlfriend and what had happened to her.

"No, not tonight. Things are looking like they might get nasty and I don't want you where you might get hurt."

"You found out something, haven't you?"

"Yes. I think Josh found out what was going on at the bank and that was why he was killed. I still don't know for sure what has been going on, but I have found out there are some very nasty people involved in it."

"But you will protect me," she said softly as she reached out and put her hand on mine.

"I can't protect you and still do what I have to do."

"This is about your former girlfriend, and the fact she died while she was with you. There was nothing you could have done to protect her," she said in a soft and understanding voice.

"That's just it. I couldn't protect her because she was with me."

Julie just sat there looking at me. I could see tears come to her eyes. I wanted to say something that would make her feel better, but I couldn't find the words.

"I want you to be with me more than anything, but I can't do what I have to do and protect you, too. I want you to stay with your brother at least until I figure what is going on and who is involved."

Julie looked at me as a tear rolled down her cheek. I reached over and gently wiped it away.

"Will you come by and tell me how things are going?" she asked.

"Yes. I will come by or call you every night. And I will miss having you in my arms at night."

"I will miss you. You could stay here with me."

"I can't come here too often. I can't always see who is following me. If they find out you and the others are here, it will make it impossible for George to protect all of you. But I will call you."

"I understand," she said, but not very convincingly. "Are you going to stay tonight?"

"I can't. I have a lot to do, but I will be in my office. I have several things I need to do. I will probably be working late," I said then we stood up and walked to the kitchen door to the garage.

Julie followed me to the door. I turned around and pulled her up to me. I held her in my arms. I didn't really want to let her go. We kissed several times, before George came into the kitchen.

"I hate to interrupt you, but are you leaving, Peter?"

"Yes. I have some work to do in the office. It will take me a couple of hours at least."

"Will you be returning tonight?" George asked.

"No. It's too easy for someone to follow me, especially at night."

"Will you call me when you get home?" Julie asked hopefully.

"Yes, but it might be late."

"That's okay. I'll be waiting for your call."

I gave Julie another kiss, then went into the garage. As soon as I was in the pickup truck, George opened the garage door and I backed out. As soon as the pickup cleared the garage door, it began to close. I turned out onto the street and headed for my office.

WHEN I ARRIVED AT THE BUILDING my office was located in, I parked the pickup in the same place I had parked it before. I took the elevator to the seventh floor and walked up to the ninth floor.

After checking the hall and finding it deserted, I started toward my office. I was about halfway down the hall between my office and the stairs when I noticed there was a light on in my office. I moved over next to the door to the restroom to think. I couldn't remember leaving a light on in the office when I left earlier.

Thinking there might be someone in my office, a drew my 9mm pistol from under my coat, then slowly moved toward my office door, staying as close to the wall as possible. When I was close enough to be able to see the door, I could see the door was slightly ajar.

Just as I was about to reach out and gently push the door open, I heard a familiar voice.

"Jake, call Mr. Blackstone at his home. It looks like someone broke into his office. Find out if he wants us to call the police."

"That won't be necessary, Fred," I said as I stepped into the outer office.

Fred turned around sharply. He had a surprised looked on his face.

"I'm glad to see you. Just a minute," Fred said, as he put his two-way radio up to his face.

"Cancel that call to Mr. Blackstone. He just walked in."

"What's going on?" I asked.

"I was making my rounds of the building like I do every night when I noticed a light on in your office. Since you rarely leave a light on, and I didn't see your Tahoe when I went through the garage, I knocked on the door. When I didn't get an answer, I used my master key and opened the door. That's when I saw this."

Fred stepped out of the doorway to my office so I could see inside. I was a bit surprised by what I saw. Someone had trashed my office.

"Do you want me to call the police, Mr. Blackstone?"

"I don't think it will be necessary. I'll take fingerprints of everything and get them checked by the police. It would be my guess whoever ransacked my office was wearing gloves. I know you have to make a report of anything you find, but I'll take it from here," I said.

"I'll need to report what I found," Fred said, looking like I might not want him to report what he found.

"I know. Report why you entered my office and every-thing you found as you normally would. Include in your report the time you discovered the light was on as well as the time I arrived. You can even put in your report I told you it would not be necessary for you to call the police. I will take care of notifying them."

"Yes sir. Do you need any help from me?"

"No, I don't think so," I said as I looked around my office. "You can finish your rounds. I'll talk to you later if I have any questions."

"Thank you," Fred said then left my office.

As soon as Fred left my office, I closed and locked the door then began looking around the room. My hope was to get some idea of what the person who trashed my office was looking for. The files from the file cabinet were still fairly well in tact even though they had been tossed out of the cabinet. It was obvious they had not been gone through page by page, or even thumbed through. My chair was tipped over, but looked more like it had been laid over than pushed over. The drawers of my desk were open and dumped on the floor. What had been in the drawers was not spread around very far from the drawers.

There was little doubt in my mind that whoever trashed my office was not looking for anything specific, like information on a certain case. He was just making it clear that someone wanted to send me a message. I had no trouble understanding the message. It was drop the case or get hurt. It was not the first time I had received such a message, and in the same manner.

As I began to pick the files up off the floor, I thought about who might have been in my office. The one person who came to mind was the guy who had tried to follow me on a couple of occasions. I wasn't sure, but my best guess would be it was Tony Williams. The only real question that came to mind was is Tony working for his father, or is he working for someone else.

Once I had things picked up and generally put away, I turned on my computer. As it booted up, I put the drawers back in the desk and arranged things back in order.

When the computer was ready, I began to look for information on Anthony Williams. As soon as the background on Williams came up, I looked to see if Rose

Williams was related to him. She was close to him in age and was probably his wife. I was a bit surprised to find out that Rose Williams was not his wife, but his sister. However, there was an indication that Anthony Williams was married.

I quickly changed over to a different program and ran a criminal record report on Rose. It showed that she had lived in Denver for the past twenty-seven years. There was no indication that she had ever lived in Las Vegas or Reno. Based on the criminal record report and what it told me, it looked like there was no proof she had anything to do with her brother's criminal activities.

Since she worked in the recovery room, and her brother lived close by, I wondered if she had anything to do with Josh's death. Being the afternoon supervisor of the recovery room, and she had been on duty the night Josh was murdered, she would have had plenty of opportunities to kill him. The question that came to mind was did her brother have enough influence over her to get her to commit murder for him, or let the person in who murdered Josh?

That little piece of information might be of interest to Mac. A quick look at my watch showed me that I was not likely to get in touch with Mac at this late hour. I would have to wait until tomorrow to talk to him.

I returned to the background program to get the name of Anthony Williams' wife. It turned out his wife, the former Betty Dahl Johnson, had divorced him shortly after his second arrest for extortion in Reno.

I looked up Betty's maiden name to find out who she was related to and if she had remarried. After Betty divorced Williams, several years later she remarried a man by the name of Edward Simmons in San Diego, California, and was still married to him. It still listed her as living in San Diego. It also showed she was currently working as a secretary at a small manufacturing firm that made special items for the handicapped. The information on her didn't seem to be relevant to my case. I could see no reason to look further into her background, at this time.

I found out some interesting and some not so interesting things over the next couple of hours. It was getting late and about time for me to go home and try to get some sleep. I could think about what I had found out in the morning.

After shutting off my computer, I shut off the lights then left my office, locking the door behind me. I took the elevator down to the main floor. I walked over to Fred who was standing near the entrance.

"Mr. Blackstone, did you find anything missing from your office?" Fred asked.

"No. Actually, it seems whoever was in my office just made a mess. I couldn't find anything missing."

"That's strange. I wonder what they were looking for?"

"No idea. I don't keep any money there."

"I'll keep an eye on your office," Fred said.

"Thanks. I'll see you later," I said as I turned and went back to the elevator.

I took the elevator to the parking garage level. When the door opened I was ready for just about anything. As I stepped out of the elevator, I noticed a car I didn't recognize. I could see someone in it, but I couldn't tell if it was a man or a woman.

Keeping one eye on the car, I walked to where I had left the pickup. I quickly got in it and started it. I backed out of the parking space and headed the long way around to the exit.

Once out on the street, I quickly made a turn at the first corner into an alley. I slammed on the breaks, put it in park and jumped out. I drew my gun as I ducked into a doorway and waited.

It only took a moment for the car to show up. It started to turn into the alley, but quickly changed direction and sped away. I moved away from the doorway. I knew it would take a few minutes for him to get to the other end of the alley.

I got back in the pickup, backed out of the alley and sped away in the opposite direction. I had no idea who was following me. It had not been the dark blue Cadillac I had seen before. It was a silver Lincoln Town Car.

There was nothing else I could do tonight. I drove home and parked the pickup in my garage then went into my apartment.

I placed a call to Julie. We talked for a few minutes, but neither of us felt like talking for long. It seemed we were both tired. After telling her I loved her and she told me she loved me, I told her I would call her in the morning, then hung up. I took a shower, then went right to bed.

CHAPTER FOURTEEN

I WOKE EARLIER THAN I HAD PLANNED. The sun was sneaking in between the gaps in the curtains letting me know it was going to be a bright shiny day. My mind was already thinking about what I had found out last night on my computer. I went into the bathroom and took a quick wake-me-up shower.

I had just stepped out of the shower when my phone began to ring. I quickly wrapped a towel around my waist and went into the bedroom. I walked over to the phone and picked it up.

"Hello."

"Peter, this is George. We've got a problem."

"What's going on?"

"Julie told me that she heard Barbara talking to someone in her room. She said it sounded like she was talking on a phone because she couldn't hear anyone else. I didn't give Barbara a phone to call anyone. She knew she was supposed to ask me for a phone if she wanted to make a call."

"She must have had one in her purse. Did Julie hear any of the conversation?"

"No. She said all she could understand was Barbara's voice, and it sounded like she was angry with someone."

"That could be a problem. Do you think Barbara might know she was overheard?" I asked rapidly becoming very concerned.

"No. I don't think so. Julie was pretty sure Barbara didn't know anyone had heard her."

"Good."

"I think I should get all the women out of here," George said. "If she disclosed where she was at, it would be hard for me to protect them here."

"I agree with you. Get them all in one room that is as secure as possible, then search Barbara's room and see if you can find the phone. If not search her and find that phone. We might be able to find out who she called."

"Got it."

"Make sure all the women are in the same room while you search Barbara's room. I'll be leaving here. Expect me in about fifteen minutes." I said.

"Got it," George said then hung up.

I hung up the phone and got dressed as quickly as possible. I left my apartment for the garage. Once in the pickup, I immediately headed for Aurora.

I HAD JUST PULLED OUT onto the street when I saw the same dark blue Cadillac I had seen before. When I was halfway down the next block, I saw it pull away from the curb. He was about a block away from me. There was no doubt in my mind that he planned to follow me in an effort to find out where I was hiding Barbara. I wasn't about to lead him to George's home.

Since my first thought was that he was trying to find out where I was hiding Barbara, it solved one question for me. If he was following me to find out where Barbara was, he was probably not the one Barbara had called. She would have certainly told him where she was and who else was there. I decided I would let him follow me for a little while.

Although it answered one question, it brought up another. If she didn't call him then who did she call? Either way, I needed to get the women out of George's home and to another secure location as quickly as possible.

While keeping an eye on my tail, I called George.

"What's up?" George asked.

"Can you get all three of the women in your car and laid down so they can't be seen when you leave?"

"Yeah, I think so."

"I want you to take them out of your house. Don't take anything with you that someone might see as you leave. Keep an eye out for anyone following you. If you see someone following you, go directly to the Precinct One and ask the Desk Sergeant for Captain MacDonald. He knows you and Julie, and he knows I'm working to find out who killed Josh Garrett."

"I'll get right on it."

"I can't come help you at the moment. I have someone tailing me."

"I'll have the women out of here in ten minutes if I have to force them into the car."

"Thanks. Call me and let me know where you are."

"Will do," George said then hung up.

I turned my full attention to the car that was following me. He was still about a block behind me. The only reason I could think of for him to be following me was he had no idea where Barbara was hiding. If that was the case, then who did Barbara call?

My thoughts were suddenly disturbed when I saw the Cadillac suddenly turn a corner. It was a bit of a surprise to me. Why had he turned if he was following me? The only thing I could think of was he had gotten a phone call. It suddenly occurred to me that he might have gotten a call from whoever Barbara had called. That call could have told him what he needed to know.

At the next intersection, I turned and headed for George's house in Aurora. The only thing I could think of was that Tony Williams was probably the registered owner of the dark blue Cadillac, and he was headed for George's house. There was little doubt in my mind that he was trying to get there before me.

I knew the streets pretty well. There were several side streets that would give me the advantage in getting to George's house before him. As I drove down the streets, pressing the speed limits a bit, I called George, again.

"What's up, Peter?"

"Are you out of the house yet?"

"No. I'm just getting the women together in the garage."

"My tail just broke off following me and is headed in your direction. If you can't get out of there in next three minutes or so, hide the women in the house as best you can and be ready to defend them. I'm on my way. I'm probably five minutes away."

"Got it. I'll be here," he said then hung up.

I placed another call to Mac. The phone was answered by Sergeant Russell. I cut him off of his usual speech and asked for Mac. He transferred me immediately.

"Captain MacDonald," - - he said but I interrupted him.

"Mac, I need you to get the Aurora Police Department to dispatch a unit to George's house as quickly as possible and hurry."

I gave Mac the address then hung up. I moved through the traffic as quickly as I could. The seconds ticking away.

I turned onto the street where George's house was located just as the Cadillac turned on the street a couple of blocks on the other side of George's house. When the Cadillac was about a block from George's he slammed on his brakes, took a sharp turn then sped off down a side street burning rubber.

I pulled up in front of George's house blocking off the driveway. As I got out of the pickup, I could hear the sound of sirens. It was only a couple of seconds before I could see a police car coming up the street toward me with lights flashing. It was clear Mac had gotten the cooperation of the Aurora Police Department.

The Aurora police car pulled up in front of George's house and two police officers stepped out of the police car with guns in hand. Although their guns were in their hands, they were not pointed at me. I put my hands up just in case.

"I'm Peter Blackstone."

"You can put your hands down, Mr. Blackstone. Can you tell us what's going on here?"

"Yes," I said, then took the time to tell them just enough for them to understand why we needed their help.

"That's about it."

"It is my understanding that Captain MacDonald of the Denver Police Department was the one who requested our assistance," the lead officer said.

"That would be correct. I don't think we will be bothering you again as it is necessary for us to move the women to another location. This location is now known by those who would like to keep those we were hiding here from talking."

"Do you want us to standby until you can leave?"

"That would be great. Maybe you can escort one of the vehicles away from here while we take them away in a different vehicle?"

"No problem. We were instructed to assist you in any way we can."

"Thank you."

I got in the pickup truck and drove it up to the garage door. It was only seconds before the door opened. I drove in and waited for George to close the garage door before I got out of the pickup.

"Thanks for the reinforcements," George said.

"You can thank Mac for that. We don't have much time. I want you to take Barbara and Mary and hide them in the backseat of your car. I'll take Julie with me. The police will escort me away from the area, back to the Denver city limits. You will go to a new location where the women will be safe then call me and let me know where you are."

"Got it. I'll wait for about fifteen minutes before I leave," George said.

"Good. We best be going."

It was only a minute or so before Julie came into the garage.

"Get in the pickup and sit in the front seat. When we leave, I want you to turn in the seat and make it look like you are talking to someone in the backseat. The backseat windows are tined very dark and no one can see in. I want it to look like the others are in the backseat."

"Okay," she said not questioning what I wanted her to do.

"You ready?"

"Yes."

We got in the pickup and waited for George to open the door. I backed out and rolled down the side window. I motioned to the police officers that we were ready. I started down the street with the police car right behind us. They turned on their overhead lights, which I thought was a nice touch. I could see the Cadillac about a block behind the police car. It followed us for a couple of blocks before it turned off.

The police followed us all the way to the Denver city limits where they waved us off. All the way, Julie had acted as if there was someone in the backseat and she was talking to them.

All the time, I kept an eye out for anyone who might be following us. Once we were inside Denver city limits there was no one following us. It looked as if the police had scared them off, but for how long I had no idea.

I drove to the dealership where I had borrowed the pickup. Julie and I went inside and returned the keys to Randy and thanked him for the use of it. I found it interesting that he didn't ask any questions. He did ask me if I might like to trade in my Tahoe for a new Ford, but I declined. I told him I would talk to him about it when I was ready for a new vehicle. I paid him for the service to my Tahoe with a little extra to cover the gas I had used, thanked him again then left the dealership.

WE ARRIVED AT MY APARTMENT shortly after one. After parking the Tahoe in the garage, I rapidly walked Julie from the garage to the backdoor while keeping my eyes moving for any danger that might be around.

Once inside, Julie turned and took me in her arms. I wrapped my arms around her and kissed her. After a few minutes of good old fashion necking, I let go of her and walked with her to the kitchen. She sat down at the table while I started getting sandwich fixings out of the refrigerator and on the table. I sat down at the table and looked at Julie.

"I thought we could talk while we eat. I didn't get a chance to have breakfast," I said.

Julie started making a sandwich while I made one for myself.

"George told me that you heard Mrs. Garrett talking on the phone. Did you hear what she said?" I asked then took a bite of my sandwich.

"No, I couldn't make out the words she said, but from the sound of her voice she was apparently angry with someone. She might have been angry about her situation, or with you for making her stay there. I'm not sure. It was clear to me that she was upset about not being able to bury her husband, but I don't think that was what the call was about."

"What makes you think that?"

"Her voice didn't sound like that was the problem. It was more like she was angry over having to stay at George's home. It was, - - I don't know how to explain it."

"Was the tone of her voice more like someone who was upset with another person or with her situation at the moment?" I asked.

"I think it was more like she was angry with someone for not doing what he or she was supposed to do," Julie said thoughtfully.

"By that, I take it you were not able to determine if she was talking to a man or woman?"

"No. I couldn't tell."

My thoughts turned to what had happened over the past few days that didn't seem to make sense. Barbara had been told that her husband would not be buried until she could safely be there to oversee it. That being the case, there had to be some other reason for her to be angry enough to risk everyone's life.

The fact she knew that placing a call from George's home could endanger everyone there caused me to wonder what was really going on. What made her call so important that she would risk the lives of everyone in the house? The bigger question at the moment was who did she call?

I leaned back on the chair and closed my eyes while I thought about what had happened so far. Julie was nice enough to let me think. She continued to eat while I thought about the situation.

The thought of Josh's car came to mind once again. Barbara had said Josh had driven his car to the café. If Josh had driven the car to the café, who had moved it from there to the parking space in the underground parking garage of my building where the police found it? Barbara had also told me that she had taken a cab to my office. If she didn't drive it to my building, then who drove her car there and why?

The only thing that did seem to make any sense was she had to have had the car all along, and she was the one who drove it to my building and parked it in the underground parking garage when she came to see me. If that was the case, why did she lie to me? Why did she tell me she used a cab to get there? What possible reason could she have for lying?

"I have to find out how Barbara got to the hospital and how she really got to my office," I said out loud to myself.

"What difference does that make," Julie asked, interrupting my thought.

"What?"

"You said you needed to find out how Barbara got to the hospital and then to your office. What difference does it make?"

"I don't know what difference it makes, but it's something that doesn't make sense. If anyone knows, I think Mr. and Mrs. Wallace know. I need to talk to them."

"Why them? She was just staying with them while they were in town."

"Was she?"

"I don't understand," Julie said looking a little confused.

"I don't either. I should place a call to Mac and find out what his people found in Josh's car."

"You can call him while I put things away, if you want," Julie suggested.

I left the kitchen and went into the living room, sat down at my desk, and placed a call to Mac. It didn't take but a minute or so for him to answer the phone.

"I've been waiting for you to call. Did you get the help you needed?" Mac asked.

"Yes, and thank you. I would like to know what you found in Josh's car. Did you find anything interesting?"

"I don't know how interesting you will find it, but we found no indication that anyone other than Josh or Mrs. Garrett drove the car."

"I do find that interesting, especially after what Mrs. Garrett told me. Are you sure of your findings?"

"Yes. The seat was in the same position it would have been if she drove it. The only fingerprints we found in the car were hers and Josh's, and we found them all over the inside of the car except on the shift lever, door handle on the driver's side and the steering wheel. We found no fingerprints at all on the shift lever, door handle and steering wheel. They had been wiped off. The cloth that was used to wipe them off was still in the car," Mac said.

"I find that interesting."

"I would think so. I think it answers one of your questions."

"Which one?" I asked.

"The one that makes it clear she didn't drive the car to the parking garage in your building."

"True, but it doesn't answer the two I really want answered. Who did drive the car to the parking garage, and why?"

"No. I guess it doesn't."

"How do you know the seat was where it should be for her?"

"The only fingerprints on the buttons used to move the electric seats were hers. We had one of our female officers who is about the same size as Mrs. Garrett sit in the car. The seat was set perfect for her."

"Did you find anything that might lead us to what was going on?"

"Nothing. Nothing that had anything to do with the bank or anything else that might be considered evidence, or a reason for anyone to want to kill Josh. In short, we found nothing you would not expect to find in a car, except for the lack of fingerprints on the steering wheel and such," Mac said.

"Thanks. I was hoping for something to help."

"So was I, but it was not meant to be."

I leaned back in my chair and thought about what I was told. I was sure there was something in the car that would help.

"Are you still there?" Mac asked.

"Yeah. I was just thinking."

"Okay. Have you got any ideas?"

"Just one. I need to talk to Mr. and Mrs. Wallace. I also need to talk to George and see if he was able to get hold of Mrs. Garrett's phone."

"What's her phone got to do to with this?" Mac asked.

"She called someone from George's place. We think she told that someone where she was, which forced George to move them to a different place. In other words, she compromised the safety of their location and everyone there."

"If you can get her phone, we can track that call," Mac said.

"I don't know if George got the phone from her. I'll have to wait until he contacts me to tell me where he took the women."

"Let me know when you get it."

"Will do," I said then hung up.

Just then, Julie came into the living room. The look on her face gave me the impression she was interested in my call to Mac.

"Mac didn't find anything in the car that would help. Mrs. Garrett indicated Josh had something to show me if I thought I could help him."

"If nothing was found, then wouldn't that tell you someone got to it first?"

"Yes, it would. Right now, the best suspect for the person removing it is Barbara," I said.

"But why would she do that?" Julie asked, the look on her face showing she didn't understand.

"That I don't know. If I find the answer to that, I'll be a lot closer to knowing why Josh was murdered."

"It's after three. What do you say we spend the rest of the day just doing nothing? It might give you a chance to clear your head and allow you to think more clearly," Julie suggested.

I had to admit that she had a very good idea. The only problem I had with it was that it was hard for me to shut down my brain and put my investigation to rest even for a little while.

Julie reached over and picked up the remote to the television and turned it on. I had no idea what was on during the day, but I had a feeling I was about to find out.

She turned on a movie channel that had old movies on it twenty-four hours a day. It just happened the movie that was on, and had just started, was one of my all-time favorites, *The Maltese Falcon*, staring Humphrey Bogart.

"I wouldn't mind seeing that. I've always liked that movie," I said.

Julie smiled then moved over close to me. She cuddled up against me while we watched the movie. I have to admit that it took my mind off my investigation for a little while. When the movie was over, we went to the kitchen to fix dinner.

We spent the rest of the evening enjoying each other's company, fixing dinner, cleaning up the kitchen and watching a couple of game shows. In short, we spent a quiet evening at home.

After the evening news, we just sat on the sofa for awhile. Julie leaned forward and looked at me.

"It might be a good idea if we get some rest. Maybe things that don't make sense now will come to you in the morning after some rest."

"I think you might be right. What do you say we take a shower before we get into bed?"

Julie agreed with my suggestion. We went into the bedroom and took off our clothes. We went into the bathroom and stepped into the shower. I must say it was a very pleasant time we shared while in the shower. We almost ran out of hot water. We got out of the shower, dried off then climbed into bed, but it was a good hour or more before we curled up together and drifted off to sleep.

CHAPTER FIFTEEN

I WOKE TO THE SOUND of the wind blowing outside my window. I didn't remember hearing anything about the weather changing, but then there were many times when a weatherman didn't get it right. I turned and looked over my shoulder to find Julie looking back at me. She smiled then reached out and put her hand on my shoulder.

"You ready to get up," I asked.

"No, but do you think we should? It's almost seven o'clock.

"I think we should."

"I'd like a kiss first," Julie said.

She didn't have to ask twice. I rolled over and pulled her up against me. Her body felt warm. I wrapped her in my arms and held her tight while I kissed her. It was a long, passionate kiss that only two people who loved each other could give to one another. As soon as it was over, Julie looked at me.

"I love you," she whispered.

"I love you, too," I said then kissed her again.

We spent the next half hour or so just holding each other and enjoying the feel of each other. Julie finally lifted her head off my shoulder and looked at me.

"I really need to get up," she said with a smile.

I let go of her and watched her as she got out of bed. I could not take my eyes off her as she walked across the bedroom to the bathroom. Her naked body moved with such grace. She was very beautiful and she wanted to be with me.

As she disappeared into the bathroom, I laid back, put my hands behind my head and looked up at the ceiling. My thoughts turned to yesterday and the things that had happened. I seemed to be thinking much clearer after a good night's sleep.

The first thought that came to mind had to do with Barbara. It was as if the thought had been lying in the back of my mind just waiting for me to wake up and look at it. It was immediately followed by a couple of questions, the first one being, what is Barbara up to? She knew that she could be risking everyone in that house if the wrong people knew where she was hiding. Why did she call someone from George's house in secret, and who did she call? What was it she was hiding?

Just then Julie came out of the bathroom and stood looking at me. I looked up at her and smiled.

"Are you going to get up, or do I come back to bed?"

"As much as I would like to have you come back to bed, I think I should get up. I have a lot to do today."

"I'll fix breakfast while you get dressed," Julie said.

I got out of bed and went into the bathroom. I took a quick shower, shaved then got dressed. As soon as I was ready, I went out to the kitchen. Julie was still in my robe and she had breakfast on the table. We sat down to eat.

"What are your plans for today?" Julie asked hoping they might include her.

"I think the first thing we need to do is have a talk with Mr. and Mrs. Wallace."

"Do you think Barbara might have called them?"

"I don't know. I guess it's possible. What I'm more interested in is if Mr. Wallace actually took Barbara to the hospital right after Josh was shot."

"Is that what she told you?"

"Yes," I said then thought for a minute. "I keep getting this feeling she is somehow involved, or she accidently said something to someone that got Josh murdered."

"So, you don't think whatever it was that got Josh murdered she did on purpose?" Julie asked.

"I find it hard to believe she would do anything on purpose that would result in Josh's death. However, she might have said something to someone who would try to discourage him from continuing to look into whatever it was he had found."

"Is it possible that she knows she might be at least a little bit responsible for Josh's death?"

"Maybe. It might be why she kept to herself at George's house and didn't want to talk to anyone. She might feel guilty about it."

Julie just looked at me for a minute. It was clear she was thinking about what I had said.

"I think you should get ready to go," I said. "I'm not leaving you here alone."

"Where am I going?"

"You are going with me. It's your day off, isn't it?"

"Yes," Julie said with a smile.

As soon as we finished our breakfast, Julie went into the bedroom while I cleared the table and put the dirty dishes in the dishwasher. I could hear the shower running while I put things away. It wasn't very long and Julie came out into the kitchen. She was dressed and ready to go. I got her coat for her and helped her into it.

"You have to do what I say when I say it. Do you understand?" I asked as I put on my coat.

"Yes," she said, suddenly looking very serious.

"I can't protect you if you don't."

"I understand. I'll do whatever you tell me to do."

I smiled at her, slipped my gun out from under my coat, put it in my coat pocket while keeping my hand on it. I took Julie by the arm and walked her to the door. After looking out and seeing that it had snowed a little, I looked for tracks near my apartment and garage. The only tracks I saw in the snow were from a couple of cars that had been backed out of the garages and left the parking lot. There were no footprints in the snow except for those leading from the building to the garages.

I opened the backdoor, looked around then took Julie by the arm. I hustled her out to the garage, all the time watching for any possible danger to us while keeping my free hand on the gun in my pocket. I continued to keep an eye out as she got in the Tahoe then closed the door.

As soon as I got in, I started the Tahoe and backed it out of the garage. I pulled out onto the street and headed for the Wallace house. I kept an eye out for anyone who might be following us. I saw no one.

IT TOOK ONLY TWENTY MINUTES to get to the street where the Wallaces lived. I drove down the street and on past their house. I didn't see any cars in the driveway, or on the street in front, or across the street from their house. I didn't see any cars parked at the corners of the block, either.

I drove a couple blocks on down the street then turned and went halfway down the block to the alley. I turned into the alley then slowly drove down the alley looking for anything that I didn't think looked right. I had no idea what it was that didn't look right, but I was sure I would know it when I saw it. I crossed two streets before I drove into the section of the alley that ran behind the Wallace house.

I was almost halfway down the alley when I noticed a dark blue Cadillac sedan. It was parked on the opposite side of the alley from Wallaces' backyard. It was partially hidden behind a couple of rather large bushes.

"Get down," I said sharply.

Julie quickly ducked down so she could not be seen by anyone outside the Tahoe. I hit the gas and we sped on by them and out the end of the alley where I turned onto the street. Just before I lost sight of the Cadillac, I saw it start to move.

"Sit up, tighten your seatbelt, it could get a little dicey. We've got a tail."

Julie said nothing, but she did as I told her. I also noticed that she grabbed hold of the hand bar above the door.

By the time the Cadillac was out on the same street we were on, we were about a block and a half ahead of it. It was obvious to me the person following us must have been there for some time because he didn't have his car running. He had to start it before he could try to catch us. That little mistake gave me just enough time to make him wish he hadn't been so lazy. There was little doubt my Tahoe could not outmaneuver or outrun the Cadillac, so I had to do something drastic.

"Hang on. It's going to be a bit bumpy. When I stop, get down," I said as I turned a corner very quickly. I sped down the street to the alley then slammed on the brakes, but didn't turn in. Instead, I shifted into reverse, then hit the gas and quickly backed the Tahoe into the alley. As soon as I was back far enough that the Tahoe could not be seen when approaching the alley, I slammed on the brakes, threw it into park then opened the door. I drew my gun from my pocket as I stepped out of the Tahoe and stood behind the door.

I had just aimed my gun toward the entrance to the alley when the Cadillac turned into the alley. The driver slammed on his brakes when he found himself head on with my Tahoe, and me pointing a gun at him. He was surprised to see me ready to take him on, but he recovered quickly. He slammed the Cadillac into reverse and threw gravel all over as he tried to back out of the alley as quickly as possible. With tires squealing on the pavement, he sped away down the street.

As soon as he was gone, I straightened up and got back in the Tahoe. I closed the door then started out of the alley.

I turned down the street in the opposite direction from the way the Cadillac had gone. In the next block, I turned into the alley, pulled off to the side and stopped. I looked over at Julie. She was still lying down.

"You can sit up now."

Julie sat up and looked at me. I noticed she was breathing hard and looked scared.

"It's all right. He's gone for the moment."

"Would you have shot at him?" she asked looking at me.

"I would have if he decided to press it and hadn't stopped."

Julie sat back in the seat and looked out the windshield. It took a minute for her to catch her breath before she looked at me again.

"Okay," she said softly. "What do we do now?"

"I think we still need to talk to Wallace."

"How are you going to do that with someone watching the place?"

"I'm going to drive right into his driveway and knock on the front door."

Julie looked at me as if I was just a little crazy. She may have been right, but whoever was watching the Wallace house already knew we knew about them.

"Do you think that's a good idea?"

"First of all, I think they were watching the Wallace house, but without him knowing it. That could mean they are hoping Barbara will be returning there since George's place is no longer safe. It could also mean they are expecting Wallace to reveal where Barbara is, and will lead them to her, or at the very least will tell them where she is."

"That last one seems like a good possibility if Barbara called Wallace from George's," Julie said.

"I agree. The only problem is we don't know if Wallace was who she called."

"So, when do we pay Mr. Wallace a visit?"

"Right now."

I shifted the Tahoe into drive and drove to the end of the alley. Once I was back on the street, I drove to Wallace's house.

AS I PULLED INTO THE DRIVEWAY of the Wallace house, I wasn't sure what to expect. I was hoping my appearance would scare the Wallaces enough that they would talk to me.

After taking a minute to look around, I opened the door and stepped out of the Tahoe. Continuing to look around, I opened the door for Julie then quickly walked with her to the front door of the house, then rang the bell. While I waited for someone to answer, I continued to keep my eyes moving just in case someone decided to put an end to my investigation.

I turned and looked at the door when I heard the door latch release. When the door opened, I found John Wallace standing there.

"It's you. What do you want?" John said rather sharply.

"I want to have a talk with you. May we come in? It's rather important."

He looked at us for a moment, then stepped back away from the door. After we were in the house, he shut the door behind us. We walked into the living room where we found Mrs. Wallace sitting on a chair looking at us.

"Okay, what is it you wish to talk to us about, and who is she?" John asked without offering to let us sit down.

"This is Julie Archer. Does the last name ring a bell?"

John looked at Julie, then turned and looked at his wife, Katheryn. From the look on his face, I got the impression he did not recognize the last name.

"To refresh your memory, Barbara was here with a bodyguard. His name was George Archer."

"Yes, we remember him," Katheryn said. "He was a very quiet man."

"That would be correct. This happens to be his sister. I would like to know if Barbara called you in the past couple of days?" I asked.

I sprung the question on them to see what kind of reaction I would get. It was obvious from their reaction that she had called the Wallaces. It was clear that the Wallaces shouldn't play poker.

"She did call here, didn't she?" I asked as I looked right at John's face.

"Yes, she did," he admitted after a moment of thinking about what he should say.

"We know that she was angry when she called. What did you talk about?"

He looked at his wife for a moment, then turned to look at me.

"She was upset because she could not make the arrangements for Josh's funeral."

"Try again. She had already been assured that Josh would not have his funeral until she could be there to arrange it."

John looked at me as if he was wondering how much I really knew.

"Sit down, please," John said softly.

Julie and I sat down on the sofa while John sat down on a chair next to his wife. I got the feeling that John was about to spill the beans. I was hoping he would spill all the beans, not just a few of them. I thought I would give him just a little more incentive.

"Don't know if you know this or not, but you have had a person of interest to me, and to the police, parked in the alley behind your house watching you. They may even have your phone tapped. It was the same man who is suspected of killing the woman who let a man into the recovery room of the hospital. That man killed Josh."

Katheryn looked like she had seen a ghost. She turned pale and gasped for air. Her eyes were big and filled with fear.

"You have to tell him, John," Katheryn said, her voice quivering a little.

"Tell us what? Please start from the beginning."

"The first we heard about Josh having any trouble at his job was when Barbara called and asked if she could stay with us while Josh went to talk to a private investigator. I assume that private investigator was you."

"That would be correct."

"When they arrived here, Josh said nothing about what was going on. In fact, he said very little, which was not like him. He did look like he was afraid of something or someone."

"Did he tell you what he was afraid of?" I asked.

"No. But Barbara said there was something illegal going on at the bank and she didn't want Josh to get involved. She wanted him to resign from the bank and get a job somewhere else. I think she was hoping that we would try to talk Josh into doing what Barbara wanted him to do," John said.

"I take it Josh disagreed with her."

"Yes. He wanted to find out if what he suspected was true. He was seeking someone to help decide what he should do about it."

"That would have been me. He had called me to meet him in the café where he was shot. Do you have any idea how the shooter found out that Josh and I were to meet there?" I asked.

"Not for sure."

"In that case, tell me what you think."

"I think Barbara might have called a friend of hers in Dillion who worked in the bank. The only thing I can think of was that the conversation Barbara had with the woman she called at the bank had been overheard, or the woman's phone was tapped," John said.

"Do you know who she called in Dillion?"

"Not for sure, but it might have been Josh's secretary. But like I said, I'm not sure."

"You mean Mary Sullivan?"

"Yes. I believe that is her name," John said.

I looked at Julie. Mary had not mentioned any phone calls from Barbara. If she had called Mary, then there was a strong possibility that Mary knew more than she was telling me. Unless Barbara just told Mary where Josh and Barbara were staying while they were in Denver and where Josh was to meet me.

"I have a couple more questions for you. How did Barbara get to the hospital when Josh was shot?"

"I took her to the hospital within minutes of the call from the hospital," John said.

"Do you know where Josh's car was?"

"He drove it to the café where he was to meet with you. I guess it is parked somewhere close to the café."

"Do you have any idea how Josh's car got to the underground parking garage at my building?"

John turned and looked at Katheryn. From the look on their faces, they knew nothing about it.

"No. I didn't know it was there," John said with a surprised look on his face.

The answer to my last question was bugging me. Someone had to have driven it to the underground parking garage, but who? And why was it parked there? It didn't make sense. It was time for us to leave. I needed a quiet place to think. I also needed to find out where George had taken Mary and Barbara.

"Are you all right?" John asked.

"Yes. I think it's time for us to go," I said as I stood up.

As soon as I stood up, Julie and John stood up. I walked to the door then waited for Julie.

"Mr. Blackstone, do you think we are in danger?" John asked.

"No. The only reason they have been watching your house was to try to find out where we were keeping Barbara. It's my guess that since George's home is no longer a good place, they might have thought we would return here thinking it would now be safe. Since they have been seen watching your house, they will probably give up on it."

"I was thinking about taking my wife and leaving town for a little while. What do you think?"

"That is up to you. But I think you are safer here. If you leave, they may try to follow you thinking you know something. I would suggest that you stay here and act as normal as possible. I'll have a talk with Captain MacDonald about having a larger police presence around your home."

"Thank you. We'll stay here," John said then looked at his wife.

"If you see or hear anything suspicious, don't hesitate to call the police. I'm sure they are still keeping a police car nearby, especially at night."

"Okay," John said then opened the door.

"You might call the police if you see a dark blue Cadillac hanging around the neighborhood."

"I will," John said.

I quickly checked up and down the street for anything or anybody who might cause us harm. When I didn't see anything, I quickly hustled Julie to the Tahoe and got her in it. I went around to the driver's side, got in and started it. I backed out of the driveway and headed for my office.

Julie sat next to me looking out the windshield. I was sure her mind was trying to digest everything we had heard from the Wallaces. I was also thinking about it, but I was also watching for anyone who might be following us.

"Well, at least a couple of my questions were answered," I said.

"Who she called from George's was one, what was the other?" Julie asked.

"Why someone was so set on getting to Mary. Someone in the bank must have overheard Barbara's call to Mary, or the phone was tapped. I still don't know how Josh's car got from the café to the parking garage."

CHAPTER SIXTEEN

WE ARRIVED AT MY OFFICE just shortly before noon. I parked in the underground parking garage, then carefully looked around before I got out. Continuing to look around, I walked to the other side of my Tahoe. As I reached to open the door to help Julie get out, I heard the squeal of tires behind me. I swung around and saw a dark blue Cadillac come racing toward us through the parking garage. I could see that there were two men in the car, and that the passenger was holding a gun.

With one hand, I pushed Julie back into the Tahoe while I drew my gun from under my coat. I ducked down behind the car parked next to mine just as shots were fired from the Cadillac. I took aim at the windshield of the car, fired three quick shots as the car went by then jumped behind my Tahoe. The Cadillac suddenly increased speed rapidly. It was going way too fast to make the turn in front of them. It made no attempt to turn.

I quickly moved to the rear of my Tahoe, I was ready to shoot again if necessary, but there was no need. I saw the Cadillac crash head-on into a concrete pillar. Glass, plastic and metal flew around as the front of the car crumbled under the impact against a concrete pillar.

"Stay down," I yelled at Julie.

I moved to a place where I had good cover and could see the Cadillac better. I could not see any movement inside the car. All I could see was steam coming from the front of the car, and oil and antifreeze draining out from under it. I could also see that the air bags had deployed and the driver of the car was slumped over the steering wheel. He appeared to be unconscious.

I could not see the passenger, but I could see the passenger's door was open. The car had hit the concrete pillar so hard that the door had flown open upon impact. I slowly worked my way around the back of the car being very careful since I was unable to see the passenger and had no idea where he might be, or if he was in any condition to shoot again.

When I got to the passenger's side of the car, I could see the body of a man hanging part way out of the car. He wasn't moving. Keeping my gun on him just in case he had any fight left in him, I moved up close. He didn't move. I reached out and touched his neck to find out if he was still alive. There was no pulse. He was dead. I walked around to the driver's side and checked the driver. With all the blood on him, I couldn't be sure if I had actually shot him. In any case, he was also dead. There was nothing I could do for either of them.

I returned to my Tahoe and opened the door, I found Julie had remained lying down across the seats. She had done what I told her to do.

"You can sit up now. It's over," I said as I looked at her.

"Are they dead?" she asked looking into my eyes.

She was trembling. I was sure she had never been shot at before.

"Yes," I said as I reached for my cell phone.

I placed a call to Captain MacDonald, but he was not in his office. I gave the Desk Sergeant my name and where I was at the moment. I then gave him a brief description of what had taken place.

"I'll get a unit out there as quickly as possible. Do you need an ambulance?"

"No. It's too late for that."

"Peter, I want you to remain on the scene until the unit gets there," Sergeant Russell said.

"No problem, sergeant. I'll keep it clean," I said, assuring Sergeant Russell I would not disturb the scene.

"I'll also be sending out a detective to start the investigation."

"Be sure you let Mac know about it. I've been working on a case with him that I believe involves the man who was driving the car," I said.

"I'll let him know as soon as I can get in touch with him."

"Thanks," I said then hung up.

I looked at Julie. She looked at me as if she was seeing a side of me that she had never seen before, and it apparently bothered her.

"Are you all right?" I asked.

"Yes. I guess I'm a little shaken by all this."

"I'm sure you are. The police will be here soon. Just tell them what you saw and answer their questions as clearly as you can. Don't offer any additional information or any opinions. That will just make it harder for them to get a true picture of what happened here."

"Okay," she said after taking a deep breath. "I really didn't see anything."

"That should be what you tell them. I know this is hard for you. You can just sit here and let them come to you."

"I've never seen anything like this. I've heard about it, but I haven't seen what it's like out here. I usually see the results in the clean, sterile confines of the operating room," she said as she looked at me in the hope I would understand how she was feeling at the moment.

"I understand. I truly do," I said as my attention was taken away from Julie at the sound of a siren.

IT WAS ONLY A MINUTE or so before a black-and-white police car came into the underground parking garage. The car pulled to a stop. As luck would have it, it was Officer Norbert and his rookie partner.

I watched Norbert and his partner get out of the car and walk toward me. Norbert turned and walked over to the car and looked around while his partner walked up in front of me. The rookie had his hand on his gun. He only glanced over at Norbert before he turned and looked at me.

"Trouble just sort of follows you around," the young officer said with a self-satisfying grin. "I've got a feeling that you are in a lot of trouble. I think you should hand over your gun. Do it very carefully," he said with a tone of authority.

I took a deep breath then handed him my gun. He looked at it, then looked at me.

"How many shots did you fire?" he asked.

"Three."

"You fired three shots at that car?"

"Yes. That's what I said."

"How many shots were fired at you, any?" he said with an air of superiority.

"I'm not sure, but probably three or four, maybe as many as five," I said calmly not willing to offer him any additional information.

"You're not sure? A man of your so-called experience, and you don't know how many shots were fired at you?" he said sarcastically.

"I can see you've never been in a firefight. In fact, you've probably never fired your gun except on the firing range. It's a whole lot different out here in the real world. Paper targets don't shoot back."

"What's going on here?" Officer Norbert asked. "And what are you doing with his gun."

"It's evidence," the rookie said.

"Give it back to him. We don't know enough about what happened here to be arresting him or anyone else."

Reluctantly, the rookie gave me back my gun. Actually, taking my gun as evidence was the only thing he had done that was right since I met him. It seemed to irritate him to have to give it back to me.

"You want to tell me what happened here?" Officer Norbert asked.

"Sure," I said then told him about what happened inside the underground parking garage. He took notes of what I told him.

"If you fired three shots at the driver, we won't have to look very far to find the slugs. Two of your shots went through the windshield and both of them hit the driver and the third one hit the door post next to his head."

"I asked the Desk Sergeant at Precinct One to contact MacDonald as soon as possible. The driver was involved in the case I have been working on, and Mac is aware of it."

"I'm sure Captain MacDonald will be notified, but we can't leave here until the detective gets here."

"I understand. When your forensic team gets here, you'll want them to go over my vehicle. It took a couple of hits in the back quarter panel and one in the rear. You can see the bullet hole in the back from here. I'm sure they will find that they came from the gun used by the shooter in the Cadillac.

"He'll also want to talk to a witness of the shooting," I said as I looked at the rookie.

The rookie's face turned pale. It showed he was sure he had made a big mistake by not checking to see if there was anyone else around.

"Yes. I have a witness, although she will probably not be able to tell you much more than the fact we were attacked by the men in the Cadillac, and my vehicle was hit a couple of times. She is sitting in my Tahoe."

The rookie glanced over at my Tahoe. Fortunately, she was not a threat to him.

"Leave her where she is," I said watching the rookie. "This whole mess has been a bit unnerving for her."

The rookie looked at Norbert. He wasn't sure what he was to do.

"Leave her there," Norbert said to the rookie.

"Thank you," I said as I looked at Norbert.

Just then we heard the sound of a siren and turned to see a dark green sedan with a single red light on the roof near the driver's door. It was obvious to me that the detective had arrived. I was hoping that it was someone who knew me. I stood there watching as the detective stepped out of his car. I didn't recognize him.

As he approached Officer Norbert, he glanced over at me, then turned and looked at the Cadillac. He didn't say a word. The detective walked over to the car and looked at the two men in the car. After looking at the damage and the two dead bodies, he walked over to Norbert and talked to him for a moment or two before walking up to me.

"I'm Detective Mendez. I want your gun," he said sharply.

I carefully drew my gun from the belt holster and handed it to him with just two fingers. I knew he would want it as part of his investigation. He would have ballistic tests run on it to make sure it was the gun that killed the two men.

"I understand your vehicle took a couple of hits, also?"

"That is correct."

"We'll have to take it in and have the forensic people go over it."

"I understand. Make sure your forensic team looks at the direction all the shots came from on both vehicles and the surrounding walls."

"I think the forensic people know how to do their job."

"I'm sure they do."

"Officer Norbert tells me you are a former police officer and are now a Private Investigator."

"That is correct."

"I will have to take you in for a statement. Should this prove to be an unnecessary shooting, you could lose your PI license and end up in jail. I understand you have a witness to this shooting."

"That would also be correct."

"Will you show us where your witness is, please? He will have to come with us to the precinct to give a statement."

"I understand," I said then turned and walked over to my car.

I helped Julie out of my Tahoe and walked with her to the detective's car. I noticed the look on Mendez's face when he saw that my witness was a woman. He seemed surprised, I'm not sure why. I opened the backdoor of the detective's car and waited for Julie to get in then knelt down to talk to her.

"When you give them your statement, don't tell them anything but what you personally saw or heard. Don't give them any opinions, or tell them things you think might have happened but didn't actually see." I said. "I will be doing the same except I will request that Captain MacDonald be called."

"Are you going to refuse to talk to them until Mac can be there?" Julie asked.

"No, but I will not get into my investigation until Mac can be there. By the way, if they get pushy ask for an attorney then don't answer any more questions or even say another word until an attorney can be with you."

"Okay," Julie said looking at me.

"You've talked to her enough. Get in the car," Mendez ordered.

I turned and looked at Mendez over my shoulder. From the look on his face, I had no idea how he felt about private investigators, but I was sure I was going to find out very soon. I stood up and walked around to the other side of the car and got in.

Mendez didn't get in the car right way. He walked over to Office Norbert and talked to him. I noticed he glanced toward his car every minute or so, but I had no idea what was going on in his mind.

It wasn't very long before the forensic team showed up. Mendez talked to them for a few minutes. He pointed to my vehicle, then to the Cadillac. I also saw him point to the walls that would have been directly behind my vehicle and the wall in front of it.

"What's he doing?" Julie asked.

"He's pointing out where the slugs from my gun and the slugs from the shooter's gun might be found."

"Don't they already know where your slugs went?"

"Yes, but they're trying to find out if I fired more shots than I claimed I fired. It's pretty routine."

"Aren't you worried about what they will find?"

"Not if they do their job like they should."

Just then I saw Mendez turn around and start toward the car. As he got in the car, Julie reached over and took hold of my hand. I looked at her and could see the concern on her face. I smiled and winked at her in the hope it would help her relax and relieve some of her worries.

WE ARRIVED AT THE PRECINCT Mendez was assigned to, Precinct Three. We were taken inside. As we passed the Desk Sergeant, he called out to Mendez.

"Detective, Captain MacDonald wants you to call him right away."

"I'll call him later. I have more important things to do right now."

It was rapidly becoming clear that Mendez wanted to interrogate us. That was not a good sign to me. I was getting the feeling that Mendez didn't like PI's very well. If Mac didn't come to the precinct where we are, it could be a long night.

Mendez took us down a long hall. When he came to an interrogation room, he opened the door.

"You can wait in here," he said to Julie. "There will be a female officer to join you shortly to get your statement."

Julie looked at me. I nodded and smiled. She turned and went into the room. Mendez pulled the door closed then turned toward me.

"Down here," he said as he took me to an interrogation room a little further down the hall.

I went inside. There was very little difference from one interrogation room to another. The only furniture in the room was a table that was bolted to the floor and three chairs. The room had painted walls, a single light hanging from the ceiling with a wire mess over the light shade, and a large glass mirror on one wall. Of course, it wasn't just a mirror. It was a one-way window that allowed someone to be watching anyone in the room without them knowing. The mirror was not a problem for me. It didn't matter if there was someone on the other side or not.

"Sit over there," he said then sat down across the table from me after I sat down.

"You're in a lot of trouble. You want to tell me what happened in the garage? What you tell me could be the difference between going to jail and losing your PI license, or you walking out of here a free man," Mendez said.

"I don't see how. It was, if nothing else, self-defense."

"We are interrogating your girlfriend as we speak," he said with a slight grin. "She will tell us all we need to know about what really happened in that parking garage."

"I take it, you do not plan to call Captain MacDonald at Precinct One. Is that correct?"

"That is correct," Mendez said with a slight grin. "You are in my precinct now. We're going to sit here and talk all night if necessary to get you to tell me why you killed those two men."

"Well, I guess you are going to have a long night of silence from me. I want a lawyer," I said then leaned back in the chair, folded my hands across my chest and just looked at him.

"You can pull that long silence bit on me if you want, but what about your girlfriend?"

I said nothing. He had not given me my rights, and I seriously doubted that Julie had been given her rights. I knew my time would come when he would wish he had called Mac right away. There was little doubt in my mind that Julie wouldn't say anything other than what she actually saw and heard.

Time passed slowly. I was sure Mendez knew he was not supposed to ask me any questions once I requested an attorney, but he continued to ask questions anyway. I continued to remain silent.

I had to admit to myself that I wasn't a hundred percent sure how Julie would stand up to a vigorous interrogation, but I was sure of what the outcome would be once I got hold of my lawyer. And since I had not been read my rights, anything I did say could not be used in a court of law.

Just the fact he didn't stop questioning me, and didn't contact my lawyer, was enough to get him fired, or suspended, or possibly be demoted and put back on the street as a police officer, at the very least. The fact he hadn't read me my rights only made matters worse for him.

The afternoon dragged on slowly. Since I still had my wrist watch on, I glanced at it and saw it was after seven in the evening. Mendez was still questioning me after almost six hours without me saying a word. I was getting a little tired of listening to him, but I was not about to talk or even ask him a question. He looked like he was getting a little impatient with me.

Suddenly, the door to the interrogation room flew open and in walked Captain MacDonald and another high ranking police officer I didn't know. Mendez turned around sharply and was about to say something when he saw a captain that I assumed was Mendez's precinct captain, and Captain MacDonald of Precinct One. It looked to me like Mendez had turned a little pale.

"What the hell is going on in here?" the captain said.

"Mr. Blackstone killed two men and damaged a building. I want to know why," Mendez said.

"Did Mr. Blackstone tell you he was working with Captain MacDonald?"

"All he said was that Captain MacDonald knows about the case he claims to be working on."

"Excuse me, Frank. Pete, this is Captain Frank Roberts of Precinct Three," Mac said then turned and looked at Mendez.

"How long has he been here?" Mac asked Mendez.

"Not very long," Mendez said.

"Pete?"

"We have been here since shortly after one this afternoon."

"What do you mean "we"?" Mac asked.

"As far as I know, they are still holding Julie Archer."

"Where is she?" Mac asked Mendez.

"She's down the hall in interrogation room two," Mendez said.

"Get out of here," Captain Roberts instructed Mendez. "Go to your desk and stay there until I get done here."

They watched as Mendez left the interrogation room. Once he was gone, Captain Roberts sat down at the table along with Mac.

"I need a little information," Captain Roberts said to me. "I need to know what happened in the underground parking garage where you supposedly shot and killed two men."

I looked at Mac before I replied. Mac nodded that it would be okay to respond to him. I looked at Captain Roberts then told him what had happened and that I had killed only one of the two men in the car, the one driving. The other occupant of the car was the one shooting at me. He died as a result of the crash into the concrete pillar in the parking garage.

"I'm sure your forensic people will verify what I'm telling you. Also, their examination of the entire scene will show that I was fired at before I returned fire. Based on the angle of the holes in my vehicle and the holes in the Cadillac, it will show that the shots came from the Cadillac before I returned fire."

"How's that?" Captain Roberts asked.

"The car was moving at a fairly good speed considering where it took place. The shooter, or passenger, began shooting well before the car went by me. Two of his shots hit my vehicle and went into the right rear quarter panel of it and a third shot hit the back of my Tahoe. Officer Norbert told me that all three shots I fired hit the car with two of them hitting the driver and one hitting the door frame next to the driver's head."

"I think it's time to get out of here," Mac said. "If you have any additional questions for Pete, I'll make sure he is available to answer them."

"One of these times, you might let me know what this is all about. In the meantime, I'll deal with Detective Mendez. By the way, did Mendez read you your rights?"

"No, he did not. He didn't stop asking me questions when I told him I wanted my lawyer. And as you can see, he didn't allow me to call my lawyer, nor did he call him for me."

"Thank you. Let's go find the young woman he brought in with you. I have a couple of questions for her before you leave."

Roberts turned and left the interrogation room. Mac and I followed him down the hall to interrogation room two.

I followed Captain Roberts into the room. There was a female officer sitting in front of Julie at a table. She immediately stood up when she saw Captain Roberts come in the room.

"I would like to ask you a couple of questions," Captain Roberts said to Julie.

Julie looked up at me. She looked scared, but I nodded that it was all right for her to answer his questions. She seemed to relax a little when she saw Mac enter the room behind me.

"What do you want to know?" she asked Captain Roberts.

"Were you given your rights?"

"No, sir."

"Were you questioned by Detective Mendez?"

"No, sir."

"Were you questioned by anyone while you were here?"

"No. This officer has been very nice. She just sat here with me and answered any questions I had. She never asked me anything."

"She didn't ask you anything about the shooting in the parking garage?"

"No."

"Thank you. You may go."

Julie stood up and walked over to me. I took her hand then walked out of the police station without saying a word.

We walked to Mac's car. He opened the backdoor. Once we were in his car, he drove us to my apartment.

WHEN WE ARRIVED AT THE APARTMENT, Julie and I got out of Mac's car. Mac said he would talk to me tomorrow then drove off. It was only a short time later that a black-and-white police car arrived and parked out in front of my apartment.

"Peter, there's a police car parked out in front."

"What are they doing?"

"Nothing. They're just sitting in the car."

"Mac must have sent them to keep an eye on us. It shouldn't take very long before the police car will leave and an unmarked car will take its place."

"I'm not sure how I feel about having a police car out front," Julie said.

"You should feel safe," I said as I walked up behind her and looked out the window. "I don't know about you, but I'm hungry. Let's see what I have to eat."

She turned in my arms and kissed me before we went to the kitchen. We found a few leftovers in the refrigerator and fixed dinner. After we finished dinner and cleaned up the kitchen, we took a shower and went to bed. Julie rolled up against me and quickly went to sleep. It had been a long and stressful day. It wasn't long before I drifted off to sleep.

CHAPTER SEVENTEEN

I WOKE WITH JULIE CURLED UP AGAINST ME. From the sound of her breathing, she was still asleep. I chose to lay quietly and simply enjoy the feel of her body against me.

While I laid there, my thoughts went to what was happening. Someone didn't want me to investigate Josh's death. From what had happened yesterday afternoon, I must be getting close to someone or something that might point to the killer or killers.

I still had no idea who the two men were in the Cadillac, but the driver could have been Tony Williams, but with all the blood on his face, I wasn't sure. I also wondered who the shooter was. If the driver was Tony, his death took one suspect out of the running for the killer of Josh, even though he could have been the killer.

I couldn't see Anthony Williams getting his hands dirty by killing someone. He was more the type to get someone else to do his dirty work. There was nothing in his past to show that he was a violent man, but I had no doubt that he could put out a hit on Josh. The fact that the visitor to Josh in the recovery room the night he was murdered was not built anything like Anthony Williams, that sort of eliminated Anthony as the killer. The visitor was taller and not near as heavy from what I had been told.

There was the possibility it was Tony Williams who had been the one to kill Josh, but I wasn't sure. Tony was built more like the man who had visited Josh in the recovery room. The only problem was the description I had of the visitor could easily fit any number of men in the Denver area.

The shooter that was killed in the car could have been the same man who was in the recovery room and claimed to be Ralph. Since he tried to kill me, there was no doubt that he was a killer. However, did he kill Josh? He was probably a hired killer from out of town. If he was from out of town, it would be harder to pin down who hired him.

It suddenly occurred to me that there was another Williams who might be involved. Rose Williams had been the recovery room supervisor on the night Josh was murdered. At the very least, she had opportunity and the means to kill him. The only thing missing was did she have a motive? She was the sister of Anthony Williams which automatically brought her under suspicion.

I had only talked to Rose briefly. Her reaction to finding out that the person who was suspected of killing Josh had been let into the recovery room by Alice Spencer, seemed to be a surprise to her. It was almost as if she took Josh's death personally, as if in some way she felt she was responsible. The question was, was she responsible?

Rose Williams had been picked up several times, but was released because there was no evidence that she had any involvement or knowledge of her brother's activities. The question in my mind was she released because she played no part in her brother's dealings, or because they couldn't prove she played a part in them? I began to think that a deeper search into her background was certainly in order.

I was just about to mentally plan my day, when Julie opened her eyes and looked up at me. She smiled at me as she reached up and put her hand against my cheek. I moved closer to her and kissed her.

"How long have you been awake," she asked.

"Not long."

"Are you ready to get up?"

"Pretty soon."

"What were you thinking about?"

"About the two men who were killed yesterday," I said.

"You couldn't help it. You only did what you had to do," she said with a worried look on her face.

"I know. I was thinking about who had hired the shooter to attack us. It's my guess it was Anthony Williams. If Tony Williams was the driver of the car, I seriously doubt Anthony expected his son would be killed. As far as their deaths are concerned, you're right, I didn't have a choice."

"Does that mean you don't think the driver was Tony Williams? Wouldn't that be kind of stupid for Tony to be driving the car? Just the fact that he was in the car would cause the police to question Anthony Williams, and I seriously doubt he would like that," Julie said.

"Yes, it would be stupid. That and the fact I couldn't be sure it was Tony driving the car leads me to believe that the driver was not Tony. If that is the case, someone hired a couple of hitmen, and hitmen don't come cheap," I said.

"What are you going to do now?"

"I thought I would give you a kiss, then get up."

"I meant, what are your plans for today? For one thing, you'll need to get a new vehicle."

"I'm going to call Mac and see if he can tell me who those two men were. Then I'm going get a new set of wheels. As soon as that's done, I'm going to find a safe place for you while I do my job," I said then leaned over and gave her a kiss.

As soon as our kiss ended, I got up, went into the bathroom and took a shower. I got dressed then sat down for breakfast. As soon as we were done eating, I went into the living room to my desk and placed a call to Mac while Julie got dressed. Sergeant Russell transferred my call immediately.

"Captain MacDonald, how may I help you?"

"Mac, it's Peter."

"Hi. How's Julie doing?"

"She's doing fine. I've got a question for you. Do you know who the two men were who attacked us in the parking garage?"

"So far all we know is who the driver was. He was a wheel man for some big thug in Detroit. His name is Charles Jones. He has a rap sheet as long as your arm. The shooter has not been identified yet, but we think he is also from Detroit and had probably worked with Jones in the past. I have a call into the Detroit Police Department to see if they might be able to tell us who he was," Mac said.

"Any idea who hired him?"

"No. We're hoping the Detroit police might be able to help us on that as well. Maybe they know who Jones worked for, if he worked for anyone. He may have worked as an independent contractor, so to speak. It may not prove anything, but it will give us a starting place. We have sent his fingerprints off to the FBI, the Detroit crime lab, and to our crime lab. Our crime lab says he's not known here. We haven't gotten anything back from the others, yet."

"You think the hitmen might have been free lancing?"

"Possibly."

"Let me know what you find out."

"Sure. I'd like to have a talk with Mrs. Garrett," Mac said with a hint in his voice that I had better let him talk to her soon or he would do something I wouldn't like.

"At the moment, I have no idea where she is. I have not heard from George yet. I'll let you know as soon as George calls and lets me know where he is hiding her."

"Okay, but it better be soon," he said.

"I'll talk to you later," I said.

"Okay," Mac said then hung up.

As I hung up the phone, I began to wonder where this was going. I still didn't know what Josh had discovered, or who might be involved. Almost everything I had was speculation. I had no proof of anything except Josh had been murdered.

Just then, Julie walked into the living room. She looked so beautiful in jeans and a sweatshirt. I stood up to greet her when the front window of my apartment exploded as bullets hit the chair I had been sitting in and shattered pictures on the wall. I dove across the room and tackled Julie taking her to the floor. I covered her with my body until the bullets stop raining into my living room.

As soon as the shooting stopped, I rolled away from her, I drew my gun and turned toward the window. I was ready to defend Julie, but all I heard was the sound of a vehicle spinning tires as it took off. I jumped up and ran to the window in the hope of seeing the vehicle before it was out of sight, but it was gone by the time I got to the window.

I turned around looking for Julie. She was still lying on the floor looking at me. Her hands were over her mouth, she had a shocked look on her face, and she was trying to catch her breath. I quickly ran to her, took her in my arms and held her close.

My first reaction was to hold her close as thoughts of my previous girlfriend came to mind. But as my thoughts began to clear, I grew angry.

"I can't take this," Julie cried.

I could feel her trembling as she hung onto me. I couldn't help thinking that I had almost lost her. No matter what the cost, I had to protect her.

It wasn't but a few minutes and I heard the sound of sirens coming closer. In a matter of minutes there were two black-and-white police cars in front of my apartment, and I could hear at least two more sirens.

Officers from the police cars seemed to be all over the place in just a few minutes. The first officer to enter my apartment stopped and looked at me. He was soon followed by two other officers. I looked up at them, but didn't take my arms from around Julie.

"Drop the gun," one of the officers said, but his voice was not demanding.

I laid the gun down on the floor beside me. Without taking his eyes off me, he stepped around Julie and bent down to pick up the gun.

"Is she injured," the officer asked.

"No. She's scared," I replied.

"Can you tell me what happened here?"

"Someone drove up in front of my apartment and opened fire. If I had to guess, he used an automatic weapon. As you can see, the place has been pretty well shot up."

Just then an ambulance pulled up in front of my apartment. The EMTs entered with a stretcher with their medical equipment on it. One of the EMTs knelt down next to Julie and looked at me.

"Is she all right?" he asked.

"No, but she is not injured. I want you to put her on the stretcher and make it look like she has been seriously injured. I want an oxygen mask on her face, and it needs to look like she has an IV running," I said.

The EMT just looked at me as if I was crazy. He then looked at the officer.

"Do as he said. He wants it to look like she was shot. There maybe someone watching," the officer said as he turned and looked at me.

"Take her to Denver General and make sure she is put in a private room with a police guard with instruction not to let anyone, and I mean anyone, in her room," I said.

"I can't do that," the EMT said. "I don't have the authority to do that."

"I do," a voice said from behind the EMT.

I turned and looked up at Mac. He had just come into my apartment.

"Who are you?" the EMT asked, not sure who was talking to him.

"I'm Captain MacDonald of the Denver Police Department," he said as he showed the EMT his badge. "She is a material witness. Do as he said."

"You go with her," Mac said to me. "I'll send an officer up to the hospital to guard her room. Wait in the room until I get there. I have a few things to do here."

"Thanks," I said, then turned to the EMT. "Put a large bandage on my head and a sling on my arm."

I stood up and had the EMT bandage me up as if I had been injured by a bullet or flying glass. When he was done, I walked out of my apartment alongside the stretcher and got in the ambulance. The driver drove away with the siren and flashing lights going.

IT DIDN'T TAKE VERY LONG to get to the hospital. As soon as we arrived, we were taken to an emergency treatment room where we waited for Mac. No one was allowed in the room, and there was a guard posted outside the door. I sat on a chair next to Julie holding her hand. She was lying on the treatment table. I could see she was still pretty shaken by the shooting. She turned her head and looked at me. It took a minute or so before she smiled at me.

"How are you feeling?" I asked.

"Okay, I guess," she said, but didn't sound like she believed what she was saying.

"Do you want to talk about it? It sometimes helps."

"No, not just yet. I just want you to hold my hand."

I sat there next to the treatment table holding her hand and gently rubbing it. She turned her head and looked up at the ceiling. I had no idea what was going through her mind. I was hoping that she was relaxing a bit to try to get her nerves settled. After a while she turned and looked at me again.

"Peter, I think it would be a good idea if I go and stay with George while you find Josh's killer. My being with you makes it harder for you to do what you have to do. I'm in the way, and by being in the way, I am risking your life. You don't need to be worrying about me."

"Right at the moment I don't know where George is. I have not heard from him since we left his home."

"As soon as you find out, I'll go and stay with him until this is over."

"I think - - -."

I was suddenly interrupted by a light knock on the door to the emergency treatment room. I quickly stood and moved close to the door.

"Who is it?"

"Pete, it's me. Can I come in?"

I reached over and pulled the door open. Mac was standing next to the guard waiting for me to let him in.

"Come on in," I said as I stepped back so he could enter.

"I'm sorry it took so long to get here. We found the car that was used in the shooting at your apartment. It was stolen only a short time before. We found it ditched in an alley only four blocks from your place. I have several police officers combing the area and talking to residents of the area to find out if anyone saw who ditched the car.

"We're taking the car in for the forensic team to go over it. I also have a forensic team going over your apartment. They will secure it after they're done."

"Thanks."

"How are you doing, Julie?" Mac asked.

"I'm doing okay. What happens now?"

"We're going to admit you to the hospital under an assumed name. We will have a guard posted at the door."

"How long will I be here?"

"Until I can safely get you to George." I said.

Mac looked at me as if it was not what he had planned. I could see from the look on his face he wasn't sure it was a good idea.

"George can protect you better than the police can even in one of their so-called safe houses. Most of the safe houses are known by the criminals in this town. That's simply because too many people know about them," I said.

"Have you heard from George?" Mac asked.

"No, not yet. I need to get to my office."

"I'll get you out of here as soon as we get Julie to a safe room." Mac said.

Mac interviewed Julie and me while we waited for word that a room was secure and a guard was ready. During that time, we told him all we knew about the shooting, which was darn little. We didn't see who did the shooting. We didn't even see the vehicle that was used. It would be up to the forensic team to find any evidence.

Mac had finished questioning us about the attack on us at my apartment when there was a knock on the door. Mac drew his gun and stepped over close to the door.

"Who is it?"

"Officer Collins, sir. We have the room ready."

"We'll be ready to move her in a moment. Wait there," Mac said.

Mac stepped out of the room and returned with a doctor and a nurse. Julie was once again placed on a gurney with what appeared to be an IV and an oxygen mask over her face. She was then wheeled out of the treatment room with the doctor and nurse, and two officers dressed as emergency room orderlies pushing the gurney.

Still wearing the head bandage and the sling, I walked alongside the gurney. She was taken to a private room on the sixth floor that had been secured by the police. Mac instructed the guard that no one was to enter her room, or the rooms on either side of her room, without his personal permission, and that included hospital personnel of any kind, doctors, nurses, staff, or police officers. He emphasized strongly that no one was to enter that room without his permission.

I stayed with Julie until she had settled down, and while I waited for Mac to make arrangements for me to leave the hospital unseen. It took Mac almost an hour to get things ready so I could leave the hospital without anyone knowing I was gone.

"It's time," Mac said as he handed me a set of scrubs including a mask.

I put them on before saying goodbye to Julie. I then walked out of her room along with the doctor and nurse. When we got to the service elevator, Mac and I got on and went down to the ground floor. There was a car waiting for me inside the loading area. I got in the car and was driven to Precinct One along with Mac.

CHAPTER EIGHTEEN

WE ARRIVED AT THE POLICE STATION and entered at the rear of the building. Using the back hallway, we went directly to Mac's office. Once in his office, I sat down in front of Mac's desk while he sat down at his desk.

"This is what we know so far about the shooting at your apartment. We think two men stole the car they used about six blocks from your place. They drove up in front of your place and opened fire on you. A fully automatic gun was used, pouring eighty to a hundred rounds into your living room before they took off. They dumped the car in an alley four blocks from your place.

"In the car, we found a good number of spent brass casings. Those and the ones we found in front of your apartment are being checked for fingerprints. Our forensic team is going over your apartment for any evidence as well as the car. We don't expect to find any fingerprints on the car except for the owners. We are sure it was a professional hit. We think that because of the way it was done. We are sure that the other attempts were also done by professionals."

"Did anyone see who dropped off the stolen car?" I asked.

"We're checking that out now. At this time, we don't have any witnesses to who might have stolen the car, or who dumped it. For now, that is all we have. We are hoping our forensic team finds something that will help, but that takes time."

"What happened to the plain police car parked out in front of my apartment last night?"

"The officers in that car are being questioned. They were there, but something was used to knock them out cold. Neither of them were hurt. We're trying to figure out what was used to knock them out. At this point, we think it was something in the coffee they ordered from down the street. Although they both claim they didn't order the coffee. The one thing they do agree on was that the coffee was delivered to them by a police officer," Mac explained.

"You will keep me informed as to what you find?"

"Certainly," Mac said. "What's your next move?"

"Since Julie is safe for the moment, my next move is to get a set of wheels. My Tahoe is in your garage being gone over by your forensic people. I don't suppose I can get in my apartment to get a gun? One of the officers who was first on the scene took the gun I had in my hand when they entered my apartment."

"Just a minute," Mac said then picked up the phone.

I only half listened to his side of the call because I had a lot on my mind, but it sounded like he was talking to someone about my gun. It wasn't very long before he hung up the phone.

"The officer that took your gun will be here in a few minutes. He still had it and is bringing it to you. Since you didn't fire the gun, it is not needed for evidence."

"Once I get my gun back, could I get a ride to my office?"

"Sure," Mac said.

We spent the next ten to fifteen minutes talking about what we knew and what we thought we knew, but were unable to come up with any real solid suspects we could pin anything on and make it stick. We came to the conclusion that we needed more solid evidence that would point to a suspect, and we hoped to get at least some of it from the forensic teams.

Our thoughts and discussion were interrupted by a knock on Mac's office door. Mac opened door. The officer who had taken my gun at my apartment walked in and handed me the gun.

"I'm sorry that I took your gun, but we didn't know if you had fired it or not," the officer said.

"No problem. Thanks for bringing it to me."

"You're welcome. We found two other handguns in your apartment, a .45 caliber and a 9mm. We have them secured. Do you want them, too?" he asked.

"No, but since my apartment is not all that secure at the moment, could you hand them over to Captain MacDonald for safe keeping?"

"Get them and bring them to me," Mac said.

"Yes, sir," the officer said then turned and left Mac's office.

"Come on. I'll give you a lift to your office," Mac said.

I followed Mac out of the police station to his car. We got in and Mac drove me to my office. He pulled into the underground parking garage and stopped in front of the elevator. I opened the car door and stepped out, looking around for any sign of trouble. I didn't see anyone.

"You want me to come up to your office with you?"

"Don't think that will be necessary."

"Okay. Be careful. Let me know when you find out where George has taken Mrs. Garrett and Miss Sullivan. I need to talk to them."

"I will," I said.

I gave him a brief wave then turned and walked to the elevator. I pushed the call button then turned and looked at Mac. He was waiting for the elevator, apparently to make sure I got in it okay. I sort of chuckled to myself when I thought of the times I had waited for my date to get safely into the house before I would leave for home.

When the elevator door opened, I stepped in and pushed the button for the seventh floor. The elevator went directly to the seventh floor without a stop. I got out and took the stairs to the ninth floor. At the ninth floor, I looked out the small window to see if there was anyone in the hall. I saw two people, but I knew who they were and where they were going.

I stepped out of the stairway and walked down the hall to my office. I unlocked the door and went inside, then immediately locked the door behind me. After sitting down in my chair behind the desk, I leaned back and took a deep breath. It had been a long day and I knew it was not over.

Getting a new vehicle was the first order of business. I placed a call to my friend Randy at the Ford Dealership. It took a couple of minutes before he came on the line.

"What can I do for you today, Peter?"

"Randy, how would you like to sell me a new Ford Explorer?"

"Are you kidding?"

"No, but there's a hitch."

"Okay, what's the hitch?" he asked wondering what kind of hitch there might be.

"I want to trade in my Tahoe, but it is currently in the custody of the Denver Police Department. I might mention that it has three bullet holes in it."

"Bullet holes?"

"Yes. There's no serious damage, just a little bodywork to fix them."

"I won't ask you how it happened."

"Good."

"If you will agree, I'll give you a good deal on the Explorer, but I don't know how much damage was done to your Tahoe, and how much it will cost to repair."

"You give me your best deal, and I'll agree to pay the cost of repairing the Tahoe. The thing is, I need a set of wheels now."

"Okay. You have a deal. Tell me what you want on your Explorer and I'll get one ready. I have several on the lot."

"Can I get one this afternoon?"

"Sure. It will be about four o'clock by the time I have it ready."

"That's fine."

We took a few minutes to talk about what I wanted in my new vehicle. He said he had two Explorers on the lot that had the options I wanted, and a little more, and he could have either one of them ready in an hour. One was red and the other was black. I picked the red one that had the options I wanted. Once we were done, we said our goodbyes and I hung up. All I had to do now was to wait for him to bring it to my office.

I had just hung up when the phone began to ring. I thought about letting the answering machine take the call, but I was waiting to hear from George. I reached over and picked up the phone.

"Peter Blackstone Investigations, how my I help you?"

"Hi."

"Is everything okay?"

"It is fine."

"Good," I said then hung up.

I quickly left my office and went down the hall to an insurance agent's office. There was a young lady sitting at the desk. I knew her fairly well.

"Hi, Marcia. I was wondering if I might use your phone for a moment?"

"Sure, Peter," she said with a smile. "I'll just step outside."

"Thank you," I said as I watched her get up and walk out of the office.

I quickly dialed the phone number of George's cell phone. It was answered on the second ring.

"I take it you think your phone is bugged," George said.

"Yes, and I left my cell phone at my apartment. I'm using the phone in an office next to mine."

"Good idea. I'm sure you want to know where I am. I have Mary and Mrs. Garrett at my friend's place in Centennial. I'm the only one with a phone. I have Mrs. Garrett's phone. She won't be calling anyone again."

"Is there some way you can get her phone to me?"

"Sure. My friend would be happy to deliver it to you."

"Not good enough. He might be followed from here back to you."

"Have him take it to Captain MacDonald at Precinct One."

"That would work. I'll send him with it within the hour."

"Is everything okay there?"

"So far, so good. I heard on the news that your apartment was shot up. Is everyone okay?"

"Yeah. Julie is currently in the hospital under heavy guard. She was not injured, but it shook her up a bit."

"I'm sure. Thanks. I was a little worried about her."

"I'm sure you were, but she is fine. I'll talk to you later," I said then hung up.

I immediately called Mac. It didn't take but a minute before he was on the phone.

"Captain MacDonald, how may I help you?"

"Mac, there will be a guy stopping by to give you a cell phone. The phone is the one Mrs. Garrett used that let someone know where she was located. I would like you to check it out and find out who she might have called over the past week or so. It could prove interesting. By the way, I know at least one of the calls was to the Wallaces, her friends where you picked up the two thugs for me."

"I remember. I'll see what I can do to find out who else she called. Are you all right?"

"I'm fine. I'll call you later. If you need to get in touch with me, you'll have to call my office. My cell phone is in my apartment. By the way, I think my office phone is bugged so be careful what you say. I'll be staying at a motel in Littleton that's owned by a good friend of mine."

"Okay. Hang on a minute."

I had no idea what he wanted me to wait for, but he was back on the line within two or three minutes.

"Pete, stop by your apartment. The forensic team is still there and said it would take them at least a couple of hours to finish up. They will give you your phone."

"Thanks," I said.

I hung up and walked out of the office. Marcia was standing in the hall about ten to fifteen feet from the door.

"Thanks, Marcia."

"Your welcome," she said with a grin, then returned to her office.

I returned to my office to wait for Randy to show up with a new vehicle of me. While I waited, I sat down at my desk and thought about what I knew and what I thought I knew. I didn't seem to be getting anywhere. I had several suspects, but no proof, nothing I could use to have Mac arrest them. There was one thing I knew for sure, I was getting close to someone who didn't want me around.

It was just a little over an hour since I had talked to Randy when there was a knock on my office door. I drew my gun then walked to the door.

"Who is it?"

"Randy."

I slipped my gun back in my holster then opened the door. Randy was standing in the hall smiling.

"Come in."

As soon as he was inside, I looked up and down the hall. I didn't see anyone so I shut the door and locked it.

"You sounded like you were in a hurry to get a set of wheels so I brought over the one you wanted. It's parked in your parking space in the parking garage. Here are the keys. You can stop by and take care of the paperwork later. Maybe after you get your Tahoe back. That way we can settle up all at once. The temporary license in the window is good for thirty days."

"That's very nice of you. Do you need a ride back to your dealership?"

"No. I have a ride waiting for me. Say, will you tell me all about this cloak and dagger stuff when it's over?" he asked hoping that I would agree.

"Sure. I'll sit down with you and tell you all about it, but right now I have to go to my apartment and get my cell phone."

"Okay. I'll talk to you later," Randy said.

I stood up and walked Randy to the door. I checked the hallway to make sure it was clear. There were several people in the hall, but I knew all of them.

"I'll talk to you later," I said, then watched as Randy walked to the elevator.

As soon as Randy was gone, I locked my office and took the stairway. I felt that the elevator was not the safest way for me to go. It was a long walk down the stairs, but it gave me time to think about who was involved and what I might be getting so close to that someone had to eliminate me.

When I reached the parking garage level, I looked out the small window in the fire door. I could see the red Explorer with the temporary license in the window. I had to admit that it looked very nice. I didn't open the fire door until I was sure there was no one out there that posed a danger to me. I opened the door and walked up to the

Explorer, opened the door and got in. After looking over the inside of the Explorer, I started it and left the parking garage for my apartment.

WHEN I TURNED THE CORNER onto the street in front of my apartment, I could see nothing but flashing red and blue lights. There were two police cars and a CSI van. There was yellow tape all over the place, and at the very least three dozen gawkers.

I pulled up behind one of the police cars and stopped. The first thing I saw was a policeman coming toward me. He didn't look very happy. I got out of my Explorer and stepped up on the curb.

"You can't park there," the officer said rather sharply.

"I'm Peter Blackstone. That's my apartment the forensic team is going over."

"I don't care if it is your apartment. - - - ."

"Excuse me," I said, interrupting the officer, "but you will care. Captain MacDonald told me I could stop by here and get my cell phone from the investigator. If you will check, you will find that he called ahead and told them to let me have my cell phone."

The officer looked at me. It was clear that he didn't know if I was telling the truth, or if I just wanted to get into the apartment for some other reason.

"Wait here," the officer said.

I nodded my head and watched him as he turned and walked over to the window where a forensic specialist was working. I didn't hear what he said, but the forensic specialist turned and talked to someone else. It was only a matter of a minute or so and I saw someone inside my apartment hand the officer my cell phone. The officer turned and walked up to me.

"Is this your phone?" he said as he held it out to me.

"Yes," I said, but he didn't look like he really wanted to give it to me.

I held out my hand, he looked at it, then reluctantly he gave me the phone. I turned around, slipped the phone into my pocket and went back to my car without saying anything to the officer.

When I got back to my Explorer, I took a minute to look at my apartment. The big window in the front had been shot out and there were bullet holes on each side of the window frame. I could see a forensic specialist working inside and another one digging slugs out of the window frame and looking for any other evidence that might give them a clue as to who shot up my place.

As I drove away, I couldn't help but think how close Julie and I had come to having our lives ended right there. The thought of it not only made me mad, it scared me. Not so much for myself, as for Julie. She came very close to being the second woman to die because she was with me, but she had nothing to do with my investigation. Or did she?

It was that question that suddenly got me to thinking about her. Was I really the one they were trying to kill? The thought that Julie may have been the target came to mind, but how could that be? Then it hit me. If Josh's killer thought Julie might have seen him in the recovery room, he might not want her to be able to identify him. I needed to talk to Julie as soon as possible.

I MADE A QUICK U-TURN in the middle of the street and headed back to the hospital. If Julie was the target all along, I had to get to her as quickly as possible. I wanted her out of the hospital and under George's protection quickly. It would not take much for someone with connections to find out where she was, and figure out a way to get to her.

It didn't take me very long to get to the hospital. I parked my vehicle and ran into the hospital. Since I knew where Julie was being held, I got on an elevator that would take me there. Once in the elevator, I pressed the button for the floor her room was located on. It seemed that it was the slowest elevator I had ever been on.

When it finally got to the floor I wanted, I stepped off the elevator. Looking down the hall toward her room, I noticed the lights had been turned down for the night. I could see the police officer sitting in a chair outside Julie's room. It looked like he was asleep. It made me mad to think that he had fallen asleep while on duty. My first thought was I would have his badge for this.

As I approached him, my thoughts began to change. I wasn't so sure he was sleeping. His position was not one I would have expected of someone who had simply fallen asleep in the chair.

I drew my gun as I approached him. When I got up close to him and was about to touch him, I noticed blood on his neck just behind his ear. I looked at the door to the room where Julie was supposed to be at the same time I reached out and touched his neck to see if the policeman was still alive. He was dead.

Moving up close to the door to her room, I slowly pushed the door open. The room was dark, not a single light was on. Being as careful as possible, and hopefully being ready for anything, I reached around inside the room and switched on the light. I'm not sure what I expected to see, but I didn't expect to see an empty bed in the room.

I quickly looked around the room, then stepped inside. I was both relieved and concerned at the same time. Julie was not in the bed and the room looked empty. My first thought was someone had kidnapped her, but I had to make sure she wasn't in the bathroom or the closet.

The bathroom door was slightly ajar. I carefully moved across the room, keeping my gun pointed at the door in case there was someone in the bathroom who shouldn't be there.

When I pushed the door wide open, I could see that the bathroom was empty.

I quickly turned toward the closet. I stepped up to the closet, reached out and put one hand on the doorknob while pointing my gun at the door. I jerked the door open and got one hell of a surprise. Huddled down on the floor in the corner was Julie.

I quickly put my gun in my holster as I knelt down. I reached out and took her by the shoulders and pulled her toward me. She threw her arms around my neck and held me tightly. She started to cry. I have to admit, I was never so relieved as I was at that moment. It took a couple of minutes for me to gather my senses and realize that I needed to get her out of the hospital and some place safe, and fast.

"Come on. We have to get out of here."

I stepped back and helped her up, all the time she was holding onto me tightly. Once I got her to her feet, I wrapped my arm around her and started walking her toward the fire door in the stairway at the end of the hall.

As we walked by the nurse's station, it seemed strange that there was no one at the desk. I stopped in front of the counter and looked over it. My worst fears were soon realized. Lying on the floor was a nurse. It was clear that there was nothing I could do for her.

I again, put my arm around Julie and took her to the stairway. I opened the door and stepped inside. Holding Julie back against the wall, I leaned out and looked over the railing, first down and then up. I also listened for any sounds that might indicate there was someone in the stairway. I heard nothing.

I looked at Julie. She looked like she was about to say something, but I reached up and put my hand over her mouth while putting my finger over my lips. I leaned close to her ear and whispered.

"Don't make a sound. We're getting out of here."

Julie nodded that she understood. I took her hand and began leading her down the stairs. It didn't take us long to get to the underground level where the loading docks were located, and where supplies were brought into the hospital. It was also where ambulances were parked when not in use. We walked to a door next to the larger overhead doors used for vehicles. It had a small glass window that had wires running through it. I looked out. I didn't see anything that might cause us harm.

"Look out the door," I said.

Julie stepped up to the small window and looked out.

"Do you see that red Ford Explorer parked next to that silver pickup?"

"Yes," she whispered.

"That's where we are going. I want you to stay as close to me as you can."

"Okay," she said looking at me.

I looked around the door to see if it would set off alarms if we opened it. It didn't look like that kind of door. I pushed the catch bar and the door opened. I tucked Julie up against me, then we started off across the open drive as fast as we could to the Explorer. I helped her in, then quickly ran around to the other side. As soon as I was in, I started the car and drove out of the parking lot.

Once out on the street, I drove at the speed limit in the hope of not drawing any attention to us. I had no idea if the hospital was being watched or not. If we had been seen, there was little doubt in my mind that we would have a tail on us in a matter of seconds.

As I drove, I didn't see anyone following us. I had to get her some place where we could spend the night. I decided to take her to my friend's motel in Littleton for the night. I would call Mac from there. I took the long way to get there in order to make sure we were not being followed.

IT TOOK US AWHILE to get to my friend's motel. I got us a room then we settled in. As soon as Julie was resting on the bed, I sat down and called Mac using my cell phone.

"Captain MacDonald, how may I help you?"

"Mac, it's Peter."

"I've been worried about you. Is Julie with you?"

"Yes. From your question, I take it you know about the guard and nurse."

"Yeah. I won't ask where you are, but do you know what happened at the hospital?"

"No, but I think someone made an attempt on Julie. She hid in the closet. The guard and nurse were dead when I got there."

"Okay. Stay where you are for now. I'll call you in the morning and fill you in on what we know. I've got to get over to the hospital."

"Okay," I said then hung up.

With all that had happened, we were both exhausted. We got ready for bed. As soon as we were in bed, Julie curled up against me. It wasn't long before she was asleep. It took me awhile longer as I had a lot on my mind.

CHAPTER NINETEEN

WHEN MORNING CAME, it was still fairly dark in the motel room. Julie was curled up against me. I knew that she had had a restless night, but I couldn't blame her. It had to be a frightening experience for her to have someone shoot at her.

My thoughts about Julie being the target for the attack on her in the hospital and at my apartment caused me to wonder what she might know. I doubt she was conscious of knowing anything important to the case. If she had been, I was sure she would have told me. I had to figure out a way to get her to dig deep into her mind and tell me what she saw or heard.

My thoughts were disturbed by her movement in the bed. I looked at her and found her looking back at me. She smiled at me. It was a smile that told me she was glad that I was holding her.

"Good morning," she said softly.

"How are you feeling?"

"I guess I'm still tired," she said as the look on her face turned serious. "Peter, I was thinking last night before I dozed off. Why would someone want to kill me?"

"I don't know. It might be you know something that could be a problem for whoever was involved in the death of Josh."

"But I don't know anything about it," she said with a hint of frustration in her voice.

"I want you to relax and close your eyes. I want you to think about the night Josh died. Start thinking from about the time the surgery was over. Take it step by step and think about everything you saw, everything you did and everything you saw someone else do. Do you think you can do that?"

"I'll try," she said.

I watched her as she rolled over on her back. She looked at the ceiling for a moment or two before she closed her eyes. After a few minutes, she began to tell me what she was seeing in her mind's eye.

"I remember seeing Josh for the first time when he was wheeled into surgery. He had been prepared for surgery. I immediately began draping his chest for the surgery. As soon as he was ready, the doctor began by opening his chest a little in an effort to find and remove the bullets. Once the bullets were removed, he then repaired the damage done by them.

"The surgery was not easy and took a couple of hours to complete, but it went very well. Once the bullets had been removed and the surgeon had repaired the internal damage, he closed up the wounds leaving a suction tube in Josh's chest to collect any drainage and keep fluids from building up in his lungs. The doctor took a few minutes to make sure Josh was doing okay before he had Josh moved to the recovery room.

"I assisted in wheeling him into the recovery room. I reconnected the drainage pump once he was in the recovery room and made sure it was working like it was supposed to."

"Did you do anything else while you were there?" I asked.

"Yes. I updated his treatment chart, took his vital signs and recorded them in the chart. At the request of the surgeon, I also instructed the recovery room nurse assigned to his care on what procedures should be used in order to care for him. There were a few extra instructions for his care because of the internal damage and the drainage tube in his chest."

"Who was the nurse you gave the instructions to?"

"Judy Dahl. She has been a nurse for a long time, but she was new to the recovery room. She knew most of what had to be done for Josh."

"Was she upset with you for telling her what needed to be done?"

"Not really, but she did seem a little distracted."

"Okay. What did you do next?"

"I went out to the changing room and cleaned up."

"I understand that you spent some time with Josh before you left for the evening. Is that correct?"

"Yes. It was a pretty busy night in the recovery room. As soon as I cleaned up, I put on clean scrubs and went back in to see how Josh was doing. Since it was busy, I spent some time taking his vital signs, checking the chest tube and drainage, and keeping watch over him."

"Is that something you usually do?"

"No. Not normally, but I sometimes do it, especially if it is a case where there is a high risk of something going wrong."

"What compelled you to do it that night?"

"I don't really know. I guess it was because they were busy, and I wasn't due to get off work for awhile. The rest of the surgeries that could wait had been rescheduled for morning."

"Why was that?"

"One of the doctors was not feeling well, and the other doctor who had just finished with Josh was pretty tired. He thought it was better to delay the remaining surgeries until morning so he could get some rest," she explained.

"Was Josh the only one you helped with while in the recovery room?" I asked, not sure where I was going with that question.

"Yes," she said thoughtfully.

"How long did you spend with him?"

"I'm not sure, probably about thirty to forty minutes."

"Were you with him all that time?"

"Yes. The only time I was not with him was when I went to clean up. It was after I cleaned up that I spent the thirty to forty minutes with him."

"While you were there, did you see anyone that didn't belong in the recovery room?"

"No, I don't think so," she said thoughtfully.

"Did anyone seem like they didn't want you there? Maybe thought you were in the way, or suggested that you leave?"

"No, ah, yes. The recovery room supervisor thought I should go. She made it sound like I was not needed. I didn't think of it at the time, but they were pretty busy. I was sure that my being there with Josh helped relieve some of the pressure."

"I would think they would want all the help they could get," I said. "Had the supervisor ever suggested that you leave on other occasions when you stayed with a patient to help out?" I asked.

"No. She had always welcomed my help."

"Who was the person who asked you to leave?"

"Rose Williams, but I think it was Judy Dahl who wanted me out of there."

"Why do you think that?"

"It was Judy's first night in the recovery room. I think she was trying to prove herself to the supervisor. She might have felt a little intimidated by me, especially since I had given her instructions on Josh's care. I only gave her the instructions the surgeon told me to tell them, which is not at all unusual. If she had worked in the recovery room before, she would have known that."

"Did you see anyone else, either in the recovery room or just outside it?"

"As I was leaving I saw a man standing at the door to the recovery room. He was looking in the window. You can't see much through that window. It's pretty small and not in a place where you can see the patients."

"Could he have seen Josh?"

"No. I don't think so."

"What did he look like?"

"Remember the car that followed you into the alley. The one where you backed into the alley and had a gun pointed at him when he started to turn into the alley?"

"Yeah."

"I got a glimpse of him after he backed out and started to speed away. That was the same man."

"Why didn't you tell me that before?" I asked a little surprised she hadn't said something before.

"I'm sorry but I just remembered it."

"Good. Now I have a couple of people to check out."

"What do we do now?"

"I think we need to get up, have something to eat, then I need to get you to some place safe."

Julie got out of the bed and went into the bathroom. I could hear the shower running while I called the motel office. I arranged for breakfast to be brought to our room. It wasn't long before Julie came out of the bathroom. She was wearing the same clothes she had on the night before, which was understandable. We had not gone to her apartment to get clean clothes, for a very good reason. I didn't want anyone to know where she lived.

"I ordered breakfast for us. It should be here at any moment."

Just then, there was a knock on the door. I motioned for Julie to go into the bathroom. As soon as she was out of sight, I drew my gun then slowly opened the door. My friend was standing there with a tray.

"It's not much, but it will have to do," he said.

"Thanks. I'll make it up to you," I said.

"I heard about your apartment being shot up. Are you going to be staying here until you can move back in?"

"I think so, but I won't be asking for room service. I have to get Julie someplace where she can have full-time protection while I find out who is trying to kill her and why."

"Okay. I'll see you later," he said then turned and walked back toward the office.

I took a quick look around, but didn't see anyone who might cause us harm. I shut the door and set the tray on the table.

"You can come out now. Breakfast is served."

After we finished breakfast, I checked outside for anyone who looked suspicious. Not seeing anyone in front of the rooms, I led Julie out to the Explorer. She got in quickly, then I ran around and got in behind the wheel.

"Where are we going?" Julie asked as I started the Explorer.

"Since I still don't know where George has taken Barbara and Mary, I think the safest place for you would be in the police station."

"You're kidding, aren't you?"

"No. I'll take you to Mac's office. It the safest place for you. I have something I need to do, and I can't take you with me."

"I understand," Julie said with a hint of disappointment in her voice.

"Besides, I need to talk to Mac," I said.

I put the Explorer in gear, took a quick look around then started out of the motel parking lot. I turned out onto the street and headed for Precinct One.

THE DRIVE TO THE POLICE STATION was uneventful. I didn't see anyone following us, and traffic was not too bad this time of the morning. It only took about twenty minutes to get to Precinct One.

As I pulled into the parking lot, I saw Mac coming out of the building and walking toward his car. I touched the horn to get his attention. As soon as he saw me, he turned and walked toward me. I stopped when he came close me.

"What's up, Pete?"

"Have you got a minute?"

"I was headed out to talk to some of the residents of the apartment building where William North lived. You want to go along?"

"I would like to, but I need a safe place for Julie to stay. Maybe she could stay in your office while we visit North's apartment," I suggested.

"Sure."

I parked the Explorer then walked around to the other side and opened the door. Mac and I walked Julie into the police station, then down the hall to Mac's office. Once inside, Mac sat down at his desk and called the Desk Sergeant. Mac told the sergeant to have a female officer come to his office, then hung up.

It was only a few minutes before a female officer knocked on the door to Mac's office. Mac told her to enter.

"Julie, this is Officer Eleanor Marcus. She will be staying with you while we are gone," Mac said, then turned to the officer.

"Eleanor, you are to stay with Julie. You are not to leave this office for any reason until we get back. You will lock the door and not let anyone in. You can call Russell to get you some coffee and maybe something to read, but you will not open the door for anyone but us or Russell. I will be telling Russell just what I've told you. Got it?"

"Yes, sir."

"We should be back by lunch time. We'll bring something for the two of you to eat," Mac added then turned to leave.

"I'll see you later," I said to Julie, then gave her a quick kiss.

I turned and followed Mac out of his office. I waited while he locked the door to his office. We made a quick stop at the Duty Desk to give Sergeant Russell his instructions, then I followed Mac out of the Precinct One building to his car.

AS MAC DROVE TO NORTH'S APARTMENT, we talked a bit about what had been going on. I was most interested in what his people found in Josh's car.

"Other than finding no fingerprints on the steering wheel, did they find anything in the car?" I asked.

"They didn't find a thing. I was hoping that they would find something that would give us, at the very least, a clue as to why Garrett wanted to talk to you and why he was murdered."

"When we get done at North's apartment, I'd like to take a look at Josh's car."

"I don't know what you think you might find, but okay," Mac said. "A second set of eyes is always welcome."

NOTHING MORE WAS SAID until we pulled up in front of the apartment building where William North was supposed to have lived. We got out of the car and walked directly to the apartment building's manager's apartment and rang the bell. It only took a few minutes for the door to open. Standing in front of us was a very nice looking woman in her mid-to-late forties.

"May I help you, gentlemen?"

"Yes. I'm Captain MacDonald with the Denver Police Department," he said as he held out his badge and ID card. "I would like the key to William North's apartment, please."

The woman looked at Mac then at me. I wasn't sure if she was going to comply with his request.

"Do you have a warrant?"

"Yes. I have a warrant," he said as he took a paper out of his pocket and showed it to her.

"Doesn't Mr. North have to be in before you can search his apartment?"

"In this case, no. Mr. North was killed in a café a few days ago."

The look on her face indicated that she didn't know he was dead.

"A key to his room, please," Mac said.

"Oh. Yes," she replied.

I watched the woman as she turned and went to a desk near the front door of her apartment. Shortly after opening the desk, she returned with a key to North's apartment and gave it to Mac. Mac thanked her for the key and told her he would return the key to her as soon as he was done.

I followed Mac to the elevator. We took the elevator to the fourth floor. We stepped off the elevator and walked down the hall toward North's apartment. Just as Mac put the key in the door, the apartment door of the apartment across the hall flew open. Mac quickly turned around as he reached for his gun. I stepped back and drew my gun.

We quickly lowered our guns and relaxed when we saw a young woman step out of the apartment. She was dressed as if she was going to the swimming pool. I happened to know there was an indoor swimming pool in the building. It was the look on her face that showed me that the guns had startled her.

"Sorry, Miss. We are police officers," Mac said.

"Oh," she said then seemed to relax a little.

Mac showed her his badge and ID.

"Excuse me, but do you happen to know Mr. North?" Mac asked.

"I know what he looks like, but that's about all. I don't know him personally. Come to think of it, I haven't seen him lately."

"Do you know anyone in this building that he might have been friends with?"

"Not really, but my roommate dated him a few times. She would know him better than I do."

"Is your roommate home now?"

"Yes. I'll get her."

"Thank you," Mac said then turned and looked at me.

"This might prove interesting," Mac said, then turned toward the door when he heard the woman returning.

"Alicia will be along in a moment," she said, then walked out of the apartment and down the hall.

It only took a minute or so before a tall slim blond wearing tight fitting jeans and a blouse walked toward us.

"May I help you?" she said as she stopped at the door and smiled at us.

"Yes. I'm Captain MacDonald of the Denver Police Department. I would like to ask you a few questions about your neighbor, Mr. North," Mac said as he showed her his ID and badge.

"Certainly," she said as she looked at his badge. "Come in."

I followed Mac and the young blond into the apartment.

"Please, sit down. Can I get you anything?"

"No. Thank you," Mac said as he sat down on the sofa.

I sat down on a chair and waited for the woman to sit down.

"What can I do for you? I understand you would like to ask me a few questions about William, is that right?"

I sat quietly and let Mac ask his questions.

"That is correct. First of all, I would like to know your name."

"I'm Alicia Gordon, I'm twenty-three years old and I'm single. I work for Elizbeth's Fine Clothing as a sales person."

"Thank you," Mac said with a smile. "I understand from your roommate that you dated Mr. North. Is that correct?"

"Yes, I did date him a few times, but we didn't seem to hit it off, if you know what I mean."

"I think I do, but can you tell me why you didn't hit it off?"

"He was a little too forceful. He expected a woman to follow him and do as she was told. In short, he was a male chauvinist. He was from somewhere back east, I don't remember where he said he was from."

"I see. You said you dated him a few times. When was that?"

"It was shortly after he moved here. I can't give you the dates."

"That's fine. We know when he moved to Denver."

"Can you tell me anything about him?"

"You mean other than he was a male chauvinist?"

"Yes," Mac with a slight grin.

"No, not really. But from the way he talked, he moved out here to meet someone. He never said who it was, but I got the impression that it might have been a woman."

"What gave you that idea?"

"I don't know, but I heard him mention something about a woman he was looking for. He was talking to one of the men who was at a party we had after I quit dating him."

"Thank you for your time. I think that will be all for now," Mac said as he stood up.

I stood and walked to the door with Mac. Just as we were about to leave, Alicia spoke to me.

"Excuse me, but do you talk?" she asked with a smile that would melt butter.

"Only when I have something to say," I said as I smiled at her.

She looked at me as if I was something strange, but didn't say anything more.

I turned and followed Mac out the door. We went across the hall and entered North's apartment.

Once inside the apartment, we closed the door and stood there just looking around the living room. After taking in the room, we began a careful search of the place. We didn't find anything that connected North to Josh or his murder. Mac did find a picture of Mrs. Franklin with the words 'with all my love, June Stevens' written across the bottom of the picture.

"Well, look what I found. It's a picture of Mrs. June Franklin, but it's signed June Stevens," Mac said.

"I'd be willing to bet that June Stevens was June Franklin's maiden name," I said. "Is there a date on the picture?"

"Don't see one. It would be my guess that she knew North long before he came out here.

"I would agree with you, but it still doesn't show us any connection to Josh or his murder. The fact that Josh was killed in the hospital points to Josh having been the target in the café."

We continued to search North's apartment but came up empty for any connection between the murders of June Franklin and William North to Josh. We closed the door to the apartment, returned the key to the manager, then walked down to Mac's police car.

As we were ready to get in the police car, I looked over the car at the apartment building. I was thinking about North, Franklin and Josh. A thought came to me, something I had not thought about before.

"What are you thinking," Mac asked.

"Just a thought."

"You want to let me in on it?"

I could tell by the look on Mac's face that he hoped I would let him in on it.

"It's a little far out, but what if all three of them were shot for the same reason?"

"Get in the car," Mac said.

I got in the car and looked at him as he sat behind the wheel. He reached down to slip the key in the ignition, but stopped and looked at me.

"Do you think they were all the target of the shooter?" Mac asked.

"I don't know, but what do we really know about Mr. Franklin?"

Mac looked at me for a minute before he said anything.

"I think it is a little far out, but it sure wouldn't hurt to see what we can find out about Franklin. Do you think he was the shooter?" Mac asked.

"I don't know, but he could have been. We have nothing to connect him to Josh's murder, but we haven't looked at him for anything other than the husband of June," I said.

"I think we should take a closer look at him. Never know what we might find."

"I agree. You use your sources and I'll use mine, then we'll compare notes."

"Good idea," Mac said then started the police car.

On our way back to Precinct One, we stopped and bought hamburgers for four along with milk shakes. We arrived at Mac's office and knocked on the door. The police woman called out before opening the door. After Mac responded, she opened the door and we went in. We spread out the food on Mac's desk then sat down to eat.

While we ate our lunch, we discussed what actions we would take. It was decided that Julie would stay with the police woman in an empty office while Mac and I did our research on Mr. Franklin.

After I kissed Julie, Mac and I left. We parted ways in the parking lot. I went to my Explorer and drove to my office. I was not sure where Mac was going.

CHAPTER TWENTY

I TURNED INTO THE UNDERGROUND parking garage of the building where my office was located, but decided not to park in either of the places reserved for me. I drove to a parking space that I knew would not be used by the person it was reserved for because he was on vacation. It was also a parking space that was closer to the stairway than to the elevator. I decided that using the stairway was probably safer than using the elevator since I would be able to see and hear anyone who might be around much sooner than in the elevator.

I parked the Explorer then walked to the stairway, being careful to watch for any danger that might befall me. When I got to the door to the stairway, I looked through the small window into the stairway. I didn't see anyone. I pulled open the door and stepped inside the stairway, quietly closing the door behind me. I listened for any noise that might let me know if there was someone else on the stairway, but I heard nothing. By walking up the stairs, it might give me a chance to think about what was going on, and a chance to get a little exercise.

When I got to the main floor of the building, I made a stop. I left the stairway and walked over to the security area. One of the security guards was sitting at a desk near the front door to the building. He looked up as I walked up to him.

"Good afternoon, Mr. Blackstone. How may I help you?"

"Good afternoon. I would like to know if you have made rounds this morning?"

"Yes, I have. I went by your office about an hour ago," he said as he glanced at his watch. "I didn't see anything out of the ordinary. I tried the door and it was locked, and I knocked to see if you might be in, but got no answer. I opened the door, took a quick look around, but didn't see anything unusual. I shut and locked the door as I left. Fred told me to check out your office even during the day. He told me what had happened. Is there a problem?"

"No. Has anyone asked for me, or asked when I would be in my office this morning?"

"No, sir. It's been pretty quiet around here."

"Thank you," I said then turned and went back to the stairs.

I again began the walk up to the ninth floor of the building. It took me awhile, but it felt good to get a little exercise. I even think it cleared my head a little.

When I got to the ninth floor, I looked out through the small window in the door. I didn't see anyone in the hall except for a couple of the secretaries I knew worked in the insurance office just down the hall from my office. I quickly stepped out into the hall and walked toward my office. As I passed the two secretaries, I nodded a greeting, but didn't say anything to them. They smiled then went on with whatever they were talking about.

After opening the door to my office, I went inside and locked the door behind me. I knew I was being extra cautious, but with what had happened so far, it seemed the right thing to do.

Once I was in the office, it was time to get to work. I turned on my computer. While it was booting up, I removed my coat, hung it up then sat down in front of my computer. It was time to find out everything I could about Mr. William North and Mr. Robert Franklin. I started with William North.

I spent the next couple of hours searching for the information I needed. What little I found on North didn't seem to be of much help. It had become apparent that he had come to Denver to be close to June Franklin. The only connection I could find was they had apparently been high school sweethearts. It was clear that their relationship had picked up again after North got out of the service and came to Denver. He had been in the Navy for six years and served on submarines. June had apparently gotten married to Robert Franklin only two years ago.

Not finding anything interesting to my investigation, I turned to checking on Robert Franklin. The report on Robert Franklin proved to be much more interesting. I discovered that Franklin was a good twelve to fifteen years older than June. The interesting part was that Franklin had been married to his first wife for almost ten years when she died unexpectedly. Based on the report, her death had been considered suspicious by the police, but they had never been able to come up with any solid evidence that her death was the result of foul play.

I began a search to find out the cause of death of Franklin's first wife. A check of her death certificate showed the cause of death was listed as 'accidental', but there was no explanation as to the kind of accident. There was a note in the remarks section of the death certificate. It simply read, "Possible drug overdose, type of drug undetermined" as a possible cause of death. I found it interesting that a death certificate would be signed off by the Medical Examiner in such a way. A look at the toxicology report sort of cleared that up, a little. It indicated that there had been cocaine in her system, but not near enough to have caused her death. It also noted that she was a known user of cocaine, but apparently not a heavy user.

The unfortunate part of all the information was it didn't prove anything, and none of it appeared to have anything to do with Josh's murder. It was clear that Josh had been killed by a large overdose of cocaine. From what information I was able to get, there didn't seem to be any connection between Robert Franklin and Josh Garrett, or anyone else who I thought might have been involved in Josh's death.

As I continued to look for something that might connect Franklin with either Josh or any of my suspects in his death, I came across a photo attached to a newspaper article. It was strictly due to luck that I came across the newspaper photo at all. The photo was a picture of a group of men who were investing in a large block of property that was going to be used for a rather large high-priced housing project on the outskirts of the Denver Metro Area, in the foothills. In the photo was Anthony Williams, of Williams Reality, several other men I could not immediately identify, and Robert Franklin.

It suddenly became clear that Franklin knew Williams. In the photo, Franklin was standing next to Williams. It appeared that they were talking and Franklin was smiling, almost as if they were joking about something. This was one piece of information that I was sure Mac would like to know, but before I called him, I thought it would be a good idea to expand my search of Franklin's background.

I did a complete background check including Franklin's past history of where he had lived. It was interesting to find that he had lived in Reno, Nevada, at the same time Anthony Williams had lived there, and he had left within a month or so after Williams. Franklin's most recent address was in Denver, and showed he had moved here about the same time as Williams had moved to Dillion. I got the feeling that they knew each other, and probably for a long time.

I decided to do a criminal background check on Franklin, as well. I had no idea what it would show me; but if I was right, I would find a long criminal history.

It didn't take long for the Criminal Record of Robert Franklin to come up on the screen. The result showed me only that he was the prime suspect in his wife's death, but that he had been let go for insufficient evidence by the Reno, Nevada, police. Other than that, there was nothing else in his Criminal Record. There were several minor traffic violations, but nothing else.

I decided to run a Criminal Report on Franklin's first wife. I was not surprised when it showed that his wife had a history of using cocaine with several arrests, each one was for relatively minor drug offences, like possession of a small amount of cocaine, and under the influence of the drug. There was no indication that she ever had any large amounts of cocaine, or had any intentions of selling the drug, or that she was completely out of control while using the drug. There was nothing to indicate that she had ever overdosed on cocaine or any other drug. Nor was there any indication that she had ever tried to commit suicide.

There was one interesting thing in the report. She had been the widow of a very wealthy man who had been part owner of a large casino in Reno. That might be how Franklin got so rich so quickly.

I decided it was time to have a talk with Mac about what I had found out. I knew what I had found out was nothing he could not find out himself, but I wasn't sure if he had looked it up. There was another reason I wanted to go to his office rather than just call him, Julie was there.

I printed out what information I had found on my computer. I put it in a folder, then shut down the computer. Once it was off, I put on my coat and headed for the door with the folder in hand.

Just as I was reaching for the door, I heard what sounded like someone was trying the front door to see if it was locked. I stepped back into my inner-office, slipped the folder behind a chair and drew my gun from under my coat. I waited to see what was going to happen.

It was a little while, maybe a minute or so, before I heard what sounded like someone picking the lock or slipping a key in the lock of the front door. I heard the lock release. I could see the door handle move through the crack between the door and the doorjamb of the door to my inner-office. The door slowly opened. All I could see was the hand and part of the sleeve of a winter coat. Whoever it was, he was being very cautious, but not cautious enough. I gave him enough time to step into the outer office and close the door before I stepped around the door.

"That's far enough," I said as I pointed my gun at him. "Well, we meet again. I wouldn't try anything stupid."

The man stood there looking at me with squinted eyes. I could see from the look on his face that he was mad as hell for letting me get the drop on him, a second time.

"Where's your partner? The last time I saw you, you were leaving the Wallaces house in handcuffs."

He just stood there looking at me, and not saying a word. I remembered how much he wanted to take my gun away from me the last time we met. If it hadn't been for George standing behind him, he might have tried. I was well aware that George was not behind him now.

"I see you're still not talking. That's okay. Turn around and put your hands on the wall."

For a couple of seconds, he just looked at me. He finally slowly turned and reached for the wall.

"Now, before I call the police and have you arrested for breaking and entering, I want a little information from you. I suggest you answer my questions because if you don't I just might have to hurt you before I call the cops. You understand?"

"Yeah, I understand," he said with a defiant tone in his voice.

"Good. We understand each other. I want to know who hired you to kill Julie Archer?"

"No one," he said sharply.

"Wrong answer," I said as I jabbed him in the back with barrel of my pistol.

He groaned with pain then took a deep breath. I gave him a moment to think about his answer before I tried again.

"You want to take another try at answering that question?"

"No. I wasn't hired to kill anyone."

"Obviously, you were hired to kill someone. Who were you hired to kill?"

"No one," he insisted.

I thought about what he said for a moment. I decided to take a different approach.

"Let's try this. Who were you hired to muscle?"

There was a long pause. The nudge in the middle of his back with the barrel of my gun ended the pause.

"All right. I was hired to make sure you stopped nosing around in someone's business."

"Who was this 'someone'?"

"I don't dare tell you that. He would have me killed."

"I want to know who shot up my apartment, who tried to kidnap my girlfriend or kill her, and who killed Josh Garrett?"

"I don't know. I don't know. I was hired to get you to stop your investigation, that's all. I didn't have anything to do with trying to kill anybody."

I looked at the man I had leaning against the wall. He was sweating and breathing hard. There was little doubt that he was scared. I wasn't sure I believed him, but he could be telling me the truth. However, I doubted that. You don't come to someone's house with guns just to talk.

"Okay, let's say I believe you. Let's start with who shot up my apartment?"

"I don't know. It was probably the two guys that came out here from Detroit."

"Wrong answer. They are dead, and were dead before my apartment was shot up."

"Then I don't know who did it."

"Well, I can see that I'm not going to get anything out of you without making a mess of my office. That being the case, I'll just have you arrested as a material witness. The police can hold you for seventy-two hours without charges that way."

I moved up close behind him, stuck my gun against the back of his head. He took a deep breath and his body tensed. I was sure he thought I was going to kill him, but that was not my plan. I simply reached around him and relieved him of his gun. I then moved to his side so he could not kick me, if he suddenly got brave, and relieved him of his ankle gun.

"You stay right there," I said as I stepped back.

While keeping an eye on him, I called Mac's office. The phone rang a couple of times before it was answered by Russell who transferred my call to Mac.

"Captain MacDonald, how may I help you?"

"It's Peter. Can you come to my office and pick up a guy who broke into my office? By the way, he's one of the guys you had taken away from Wallace's house."

"You're kidding?"

"Afraid not. You might want to hurry. I don't know if he's alone. If he tries to get away, I might have to shoot him."

I added that last bit of information more for my prisoner's benefit than for Mac's.

"I'm on my way," Mac said then the phone went dead.

"You can relax, but stay right where you are," I said.

After I hung up the phone, I sat down on a chair behind him while keeping a close eye on my prisoner.

"It won't be long before the police will be here to take you to jail."

"I won't be in jail very long," he said with a slight ray of hope in his voice.

"I don't think I would be in any hurry to get out of jail, if I was in your shoes."

"Why? You going to hunt me down and kill me?"

"I won't have to. Just the fact that I had you alone for over a half hour would be enough for the people who hired you to think that you might have talked. I wouldn't give you more than, ah, about seventy-two hours at the most after you're out of jail before they find you and kill you."

From his body language, I could tell he was thinking hard about what I said. His breathing increased in speed and he couldn't seem to stand still.

"You think they are going to let you live knowing what you know?" I asked, but didn't expect an answer.

He didn't say a word, but it was easy to see that he was very nervous. I wondered what he would do once the police showed up.

It was about twenty minutes before there was a knock on my outer office door. I had a pretty good idea who it was, but I was ready for anything.

"Who is it?"

"It's me, MacDonald. I have a couple of officers with me."

"Just a minute."

I stood up and moved around to the door. I unlocked the door and opened it while still keeping an eye on my prisoner. I stepped back and watched while Mac came in my office. He was followed by two uniform officers.

"What do we have here?" Mac asked while looking at the man leaning against the wall.

"We have a man who broke into my office. You'll find a set of lock picks on his person. He got as far as my outer office when I stopped him at the point of a gun."

"Cuff him," Mac said to the officer standing next to him.

Once he was cuffed, the officer turned him around. Mac looked at him for a minute before he said anything.

"You were the hired gun at the Wallaces' house. It sure didn't take you long to pay us another visit," Mac said then turned to me.

"You pressing charges on this guy?"

"I will, but if you get him to talk, I might drop the charges. I'll be down in a couple of hours to press charges."

"Since he was picked up only a few days ago, I'll keep him as a material witness. I can keep him for seventy-two hours that way. Has he talked?"

"Nope, but I think he's scared that if we let him go, he will be dead in less than seventy-two hours."

"Maybe I should keep him under protective custody," Mac said with a grin.

"Sounds good to me."

"Get him out of here. He's to be locked up under protective custody. I don't want anyone talking to him, and I want him locked up away from any others in the jail, you understand?" Mac said to the lead officer.

"Yes, sir," the lead officer said.

The lead officer reached out and took the man by the arm. With an officer on each side of the man, they led him out of my office.

"What's your next move?" Mac asked as soon as they were alone.

"I'm going out to have a talk with Franklin."

"You want company?"

"You've already talked to him, haven't you?"

"Yeah. He wasn't too cooperative."

"With what I've found out about him, I can see why."

"What do you mean?" Mac asked.

"He was the prime suspect in the death of his first wife."

"So? There wasn't enough evidence to charge him."

"He had to have been questioned a good many times by police. I would think that he would be very cautious anytime a policeman questioned him. I'm sure he would be on his guard around policemen," I said.

"I suppose you're right," Mac said. "I take it you think it would be better if I didn't go with you."

"I think it would be best if you didn't. I will certainly tell you anything I find out."

"I would sure hope so."

"Do you happen to know where Franklin works? I couldn't find anything that would tell me."

"I'm not sure what he does for a living. All I know is that whatever it is it pays well. He lives in a big house in the foothills above Denver. It would be my guess he works from home."

"What makes you think that?" I asked. "Have you had him under surveillance?"

"Yes, and the only places he has gone were to grocery stores and restaurants, and places like that."

"Has he met anyone at those places?"

"Not that we've seen."

I took a minute to think about what Mac had told me. There was something that just didn't seem right. He had just lost his wife. Maybe he ate at restaurants because he didn't like to cook for himself. Yet, he went to grocery stores which would indicate that he didn't mind cooking, or he had someone who cooked for him.

"In your surveillance, did you see anyone who might be staying at the house," I asked.

"We didn't see anyone, but with the size of his house, it wouldn't be hard for someone to live there without being seen. That house has everything a person would need to never have to go out, except for groceries."

"In case you didn't know, he inherited a lot of money from his first wife when she died. She was very wealthy, having been the sole heir of her father's estate. Her father was one of the owners of a large casino in Reno. From the looks of things, the other owners bought her out."

"I didn't know that," Mac said. "I knew that Franklin and his first wife had money. I didn't know where it came from."

"I think I'll go pay him a visit," I said thoughtfully.

"I've seen that look before. What are you thinking?"

"I'm thinking, I'll pay him a visit and see if I can find out if he is really living there alone. I'll also ask him a few questions," I said.

"Okay, but you be careful around him. We don't know what's going on, and how much he is involved, if at all."

"Oh, I'll be careful," I assured Mac.

Mac just nodded, then turned and left my office. I had a pretty good idea of not only where he was going, but what he was going to do. He had a man to book into jail. I also had a pretty good idea that he would let his surveillance team know that I would be paying Franklin a call.

As soon as he left, I closed up my office and headed for the parking garage. It was time to visit Robert Franklin.

CHAPTER TWENTY-ONE

THE DRIVE INTO THE FOOTHILLS above Denver was uneventful. I didn't see anyone following me, and I didn't see anyone I knew. I turned off Interstate 70 onto a two-lane road that wound its way around a number of hobby ranches in the foothills. It wasn't long before I came to a turn off that led into a large housing development. I turned in and quickly found myself looking at a few very large and very expensive homes. It didn't take me long to find Franklin's house.

The house was set back away from the road about a hundred yards. There were very few trees anywhere near the front of the house which would make it very hard for anyone to get close to the house without being seen. From the look of it, it was planned that way.

I began to wonder how Mac could keep the place under surveillance without his surveillance team being spotted. From what I could see on the road out front, I could tell that the land the house was built on sloped down behind the house and into the woods. It didn't look like it would be very difficult for people to leave or come to the house without being seen.

All the time I was looking toward the house, I was moving along the road. Once I was past the house, I started looking for a place where I could turn around. I found what looked like it was an old fire lane that ran back into the forest indicating it was on Federal Forest Service land. I had no idea where it went, but there was a possibility that the fire lane was crooked and looped around behind Franklin's house.

I pulled onto the fire lane and stopped. I spent a few minutes just looking down the fire lane. I could see that it turned about fifty yards further down, but couldn't tell where it went from there. Was it possible for someone to use the fire lane to come and go from Franklin's house without being seen?

I put my Explorer into park, then stepped out of it. I walked around in front of the Explorer then bent down and looked at the tracks in the fire lane. I was surprised at what I found. There were a good number of tracks from different vehicles where the grass had not grown over the fire lane. Most of the tracks seemed to be fairly fresh. Some were from trucks, but several were from cars. It seemed that there had been an unusual amount of traffic for a fire lane.

My thoughts were suddenly disturbed when I heard a vehicle turn in behind my Explorer. I didn't think whoever was in the car could see me. I quickly stood up and stepped in among the trees. I stood next to a tree and decided it was time to relieve myself.

I could hear someone get out of a vehicle and walk toward me. I didn't stop or look back, until I heard him stop moving. I looked over my shoulder and looked at him and smiled. He didn't smile back. He just stood there. When I was finished, I zipped up and turned around.

"Good afternoon, officer," I said. "I'm sorry if I'm parked somewhere I shouldn't be, but when you have to go, you have to go."

"I take it you're done?" the officer asked, looking very serious.

"Yes. Did I do something illegal?" I asked.

"No. I just stopped to see what you were up to. Do you have some sort of identification?"

"Certainly," I said, then I took my wallet out of my back pocket.

I showed him my driver's license but didn't show him my PI license or concealed weapons permit. I was in no hurry to let him know what I did for a living or get him all excited about me carrying a gun. However, if he asked, I wouldn't lie to him.

He took his time looking at my driver's license. I couldn't tell what he was thinking; but if he knew anything at all, he knew he could not ticket me for anything.

"Is this your vehicle?"

"Yes, it is. It's new so I don't have anything but the paper license in the rear window."

"How long have you had it?"

"Just a couple of days. There's a temporary registration in the rear window. Is there a problem, officer?" I asked after waiting for him to make up his mind about what he was going to do.

"Well, no."

"In that case, I will be on my way. Would you please give me my driver's license, then move your vehicle so I can go?"

He looked at me for a second. He handed me my driver's license, then turned around and returned to his vehicle. I got in my Explorer then waited while he backed out onto the road so I could leave. As soon as he drove away, I backed out onto the road and headed back the way I had come.

When I got to the driveway leading to the front of Franklin's house, I turned in. I had just turned in the drive and headed toward the house when a man in a dark suit stepped out onto the front porch. If I had to guess, he was a bodyguard for Mr. Franklin.

As I pulled up in front of the house, I noticed he unbuttoned the suit coat he was wearing. That told me he was probably armed and didn't want his coat in the way if he felt he needed to grab his gun.

I stopped in front of the house, shut off the engine, then got out. Since the bodyguard didn't step off the porch, I walked around in front of my Explorer and stepped up on the porch.

"May I help you?" the bodyguard asked politely.

"My name is Peter Blackstone. I would like to speak to Mr. Franklin, if I may."

"Is he expecting you?"

"No, but you already know that."

"Yes, I do," he said with a slight grin.

"I still would like to talk to him."

"What do you wish to talk to him about?"

"I don't really think that is any of your business, but since you asked, I would like to talk to him about the death of his wife," I said knowing full well that I would not get to see him if I said 'I just want to ask him a few questions'.

"Wait here. Oh, I wouldn't step off the porch if I were you."

I watched him as he turned and went into the house. I had no idea if my request to talk to Mr. Franklin was going to be honored or not. While I stood on the porch, I noticed another guard step around the corner of the house and stop. He just stood there looking at me. At his side was a rather large Doberman on a fairly heavy leash. As soon as the guard stopped, the dog sat down at the guard's side and simply looked at me. The dog didn't growl or bare his teeth. In fact, he looked bored. I had a few experiences with large dogs in the past. Many did not get nasty if you simply did not act scared of them, or didn't do anything they might decide is a sign of aggression. However, there were exceptions, and this dog just might be one of them.

It was only about three or four minutes before the bodyguard returned. From the look on his face, I had no idea if I was going to be able to talk to Mr. Franklin.

"Mr. Franklin is very busy, but since you have come all the way out here to see him, he will give you a few minutes of his time. Follow me."

I followed the bodyguard into the house. The entryway looked like it was large enough to hold a banquet. There were several doors off both sides of the hall. From what little I could see as I passed one of the doors, it looked like a room full of televisions. The only one that I could see showed an area that looked like it might be behind the house, but someone inside quickly closed the door before I could see much else. If I had to guess, the entire property was probably under continuous surveillance from the house.

The walls of the entryway had a good number of paintings which many, if not all, were originals. I continued to follow the bodyguard down a long hall that had to be at least twelve feet wide and fifty feet long. When we got to the end of the hall, we turned and he stopped in front of a large oak door; he opened the door and motioned me to go inside.

I stepped into the room then heard the door close behind me. The first thing I saw was Franklin sitting behind a very large oak desk that had two computers on it, two telephones, and a large silver pen set. There were several papers on the desk, but I could not see what they were. Franklin was looking at me.

Franklin stood up and walked around in front of the desk, then motioned for me to have a seat on one of the chairs in front of the desk. He sat down on a chair next to the one I sat down on.

"Now, what is it I can do for you, Mr. Blackstone? I understand that you have some questions about my wife."

"That would be correct. Do you have any idea what your wife was doing in the café with Mr. North?"

"I believe I have answered that question when a Detective MacDonald visited me a few days ago. Since you have come all the way out here, I'll answer the question, again," he said with a hint of frustration in his voice.

"No. I have no idea why she was in the café. I have to take your word for it that she was actually in the café with this Mr. North."

"Had she told you why she was going into Denver?"

"She said that she was going to do some shopping, which was one of her favorite past times."

"So, you didn't know she was going to the café."

"That would be correct."

"Did you know Mr. North?"

"I've never met him."

"But did you know of him?"

"I knew he was, at one time, June's boyfriend. I believe it was when she was in high school. June told me about him before we were married."

"Did you ever see him?"

"No. As I said, 'I've never met him'," he replied rather sharply.

"It is my understanding that you were married before, and that your first wife died rather suddenly. Is that correct?"

He looked at me as if he was wondering how much I knew about his past. I noticed his body language changed at the mention of his first wife.

"Yes, that is true. What does the death of my first wife have to do with the death of June?"

"Nothing that I know of. Do you think it might have something to do with it?"

"No, of course not. My first wife died a long time ago. She died of an accidental overdose of cocaine. At least that is what the coroner told me."

"That's not what the Death Certificate reported. In fact, the police thought the cause of death was foul play."

"They could never prove it."

I noticed he didn't deny it. Franklin's body language told me he had murdered his first wife, but proving it was a whole different story. From the tone of his answers and comments, he was afraid that the death of his first wife was going to be looked into again.

"Do you know a man by the name of Williams, Anthony Williams?" I asked, changing the subject in the hope of putting him off guard.

"Yes. He's a real estate broker in Dillion. We've been working on a housing development in the foothills. We've been working together on it for several years."

"It doesn't seem to be going very well. You haven't built a single home, yet you have been taking in large amounts of money. How do you explain that?"

I knew I was guessing, but from what I had been able to see there had not been a new house built in this development for at least the past ten years. This was the only housing development anywhere near the area where they claimed to have property.

"I don't see what this has to do with the death of my wife?" he said then stood up. "This interview is over."

He reached over and pressed a button on his desk. Almost immediately the bodyguard who had met me at the front door, opened the door and stepped into the room.

"Escort this man out of here. I don't want him on this property again. Do you understand that?" Franklin almost yelled.

"Yes, sir."

I stood up and walked toward the door. I stopped, turned around and looked at Franklin. He appeared to be very upset, or maybe he was worried.

"It was nice talking to you," I said, then turned and walked toward the front door.

When I got to the front door, I stopped and waited for the bodyguard to open the door. As soon as he opened the door, I walked out of the house and down the steps. I got in my Explorer, started it then drove down the driveway to the road. As it turned onto the road, I glanced back at the house for a second before I headed back to town. The bodyguard was still standing on the front porch watching me as I left. Just before I lost sight of the front porch, Franklin stepped outside. There was little doubt that I had shaken him up, just a little.

WHILE I DROVE BACK TO MY OFFICE, I thought about his reaction to my suggestion that the land development he and Williams were involved in was not going anywhere. I knew I had touched a nerve when I mentioned the large amount of money that was being poured into it without any progress. It had been a guess on my part, but the more I thought about it, the more I was sure I had hit the nail on the head.

I believed I had accidently discovered what was going on at the bank. The money was supposed to be for the sale of lots and for building homes, but it went through the real estate office of Anthony Williams who deposited the money into the bank in different investments. The real question was where did the money come from?

A thought ran through my mind reminding me that Josh was murdered using cocaine, a large amount of cocaine. When I added up what I knew with what I thought I knew, it brought to mind the thought that Franklin and Williams were laundering drug money through the bank by way of real estate sales, when there were no sales. The money was then put into investments that could be cashed out in any number of locations under any number of names. Not the most sophisticated plan I'd ever heard of, but simple enough that it had apparently worked. This was something that I needed to talk over with Mac.

It was at that moment when I heard a loud bang and felt the Explorer start to shimmy. I thought I had blown a front tire. I took a quick look around to see if anyone was near that could be hurt if I lost control of the vehicle. At that moment, I heard a second loud bang. I saw someone in a Black SUV had fired a shot. It went through the side rear window. I could only see part of the car. I could not see the person who had fired at me because he was in my blind spot, but they had dropped back behind me. The third shot I heard took out the rear window and I immediately felt a sharp pain in my side. The bullet had apparently gone through the window and through the seat hitting me in the side. There was no way I could get away from the black SUV.

I was rapidly losing control of the Explorer. I couldn't hold it on the road. The Explorer suddenly veered to the right and hit the end of the guardrail. It rolled the Explorer over and sent it down into a steep ravine. The last thing I saw was my new vehicle coming to a sudden stop against the side of a rocky cliff. Then everything went black.

CHAPTER TWENTY-TWO

I FELT GROGGY AND DISORIENTED, even a little uncomfortable, yet I could hear something that sounded like a steady beeping noise. It sounded familiar, but I couldn't place it. I could even hear someone talking, but I didn't think it was anyone I knew. I listened very carefully hoping to find out who it was. I also began to realize that I was lying down in a bed, but it didn't feel like it was my bed.

"You should really go home and get some rest. It could be a long time before he comes around. His vital signs are very good. He just has to wake up."

"I'm staying right here until he wakes up."

The second voice I recognized. It was Julie's voice. What was she doing here? For that matter, where was I?

It was at that moment I began to realize I must be in a hospital, and the beeping sound was a heart monitor. I was also beginning to remember what had happened. I slowly opened my eyes, then slowly turned my head. I could see Julie talking to a woman in scrubs, but Julie was in a nice blouse and slacks. She also didn't look all that happy about being told to go home.

"Hey, what's a guy have to do to get some sleep around here?"

Julie turned and looked at me, then jumped out of the chair and leaned over me and kissed me several times on my face. She quickly straightened up when I groaned in pain.

"I'm sorry," she said looking as if she was in pain. "I thought I was going to lose you."

"Am I going to be okay," I asked Julie as I looked into her eyes to see if she was going to tell me the truth.

"Yes, you're going to be fine, but it will take awhile."

"I guess I'll leave you two alone. I'll tell the doctor you've come around," the nurse said with a grin, then turned and walked out the door, closing it behind her.

Just as the door was closing, I saw what looked like a police officer sitting outside my room. It wasn't hard for me to figure out that Mac had put a guard outside my room. He must have found the bullet holes in my new Explorer.

Julie sat down next to the bed and held my hand. She looked like she had been up for a long time. I could not only see the relief in her eyes that I was going to be okay, but I could see just how tired she was. I wondered how long she had been at my side.

"How long have I been here?"

"Three days," she said softly.

"Have you been here all the time?"

"Almost all the time. I did go home to shower and get a change of clothes."

"I love you," I said.

"I love you, too."

"Has there been an officer outside my room all the time?"

"Yes. Mac thought it was a good idea, and I agreed with him. I've had a police woman with me all the time, too."

"Would you give Mac a call and tell him I need to talk to him?"

"Do you think you are up to it?"

"Yes. The sooner he knows what I found out, the quicker this whole mess will be over," I said.

"Okay, I'll go call him," she said.

"After you call him, call your brother. I want you to go stay with him. It will be a lot safer for you."

"But I want to stay with you," she said in protest."

"I would feel better knowing you are safe with him. I already have a guard here."

"Okay," she said reluctantly. "I would still rather be with you."

"I know. I would like you here, but it's too dangerous. Please call George and ask him to have someone come to get you. You should wait in the receiving area where you can see who he sends before he sees you. I'm sure he will send one of the men he often has helping him when he is protecting someone. It would be someone you would recognize."

"I'll do as you ask, but I still wish we could be together," she said.

Julie stood up, leaned over me and kissed me, then turned and left the room. I thought I saw a tear run down her cheek. I didn't want her to leave any more than she wanted to leave, but I had to be sure that she was safe. I couldn't be sure she would be safe if she was with me.

I still didn't know how badly I was hurt, but I was sure I would be finding out very soon. I tried to move a little, but found it was difficult. There was not only the pain in my side from being shot, there was stiffness and pain all over my body. Remembering the Explorer rolling over several times and hitting the side of the ravine, it was easy to understand why I was so stiff and sore. I had to have been banged around inside the Explorer. I wondered what my Explorer looked like. If the way I felt was any indication, it was probably totaled, and I hadn't had it long enough to have its first oil change. I wondered what my insurance company would think about it.

My thoughts were disturbed when I heard the door open. I turned to see who was coming into my room. It was a man I didn't know, but he was wearing a white coat and looked like he might be a doctor. I noticed that he had a stethoscope around his neck and one hand in the pocket of the coat.

"It's good to see you awake," he said with a pleasant smile.

"I'm glad to be awake."

"I'm sure. From what I was told about your accident, you're lucky to be here."

The fact that he called it an accident meant one of two things to me. Either he was not the doctor who treated me when I was first brought in, or he wasn't a doctor at all. If he had treated me, he would know it was no accident and that I had been shot. That was when I noticed he didn't look at my chart at the end of the bed.

"Officer," I called out. "Get in here."

The officer at the door quickly stepped into my room. He was looking at the doctor.

"I want you to verify that this guy is a doctor."

The officer immediately drew his gun and pointed it at the doctor.

"What's going on?" the doctor asked.

"Sorry, doc, but I have no intentions of becoming the second patient to be murdered in this hospital."

"You are crazy," he said with a look of anger in his eyes.

"Officer, lean him up against the wall and search him."

I watched as the officer did as I told him. He didn't find a gun on the doc, but he did find a syringe with a clear liquid in it. There was a plastic cap over the needle on the syringe. Just then a nurse came into my room. It was the same nurse who had been here when I woke up.

"What's going on here?" she said as she looked at the officer with a gun in his hand, and the doctor with his hands on the wall.

"Nurse, do you know this man?"

She looked at me as if I was crazy before she leaned closer to the man. She took a good look at the man leaning against the wall. She turned and looked at me.

"I've never seen him before," she said with a worried look on her face.

"Is it common practice for doctors to run around carrying a loaded syringe in their pocket?" I asked, knowing the answer.

"No, of course not," she replied.

"I want you to go out to the nurse's station and call the police at this number," I said as I wrote the number on a pad of paper on the bedside table. "I want you to talk to Captain MacDonald. Tell him - - -."

"That won't be necessary, Pete," Mac said as he stepped into the room.

"I'm glad to see you," I said.

"I'm glad to see you alive. Julie called and said you were awake. What do we have here?"

"A doctor who apparently is not a doctor."

"Officer, cuff him," Mac said as he drew his gun to cover the man.

"You might want to take the syringe to the lab and find out what is in it," I said.

The officer handed the syringe to Mac, then cuffed the man. Once he was cuffed, Mac had him sit down on a chair.

"You want to tell me your name?" Mac asked the man.

The man just sat there looking at Mac. Keeping quiet probably wouldn't make much difference.

"Have it your way," Mac said.

Mac read him his rights then asked him if he understood them. The man just nodded that he understood his rights.

"Do you want a lawyer?"

The man shook his head that he didn't want a lawyer.

"Okay. Once we get you downtown and fingerprint you, it won't be long and we will know who you are, where you're from, and probably who you work for. We will also find out, in a very short time, what is in the syringe. I have a feeling I know what is in it, but we'll let the lab tell us just to be sure. If I'm right, it might very well connect you to the murder of Josh Garrett," Mac said.

The man remained quiet, but his change in body language showed that Mac's last statement caused him some concern. He just looked at Mac as if he didn't exist. He probably knew that his days were numbered. When a hitman fails to do his job and is caught alive, he usually ends up with a contract out on him.

"Do you have anything you would like to say?" Mac asked.

He shook his head again.

"Okay, have it your way," Mac said.

Mac turned to the officer and said, "Call for a unit to come and get him."

"Yes, sir."

I watched the officer leave the room. I wondered what they were going to be able to find out from the man. Probably nothing, but I was more interested in what was in the syringe.

Nothing much was said while we waited for the officers to come and take the man to jail. Mac didn't question him or say anything to me. He probably didn't want the man to overhear him.

I had a lot to tell Mac, but I didn't want to tell him in front of anyone. I tried to remember if I had ever seen this guy before. I could not remember ever seeing him before which got me to thinking that maybe he was someone from out of town sent here to get rid of me. It would not surprise me since two out of town hitmen had already tried to kill Julie and me, and were now lying in the morgue.

It didn't take long for the police officers to arrive at the hospital. Once Mac had given them their instructions to lock him up and not to let anyone talk to him until he returned, the man was taken away. Mac sat down on the chair next to my bed. I spent the next half hour talking with Mac about my visit to Mr. Robert Franklin.

I told him about the security at the Franklin house. He was not surprised that I had come to the conclusion that Franklin and the Williamses were running a drug operation and laundering the money through the bank with the help of at least two others. I could see by the look on Mac's face that he was thinking about what I told him. After a couple of minutes thinking about it, he nodded his head.

"My men reported you going inside Franklin's house, but never saw anyone else go in or out except the bodyguard who came out on the porch."

"I didn't see anything that would indicate there was anyone else in the house other than his bodyguards. However, there may be others who were in the house before you started your surveillance of the property. There is always the possibility that there is a way in and out of the house," I said.

"Did you find such a place?"

"I may have. There's a fire lane just down the road from Franklin's home. I have no idea where it goes or where it might come out. It does look like it could go directly behind the house. If your surveillance team didn't have both ends of it covered, someone could easily go in or out of the house using the fire lane."

Mac looked at me. It was obvious that he had not thought of a fire lane.

"I think it might be a good idea if I check it out with the forest service. I wouldn't want him to escape if I have to go arrest him."

"Mac, have you heard anything about how long I might be here?"

"No, but I'll check with the doctor," he said.

Just then the phone next to my bed began to ring. I reached for it, but found it difficult to move very much. Mac was nice enough to reach over and pick up the receiver and hand it to me.

"Hello?"

"Hi, honey."

"Hi, where are you?"

"I can't say, but I'm with George. I thought you would like to know that I am safe," Julie said.

"I'm very glad to know you are safe with him."

"George doesn't want me talking to you very long. He said to tell you that the others are also safe."

"Thank you. I'm a bit tired so maybe we best get off the phone. I love you," I said.

"I'll try to call you tomorrow. I love you, too. You should get some rest."

"I will. Goodnight."

"Goodnight," she said then hung up.

"That was Julie. She is safe with George."

"I gathered that," Mac said with a grin. "I need to be going so you can get some rest. I'll probably talk to you tomorrow."

"Okay," I said.

Mac stood up and walked out the door. Just before the door closed, I could see he was talking to the guard at my door. I looked up at the ceiling for a few minutes before I closed my eyes and drifted off to sleep.

It was around six o'clock when I was awakened by the door to my room opening. I looked toward the door and saw a nurse walking toward me with a tray.

"Time for dinner, Mr. Blackstone. Do you think you can sit up?"

"I'll give it a try."

It proved hard to sit up, but I did manage to sit up a little. The nurse helped me eat the dinner. The food was edible, but that was about all anyone could say about it. When I was done, she took the tray and left the room. I again dozed off.

THE DAYS PASSED SLOWLY in the hospital. The only visitor I had was Mac. He kept me up to date on his investigation of Franklin and Williams. The more he found out, the more he agreed with my assessment of what was going on at Franklin's home and at the bank. With each visit, I could see it was getting closer to the time when Mac would be ready to pick up Franklin and Williams.

My days were also marked by the progress I made in being able to move around. By the fourth day, I was able to get in and out of bed without very much pain, and without any help. Most of the stiffness was gone and the minor cuts had healed pretty well, and the bruises were starting to look better. I still had a dressing over the gunshot wound, but it was healing well.

I couldn't have been happier when the day came for me to be released from the hospital. The doctor removed the stitches from the wound in my side, and placed a clean dressing on it.

As soon as that was done, Mac came by to make sure I got home safe. He took me to my apartment, then stayed with me until an officer could get there to keep me safe. I noticed the officer had driven up in a car that was probably his own. It was certainly nothing like what the police department would use. It was a 1958 Chevy Impala hardtop with a candy apple red paint job and chrome wheels. It was a beautiful car. He also came in street clothes. Mac introduced him.

"This is Bill Smith. He's a cop I borrowed from Precinct Six. He's a street cop and very good with a gun and very savvy when it comes to spotting people who don't belong there. By the way, he is a sergeant."

"Nice to meet you, Officer Smith."

"Just call me, Bill. I'm sure we will get along just fine."

"I'm sure we will," I said.

After Mac left, Bill and I sat at the kitchen table and talked. We didn't talk about Josh's murder very much. He seemed to have been filled in on it, probably by Mac. We talked about sports and cars, mostly cars. He seemed like a nice guy.

With each day that passed, I felt like I was getting stronger. I spent a good deal of my time trying to get back in shape. Bill was very helpful. He encouraged me, and made sure I ate good solid and healthy meals. He also made sure I got plenty of rest. By the end of the week, I was feeling pretty good. In fact, good enough to get back to work.

I was also missing Julie. I talked to her every evening before I'd go to bed, but it wasn't the same as having her near me.

"I think it's time for me to get back to my job," I told Bill.

"I'm supposed to let Mac know when you feel up to getting back to work."

"Okay. Why don't you give him a call? In the meantime, I'm going to make arrangements to get me a new vehicle."

Bill walked into the living room. I could hear he was on the phone, but could not hear what he was saying. I assumed he was talking to Mac.

I sat at the kitchen table and placed a call to my insurance company. My agent told me he had already taken care of the paperwork based on the report from the sheriff's deputy who had done the initial investigation of the 'accident'. Apparently, it had been reported that the front tire had blown which caused the 'accident'. Since the Explorer was a total loss, they had covered the loss of the Explorer. He told me that he had a check for the Explorer in his file. All I had to do was stop by, sign for it, pick it up and deposit it. Once that was done, I could go out and find a new vehicle.

Bill came into the kitchen just as I was hanging up. I smiled up at him, but my smile quickly faded when I noticed that he had a gun in his hand and it was pointed at me.

"I take it I won't be going to look for a new car today," I said.

"Not today, not ever."

"You know you won't be able to get away with this."

"I think I will."

"You kill me, then someone comes here and knocks you out. The police arrive and find you out cold and me dead. Does that sum up what is about to happen?"

"You're pretty smart. It's too bad you won't be around to see how well it works."

"You have got to be stupid. Do you think they are going to just knock you out? They can't afford to have you questioned by the police, which the police will do. When you called them to come here and knock you out, you wrote your own death certificate."

Suddenly, there was a knock on the backdoor. Bill seemed a bit surprised. He hesitated a moment, trying to decide what to do. Then there was another knock on the backdoor only harder and louder. He glanced at the door wondering who was there. Just as he was turning back toward me, I tipped the kitchen table over against him, knocking him off balance. I grabbed a knife off the counter and dove at him, knocking him to the floor. I landed on top of him. I had the hand he had the gun in pinned to the floor. I put the knife against his throat with the point of it digging against the underside of his chin and into his skin. I knew I couldn't fight with him for very long. I still was in no shape to do any fighting. If he tried to fight back, I would have to kill him.

I looked up at the backdoor. Jimmy, a neighborhood kid, was standing there casually looking around. The look on his face told me that he didn't have a care in the world.

He looked like he was trying to decide if he should leave, because I didn't answer him. He was my only chance to get help.

"Jimmy, come inside," I yelled.

I heard the door open. Jimmy stepped inside, quickly shutting the door behind him. He then turned and looked at me. He had a shocked look on his face when he saw me on the floor, on top of a man, and I was holding a knife against his throat.

"Jimmy," I yelled to get his attention.

I had to call to him again before he seemed to become aware that I needed his help.

"Jimmy, call 9-1-1. Tell them to send a police car here, and fast."

Jimmy didn't move.

"Jimmy, do it now. Call 9-1-1."

Jimmy finally got the message and placed the call. I could hear him give the operator the address. The only thing I could hope for was that the police got here before whoever Bill called arrived.

"Jimmy, I want you to go to my bedroom and hide in my closet. Don't make any noise, and don't come out until I call you. Do you understand?"

Jimmy didn't say anything. He nodded his head, but he didn't move.

"Go, go now," I insisted.

Jimmy ran toward my bedroom. I could only hope he would stay there until it was safe to come out.

It was only a few minutes before I heard a car door shut out in front of my apartment. Since I had not heard any sirens, I could only assume it was not the police. Just as the front door started to open, I heard sirens and they were getting close fast.

"Let's get out of here," I heard someone at the front door yell.

The front door slammed shut. The next thing I heard was the squealing of tires as a car quickly pulled away from the curb. I was afraid to move off of Bill. If I let him up, he would tell the police I had attacked him. I had no idea how the police, who had just arrived, would react when they saw us on the floor. Just then, I heard the policemen come into the living room.

"Out here in the kitchen," I called out.

The two officers entered the kitchen. The look on their faces told it all. They were surprised to see me holding down a man.

"I'm Peter Blackstone. He has a gun under my arm and against his body. I need one of you to get it before I get off him."

One of the officers moved over next to me, knelt down and reached under my arm. He quickly found the gun and pulled it out, then stepped back.

"You can take the knife away from his throat now. We have him covered," one of the officers said.

I quickly rolled away from Bill, sat up leaning against the kitchen cabinet.

"You want to tell me what's going on here, Mr. Blackstone?" the lead officer asked.

"This guy is crazy. I'm Sergeant Smith from the Sixth Precinct. If you let me reach in my pocket I'll show you my badge and ID."

"Call Captain MacDonald at Precinct One before you trust him. This man is who he says he is, but he is also a hired killer. Hired to kill me," I said hoping they would listen to me.

The lead officer looked from one of us to the other. It was clear that he was wondering who to believe. He didn't want to pick the wrong one.

"Let me tell you this, this is my apartment. What would he be doing here if he is from the sixth precinct, which is on the other side of town?"

"Juan, call Captain MacDonald at Precinct One. Call from the phone over there," he said as he pointed to the kitchen phone.

"Yes, sir," the rookie said.

"You two, just stay where you are. I would hate to have to shoot either one of you."

I sat there and watched Bill. I had no idea what he might do since I was pretty sure he was feeling trapped.

I could only hear the rookie's part of the conversation, but he asked for Mac. It was only a minute or so when the rookie sounded like he was talking to someone of authority, probably Mac. It was also clear that Mac was having another police car sent to my house. It was clear that Mac had given additional instructions to the rookie before the rookie said, 'Yes, sir', and hung up.

"Captain MacDonald said that we are to relieve Smith of his weapons and handcuff him. We are to keep him here until the captain arrives. He's also sending another police car for back up."

"Are you sure that's what he said?"

"Yes, sir. He was very clear about what we are to do. We are to relieve Smith of his weapons and handcuff him, then keep him here until he arrives."

"Okay," the lead officer said, then looked at Smith.

"Standup, and do it very carefully," the lead officer said, his gun still pointed at Smith.

As soon as he was standing, the officer had him turn around and put his hands on the wall. He was searched and cuffed by the rookie while his partner kept a gun on him. As soon as he was cuffed, Smith was sat on a chair.

"Excuse me, but I need to tell the young man in my bedroom that he can come out now."

"What's he doing in there?"

"I had him hide there when we knew there were others coming to make sure I was killed. I'm sure Mac, Captain MacDonald will explain it to you."

"Go with him to the bedroom," the lead officer said.

The rookie followed me to the bedroom. Once I was inside, I called out to Jimmy.

"Jimmy, you can come out now."

Jimmy came out of the closet and stood up.

"It's okay now. I'm sure they will want to talk to you so you can tell them what you saw and what you did, okay?"

"Yes," he said nervously.

We returned to the kitchen where we waited for Captain MacDonald. It was a very quiet wait. No one wanted to talk. Jimmy sat next to me. It was clear he didn't know what was going to happen.

"Jimmy, you can relax. All you have to do is answer Captain MacDonald's questions as best you can. Just tell him what you saw and heard. Don't add anything you didn't actually see yourself or hear yourself, but might have thought happened. It's a lot easier for the police if you are straight forward with them. Okay?"

"Okay, Mr. Blackstone," he replied.

"By the way, what brought you to my door?"

"I was selling chocolate candy bars to raise money for the football team at school."

"I'll take a dozen," I said with a smile.

After Mac arrived, he questioned Jimmy, then thanked him and let him go. The rest of us went downtown to Precinct One. Smith was questioned, but wouldn't talk without an attorney.

After I made my statement, I was sent home to get some rest. Mac said he had a lot to do, but he would like it if I would come in tomorrow morning by nine. I agreed but was interested in what he was planning.

I knew he had been working on the idea that it was a drug ring and that they were filtering their money through the bank in Dillion. He might have even gotten the Feds involved. I had told Mac after my visit to Franklin that I had a feeling that was what was being done, and that Franklin was probably the head man. He had agreed with me.

It is my guess that Josh had found out about what was going on and was murdered to keep him from telling anyone. It was good to know that Mac had come to the same conclusion. It was now time for me to get some rest.

One of the officers drove me back to my apartment. As soon as I was in the apartment, I locked it up and got ready for bed. I went to bed with a gun under my pillow. It didn't take me long to fall asleep.

CHAPER TWENTY-THREE

FOR THE FIRST TIME in what seemed like a very long time, I managed to get a full night's sleep. I didn't have a nurse waking me to take my vital signs every few hours or being woke up by the noises that are often found on a hospital ward. It was six-thirty when I woke. I was feeling pretty good. I was no longer feeling stiff and sore, and the wound to my side was not hurting me unless I bumped it.

I took a quick shower, then went to the kitchen to fix breakfast. It was a simple, yet a good breakfast consisting of a bowl of cereal with a banana on it, a glass of orange juice, and a cup of coffee.

While I ate my breakfast, I thought about what Mac might have planned for this morning. Although he didn't say anything about it yesterday, I got the feeling he was going to get a warrant to search Franklin's home and grounds. If he was thinking the same thing I was, he would have to have a lot of help. Anything I thought of now would be nothing but speculation; and I had found I did a lot of that in the past, even though speculation often proved to be a waste of time. However, it often kept me from being surprised, too.

As soon as I was finished with breakfast, I rinsed the dishes and put them in the dishwasher. I got my coat and started for my garage, but remembered that I didn't have a vehicle. I returned to the kitchen and went to the phone. I placed a call to Randy at his dealership. It was answered rather quickly.

"Hi, Peter. How's it going?"

"Not so good. Remember that Explorer you sold me?"

"Yeah, sure. Do you have a problem with it? If you do, I'll take care of it," he said.

"Well, I do have a problem with it. The last time I saw it, it was in the bottom of a ravine up in the foothills. Outside of the bullet holes in it, it was totaled."

"You totaled it?" Randy said with surprise.

"Yeah. I was wondering if you still had the other one, the one I didn't choose."

"You haven't paid for that one, yet."

"I know. As soon as I can get to my insurance agent, I'll get the check to pay full price for that one. Then I would like the same arrangements we made on that one to apply to a new one. Can we do that?"

"Ah - yeah, but I don't have the other one any more. I got a blue one in yesterday with the same options as the red one had, would that be okay?" Randy asked.

"Sure. That would be great. Could you bring it by my apartment, say in the next hour?

"Ah - Yeah, sure."

"Okay. I'll settle up with you later."

"Okay," Randy said, and I hung up before he could change his mind.

Randy arrived about forty-five minutes after I hung up. He had several papers for me to sign. After I signed the papers, he turned to leave but stopped and looked at me.

"I really hope you don't wreck this one, not that I mind selling you two vehicles within a few days. I hate to see such a good customer covered in bruises," Randy said.

"I think I'll try to keep this one for awhile," I said with a grin.

"Good. By the way, do you have any idea when you will get your Tahoe back?"

"No, but it should be soon. I'll stop over tomorrow with a check to pay for the one I wrecked."

"I'll be around all day."

"Thanks, Randy."

"See you tomorrow," he said then turned and left my apartment.

I followed him out the door, locking it behind me. He got into his fancy pickup and drove away. He had someone with him. I assumed it was one of his employees who had driven the new Explorer to my place.

A quick glance at my watch told me it was time to get over to Precinct One if I wanted to be there by nine. I got in my new Explorer and drove to Precinct One, arriving at eight fifty-five.

AS I WALKED IN THE DOOR, Russell saw me. He didn't say anything, he simply pointed in the direction of Mac's office. I sort of waved at him and went down the hall. I knocked on Mac's office door and was immediately told to enter. Upon entering, I noticed there were five people in the office, not counting Mac. I was introduced to them. Each of the drug enforcement agents nodded when Mac mentioned their name, Dave Morgan and Matt Warren. The two drug enforcement agents were from the Denver office.

It seemed that Mac had things pretty well worked out. There were two men, Walter Shale and Hank Smart, from the Banking Commission. One was an auditor, the other an enforcement officer.

There was also one of Mac's local lieutenants, Lieutenant Jameson. Mac also had Sheriff Tom Stillwell on the speaker phone.

"Gentlemen, now that we are all here, it's time to get this joint operation going. The two men from the Banking Commission will leave first and meet Sheriff Stillwell at the edge of Dillon. Sheriff Stillwell will take them to the bank, secure it and arrest Mr. Routh and Mr. Sheridan, as well as Mr. Williams if he happens to be there. If he is not there, Sheriff Stillwell's deputies will go to Williams Reality and arrest him there and secure his office taking charge of everything in the office. If he is not there, the deputies will secure his office and remain there until he shows up or is picked up someplace else.

"Once they are ready to take control of the bank and the real estate office, the drug enforcement agents will go with the rest of us to Franklin's home in the foothills. Those of us going to Franklin's place will secure the property and arrest all those on the property.

"When those going to Dillon are in place, we will all make a coordinated attack on the three designated locations.

"For your information, Pete, I checked with the Forest Service about the fire lane that runs behind Franklin's home. The fire lane runs from where you saw it and comes out on another road about a mile and a half on the other side of the development. You were right when you said it might be a way for people to get in and out of Franklin's place without being seen," Mac said.

"Do we have someone covering it?" I asked.

"Yes. The state police officers are in the area and will move in when I call them. They are meeting at a little café for their usual coffee break, something they do almost every day. No one will think anything of it. Are there any questions?" Mac asked.

No one had any questions.

"In that case, you guys from the Banking Commission need to get going. You have the furthest to go."

Nothing was said as the two men from the Banking Commission left the room. They got in their car and headed for Dillon.

"Stillwell, did you hear me?"

"Yes, I did. I'll meet them at the first exit to Dillon as planned and will call when we start for the bank."

"Where do I fit in?" I asked.

"You, Dave and I will go in the front door of the Franklin home, arrest Franklin and anyone else in the home. Matt and Lieutenant Jameson with cover the back and arrest anyone in the small building behind the house and anyone who tries to escape from the house. As soon as we are in the house, there will be several black-and-white units sent in as back up. They will arrest anyone who might be around and transport them and anyone we arrest to jail. As soon as the house is secure, we will start a complete search of the entire house, garage and any other buildings on the property," Mac explained.

"Oh, you might want one of these," Mac said as he opened a desk drawer and pulled out the two guns that had been left with him after my apartment was shot up.

I took the .45 caliber pistol, but decided to leave the 9mm pistol. I thought that under the circumstances the .45 was a better choice. I slipped the gun into my coat pocket.

"Excuse me, Captain MacDonald. I mean no disrespect, but I like to know who is going to be covering my back." Dave said. "I don't know Mr. Blackstone other than he is a PI."

"Mr. Blackstone is as qualified as anyone here. Mr. Blackstone was a former policeman, and I might add a very good one. He is now a private investigator, and also a very good one. I have worked with him when he was a policeman and with him as a PI. I would trust him with my life, and I have," Mac said.

"Sorry," Dave said as he looked at me.

"No apology necessary," I said as I smiled at him.

"Any other questions?" Mac asked.

No one had a question.

"In that case, it's time to do what we came together to do."

We all walked out of Mac's office and out into the parking lot. As we started across the parking lot, Mac walked beside me.

"Dave, you and Pete will go with me."

I simply nodded. Once in the cars, we left the parking lot and headed to the place where we would wait until Stillwell called to tell us that he and the Banking Commission guys were in position, and ready to take control of the bank and Williams Reality. Lieutenant Jameson and the other drug enforcement agent followed us.

WE DROVE TO A PLACE where we could get off the road and wait for the call from Stillwell. It was a time to wait and mentally prepare for what was to come. Waiting was something I didn't really like to do, but it was often necessary.

"Mac, did you ever get a report on what was in the syringe that guy brought into my room in the hospital?"

"Yeah. It was cocaine. It looked like he was going to murder you in the same way Josh was murdered."

"I take it you still have him in custody?"

"Yeah. He hasn't talked so far, but if this raid goes well, we may not need him to tell us if he killed Josh. I suspect he did it."

I sat in the car just looking out the window. I was watching cars go by on the road. I noticed a car that had a light bar on the roof go by. It also had a sign showing it was security from the housing development where Franklin's home was located. I noticed that the passenger turned in the seat and looked at us.

"Mac, I think we've been made. The guy in the car was the same guy who stopped me when I visited Franklin. I think he might have recognized me."

Mac looked at me for a second before he got on the radio.

"Everyone move in. We've been spotted. Move in. Move in."

Mac started the car and put it in gear. Not wanting to give those in Franklin's home any more warning than necessary, we raced up the road toward Franklin's home without the sirens. He turned into the drive to the front of the house with three other police cars behind us. The security car was in front of the house.

As we approached the house, a guard stepped around the corner with the big Doberman on a leash. The dog was excited. He was pulling on the leash, making it hard for the guard to control the dog.

The first car behind us had stopped at the corner of the house, and the two men in the car jumped out and ran around to the back to the house. We heard a couple of shots from around back, but we had our hands full.

We came to a stop in front of the house, and piled out of the car. Mac and I ran to the front door while Dave confronted the guard with the dog. I heard Dave yell at the guard.

"You come any closer with that dog and I'll shoot both of you."

Mac and I hit the front door at the same time. The door flew open and we dove inside. A shot was fired at us, but I was the only one in a position to shoot back. I shot the guard, dropping him on the floor of the hall. He was out of the fight, but he wasn't dead.

Mac looked at me. He motioned for me to move toward the door to Franklin's office. I moved along the wall using what furniture there was as cover. It didn't take me but a minute or so to get to the door to the office.

As soon as Mac joined me next to the door. I was about to kick the door in when I noticed something that looked like some kind of electric switch. I had no idea what need there was for an electric switch there except as the trigger for a trap.

"Wait!"

"What's the matter? Kick it in," Mac said.

"I think it's a trap," I said as I pointed at the switch.

When I looked around, I could see several uniformed officers rush into the room where I had seen the televisions. While looking around, I noticed a rather heavy looking four-wheel cart up against the wall on the other side of the hall. Next to it was a small, heavy looking, sofa. I motioned for Mac to help me.

We pulled the cart away from the wall and pointed it toward the door, then we picked up the sofa and put it on top of the cart. I had no idea if what we were doing would work or not, but there was only one way to find out. I got behind the cart and motioned for Mac to move down the hall and lean against the wall.

As soon as he was ready, I put both hands on the cart and moved it back and forth to get a feel of how easy it would roll. It rolled fairly easy. After taking a couple of deep breaths, I pushed the cart toward the door. When the cart was just a few feet from the door, I gave it a final push, then dove off to the side and rolled under a table.

There was one hell of an explosion when the cart hit the door causing the door to open. Pieces of the door and door frame flew all over the place.

As soon as the dust cleared enough so we could see, we got up and moved up close to the door. Dave came running in when he heard the explosion and saw us standing at the door to Franklin's office.

"You all right?"

"Yeah. What did you do with the guard and his dog?" I asked.

"Hand cuffed the guard to the porch railing. The dog didn't like the pepper spray. I think he headed back to the kennel."

"Good. I think we can go inside," Mac said.

Mac went in first and quickly moved to one side. I went in second and quickly moved to the other side of the door. Dave stood outside the door, but in a position where he could cover us. I looked around the room but didn't see anyone. I looked at the desk and found one of the phone receivers was hanging off the desk as if it had been dropped there, as if someone had left in a hurry.

"I think he was in here when we came in the front door," I said as I pointed to the phone.

Mac simply nodded that he saw the phone. If he had left in a hurry, there had to be a way out of the room. I looked around but didn't immediately see any way out. All the windows had bars on them. It wasn't until I took a serious look around the room that I noticed there was one picture on an inside wall that was hanging crooked. I moved over toward the wall where anyone behind the wall would not be able to see me. Moving slowly toward the wall and closer to the picture, I looked for some evidence that there was a door of some kind on that wall. I noticed a slight scratch on the wood floor that ran from the wall out into the room in sort of a quarter circle.

I snapped my fingers and both Dave and Mac looked toward me. I pointed to the scratch on the floor then pointed at the wall. They both nodded that they had seen it. I began to look for some way to open the wall panel, but I didn't find any way in.

It took me a minute to think about how the wall would open. As I thought about it, I remembered that Franklin had pressed a button on his desk and the guard stepped into the office almost immediately. I wondered if there was a button somewhere in or on the desk that opened a portion of the wall. I moved over to the desk and began running my hand around the edge of the desk top. It didn't take but a few seconds to find a small switch.

The last switch I found caused the door to explode. I wondered if it was there to cause the desk to explode and destroy everything in and on the desk. I bent down and looked at the switch. This switch was different. It was a small button. It was the kind that would not be used to detonate an explosive. I decided it was probably the button that would call someone to the office or possibly open a hidden door in the wall. I looked toward the wall where the hidden door was located, then pressed the button.

A small part of the paneled wall opened, but only a few inches. Dave and Mac moved up close to the opening in the wall, one on each side. From the desk, I was able to look straight at it. I knelt down behind the desk, then motioned for Mac to pull the wall panel open.

Suddenly there were three shots fired from inside the wall. I returned fire immediately. I heard a slight groan then what sounded like footsteps running away.

"I think we have a rat trapped in there," Dave said.

"I wouldn't count on it. Who knows where that goes. It could come out almost anywhere," I said.

Suddenly there were several shots outside. Dave ran over to the window to see what was happening.

"It looks like they've found a couple of Franklin's men in the building out back," Dave said.

"You think that might be where this tunnel goes?" Mac asked.

"I don't know, but if I have to guess, no. If people were able to get in and out of here without being seen, going to that building wouldn't be the place. It's too close to the house, and it's too easy for people doing the surveillance to see anyone trying to leave from it," I said.

"Where would Franklin go?" I asked myself out loud.

"What's on your mind?" Mac asked me.

"Franklin would know by now that we know he has been running a drug operation from here, and running the money through the bank in Dillon. He would most likely want to get as far away as possible as soon as possible. Does he have a plane?"

"I believe he does," Dave said. "But I have a no idea where he keeps it."

"Since he has been working with Williams, and with the bank in Dillon, it would be my guess that he has a plane in or near Dillon. And if I had to guess, he has money stashed where he could get at it quickly."

"There is a small airport near Dillon," Dave said.

"Call Stillwell and see if he can get someone out to the airport. Have him ground all aircraft wanting to leave that airport until you know who is on board, and tell him we are on our way," I said.

Mac picked up a phone, but the line was dead. He ran out to his police car and called Stillwell from there. I went with him. I could hear him on the phone. They had the bank auditors working in the bank and had arrested Mr. Routh and Mr. Sheridan at the bank. Stillwell's deputies had arrested both Tony and Anthony Williams in the reality office. It looked like the only one left was Robert Franklin, and we had no idea where he might be.

We immediately headed for Dillon. We were only a few miles from the exit to Dillon when we received a call telling us that Franklin just flew out of the small airport in a twin engine private plane.

We arrived at the small airport when we saw a ball of fire and smoke rise up into the air. We parked in front of a hanger next to a sheriff's car. There were two deputies standing next to their police car looking toward the column of smoke. One of the deputies turned and saw me. He smiled.

"Hi, do you remember me?"

"Sure. Your one of Stillwell's deputies. What's going on?" I asked.

"We didn't get here in time to stop the plane from leaving, but we got several shots at it. I think we hit it a couple times. It suddenly started to smoke, then crashed where you see the smoke. We have the forest service taking a couple of fire trucks up there to make sure it doesn't start a forest fire."

"Can you take us up there?"

"Sure," he said. "Get in my truck"

Mac and I got in the deputy sheriff's truck and headed across the airfield to an old logging road that went up into the hills around the airport. We bounced along for what seemed like forever. We arrived on the scene of the fire, but the fire fighters had the fire under control. I looked around but didn't see a body in the wreckage. I slowly walked around the wreckage. I had no idea what I was looking for, but I looked just the same.

Suddenly, my eyes spotted something that looked a little strange. In the dirt, several feet from the plane, I noticed what looked like something had been dragged along the ground. I also noticed that it seemed to go from the wreckage toward a rough area of rocks. A closer look, showed what looked like shoe marks alongside the drag marks. I looked over toward some of the rocks. Someone had either been dragged into the rocks, or someone was hurt and had dragged a limp limb into the rocks.

"Mac," I called to him.

Mac looked at me, then walked over to me.

"What's up?"

"I think Franklin got out of the plane before it burned. Look here," I said.

I showed Mac the tracks.

"Let's go find him," Mac said as he drew his gun.

I drew my gun and slowly started toward the rocks where the tracks led. As we got into the rocks, we found fresh blood on several rocks. Being careful as we moved around the boulders, we followed the tracks. We hadn't gone very far when I found a couple of hundred-dollar bills.

As I picked up the bills, I thought I heard a moan. I stopped and listened. I put my finger over my lips so Mac would not make a sound. I pointed to a large boulder. Mac moved up close to me.

I pointed at myself, then pointed out that I was going to work my way around the boulder. I pointed at him, then pointed the way I wanted him to go. He nodded that he understood.

As soon as we were ready, I began working my way around the boulder. It didn't take me very long before I could see Franklin lying on the ground. He looked as if he was trying to work his way under a large bush. I also noticed that he had a briefcase. It looked like he was trying to bury it under the bush. I was behind him.

"Give it up," I said.

He turned over and pointed his gun at me, but he never got a chance to pull the trigger. There was one shot that hit him square in the chest. I looked toward where the shot had come from and saw Mac. We both let out a sigh of relief.

"He was burying a briefcase. My guess is it was his travel money," I said.

"I think we have the leader, and some of his money. Now all we have to do is figure out who killed Josh," I said.

We turned and looked at the two deputies who were standing on the thin trail looking at us. They had their guns in their hands.

"It's all over here. You can put your guns away. You can take care of the body. We'll take care of the briefcase. Would you be so kind as to take us back to the airport?" Mac said.

"Sure," one of the deputies said.

"One of you should stay here until you can get the body out of here."

"No problem, I'll stay," the other deputy said.

"Thanks."

Mac and I got in the sheriff's truck and rode back to the airport. Once we arrived at the airport, we drove into Dillion and checked with Stillwell. Since he had everything under control, Mac and I went back to Precinct One in Denver. As soon as we were in Mac's office, I called Julie. George answered the phone.

"Hi. How's it going?"

"It's all over, well, at least my part in this is. I'd like to talk to Julie."

"Sure. She's right here."

"Hi," she said.

"It's over. All that's left is to give Mac my statement. As soon as I'm done, I'll call and come and get you," I said.

"Okay. How are you feeling?" she asked.

I could hear the concern in her voice.

"I'm doing okay. I'm a little tired, but feeling pretty good otherwise. Honey, I have to go. The sooner I get done with my statement, the sooner I can come get you."

"Okay. I love you," Julie said.

"I love you, too," I said then hung up.

I had just hung up when a woman came into Mac's office. She had a stenographer's recorder. She sat down next to Mac's desk.

"This is Nancy. She's here to take down your statement. I figured it would be faster. Once you are done with your statement, she will type it up and have it ready for you to sign in the morning. She will also be taking my statement."

"Are you ready, Mr. Blackstone?" Nancy asked.

"Yes. Where would like me to start?"

Nancy looked at Mac, apparently not sure how to answer me.

"Start with your arrival at my office this morning."

I nodded that I understood, then tipped back in the chair and took a couple of minutes to think about how this day had started. As soon as I was ready, I told her about my day.

It was a good half hour before I got to the part where Mac and I returned to his office.

"I guess that's about it," I said.

"Is there anything else you would like to add or change?" she asked, her voice showing how professional she was at her job.

"No. That covers it."

"That was very good, and very detailed" Mac said. "I think you can go now. I would like you back here in the morning to review your statement and sign it if it is correct," Mac said.

I thanked Nancy for letting me dictate my statement. Then told Mac I'd see him in the morning.

I left Mac's office and went out to my Explorer and got in. I placed a call to George to find out where Julie was. The phone rang only two times before it was answered.

"How's it going?" George asked.

"Good. I need to know where you are so I can come get Julie."

"I take it, it is safe now and we can let the women go about their business."

"That would be correct."

"I'm sure they will be glad to hear that," he said.

He gave me the address where Julie and the others were being held. I told him I would be there in a few minutes.

WHEN I ARRIVED AT THE HOUSE where Julie was, I was greeted with hugs and kisses. It was nice to be welcomed with such enthusiasm. I was told that Mr.

Wallace was on his way over to pick up Mrs. Garrett. When I asked about taking Mary back to Frisco, George said he would be taking her back himself. The grin on his face told me that he was pretty happy about taking her home.

Julie and I left and went directly to my apartment. She was happy to see that it had been repaired. We had a light dinner, then took a shower and went to bed. It was well over an hour before we drifted off to sleep.

CHAPTER TWENTY-FOUR

IN THE MORNING, Julie and I had breakfast then went to Mac's office. I reviewed my statement and signed it.

"It looks like everyone we arrested yesterday has gotten an attorney. However, I think there are two who are looking for a deal," Mac said. "They know we have a pretty solid case. The 'doctor' who brought the syringe into your room at the hospital is the one who killed Josh. He has been singing like the proverbial canary in order to avoid the death penalty. From what a couple of them that we arrested have told us, he was hired by Tony Williams. Those who have said anything at all, say Franklin was the top man, and Anthony Williams worked for Franklin, and was the go-between with the bank."

"I guess that wraps things up for now," I said.

"Pretty much, at least until their trials."

"Good. I'm sure you will let me know when they go to trial."

"Right. Take care. I'll see you later," Mac said.

"Wait. I have a question," Julie said.

"What is it, Honey?"

"I want to know what happened in the café. Mrs. Franklin was killed along with the man that was assumed to be her lover. Josh was also shot at the same time by the same shooter but for a different reason. How did the shooter know the three of them would be in that café at the same time?"

"That's just it, he didn't. From what I have been able to find out from those we arrested was the shooter didn't know the three of them would be there at the same time," Mac said.

"I don't understand," Julie said.

"Let me explain. The shooter, who by the way it turns out was Tony Williams, went to the café to shoot Mrs. Franklin and Mr. North. He had been hired to do it by Mr. Franklin. Tony had been told by Mr. Routh that Josh had discovered some irregularities in a couple of accounts in the bank, so he knew that Franklin and his father wanted Josh out of the way.

"When Tony arrived at the café all dressed in black and wearing a ski mask, he saw Josh. He quickly made the decision to kill all three of them hoping it would confuse the police. It did do that for a little while," Mac explained.

"So, the shooting of Josh was a shooting of opportunity?" Julie asked.

"Yes, but it caused an additional problem for Tony Williams. Since the shooting of Josh didn't kill him, he had to make sure the job got finished. Tony got one of Franklin's thugs to do it for him because he was afraid that Rose Williams, his aunt, might recognize him and stop him or tell the police. He couldn't wait to kill him until his aunt would not be on duty for fear that Josh might wake up and talk before he could silence him.

"Does that answer your question?" Mac asked with a grin.

"Yes," Julie said. "I have another question, though. Did you ever figure out how Josh's car got to the parking garage?"

"No, we didn't. I guess that will remain a mystery. It's also not important anymore," Mac said with a grin.

"It is time we leave and let Mac finish up," I said taking Julie by the hand.

Julie and I left Mac's office. We walked hand in hand out to parking lot and got into my Explorer. We drove to my apartment without saying much of anything. Once we were inside, Julie turned toward me and put her arms around my neck. I slipped my arm around her and pulled her up against me.

We spent the rest of the day relaxing, and watching movies and enjoying being together without any worries about being disturbed.

After dinner, we cleaned up the kitchen. With all the stress we had over the past weeks, we decided to get some rest. It wasn't long and we were in the shower.

When we started to run out of warm water, we got out, dried off and went right to bed. We spent some time loving each other, before we curled up together.

"I love you," Julie whispered.

"I love you, too," I said.

I was about to doze off when I remembered that Julie's car was still at the hospital and had been for some time. I turned my head and looked at her. She was asleep and resting peacefully. "The car can wait," I said silently to myself, then, closed my eyes and dozed off into a peaceful sleep.

www.ingramcontent.com/pod-product-compliance
Lightning Source LLC
Chambersburg PA
CBHW071123170626
46809CB00002B/479